The Lycan's Daughter

Jazz Ford

Jazz Ford

ISBN: 9798353261469

Don't be afraid to be your own hero
Sometimes only you can save yourself.

Chapter 1

Exiting the school gates, I see my older twin brothers, Theo and Leo, waiting for me. They appear bored but straighten up and smile as a group of she-wolves giggle and walk by.

'I wish you would both stop waiting for me after school. I'm almost eighteen, yet you make me feel as though I'm nine,' I growl.

'Well, you do have the mentality of a nine-year-old,' Leo says.

Theo elbows him in the gut, 'What Leo is trying to say is, you know we don't have a choice. It's Mum and Dad you need to convince, not us,'

I sigh, 'Fine, but I bet I'll beat you home again,' I reply, breaking into a run.

We race through the dense woods. Finally, I'm almost home, beating Theo and Leo from school.

'I won, again,' I say proudly with hands on my hips.

'You cheated, Lyla,' Theo says.

'How did I cheat? You saw me running in front of you the whole time?' I argue.

'You probably used magic,' Leo replies.

'You both know I wasn't gifted with magic like Mum and Grandma, so stop being sad losers and admit a girl defeated you.'

'Never,' they say in unison.

We enter our home, which happens to be a medieval castle and notice we have guests.

'Alpha Maximus, don't tell me this is your daughter Lylah?' The unfamiliar Alpha says.

I can tell he's an Alpha based on his powerful aura, but it's not as strong as my father's or my brothers.

'Yes, it is Lylah. I suppose it's been many years since you came to visit us, Alpha Greg,' my father says.

'Well, Alpha Maximus, given the recent happenings at the human borders. I needed to see you to figure out what we are going to do about it.'

My Dad pulls a glum face.

'What happened?' Theo asks.

'Over the last week, human bodies have been found dismembered and drained of blood. There were reports of wolves seen not far from the scene. The humans think a pack of wild wolves killed them, but we're still investigating it. We aren't certain wolves are what killed those people, though, as wild wolves never roam near human land. Also, they hunt wildlife, not people. The photos Greg had shown me reveal they all had two fang marks on their napes and were drained of blood before they were dismembered. It looks as though… vampires may have been the cause.'

We all stiffen and stare at one another with worry.

I step towards my Dad, 'But vampires have always kept to themselves. Even we have never met one,'

'And I hope we never meet one. They are hostile towards everyone, werewolves included. They are deadly creatures, and they need to remain in their territories. Hopefully, there won't be a repeat of this incident again.'

'What if it does happen again?' I ask.

'Whether it is or isn't vampires, if it happens again, we will have to hunt whatever it is down ourselves before they get any closer to our territory or further into the human territories,'

'We will go with you, Dad,' Leo says.

'I want to help too,' I say.

Theo and Leo laugh while my Dad gives me a look of pity.

'Why are you laughing? It's not funny,' I yell.

'Because you haven't even learnt to use magic yet,' Theo says,

'And you haven't shifted either,' Leo adds.

'That's not my fault! I've been training every day, and you both know it,' I growl.

'We'd have better luck bringing a human girl along,' Leo laughs.

'Argh!' I race towards Leo, jump high in the air, and extend my leg, kicking him square in the jaw. As my foot makes contact, you can hear the bone break. I roll when I land and keep one knee on the ground, swinging my other foot under Theo this time, knocking him over. As I pounce on his chest, I pull a small blade from my boot and hold it against his neck. He holds his hands up in defeat.

'Lylah!' I hear my mother growl. 'What have I told you about fighting your brothers?'
'Mum, they started it!'
'She's right. They did start it,' my Dad says.
'Don't encourage her behaviour, Maximus. Lylah should be practising magic in the spell room, like the good little Witch I know she is. Not getting into fist fights with her brothers.'
'I'll be eighteen soon, Mum. I'm not little anymore, and while I'm at it, stop making Theo and Leo walk me home from school. I can look after myself. Besides, it's darn embarrassing,' I say, deeply annoyed.
Mother looks away.
I withdraw my knife from Theo's throat and place the knife back in my boot. When I look up, my mother stands before me and holds her hand out for the blade. Sighing, I place the knife in her hand. Then, our attention turns to Leo as he cracks his broken jaw back in place.
'That's some great fighting talent you have there, Lylah. Have you considered becoming a warrior?' Alpha Greg asks.
'Fighting is the only thing I'm good at. I can't even cast a simple spell,' I mumble, 'It's the only skill I have to help protect the pack.'
'You don't need to protect us,' Theo says.
'Then what good am I to the pack if I have nothing to offer? I can't shift, and I can't cast magic?'
'You're our sister. We love you just the way you are, regardless of your lack of abilities. Besides, Micah doesn't seem to mind. I think he secretly enjoys your lunchtime fighting sessions,' Leo says, wiggling his eyebrows at me.

My cheeks redden, 'Have you two bogus brains been spying on me too?' I growl, glaring between Theo and Leo.

'It's obvious to the whole school you two are crushing on each other,' he smiles.

'And who told you that?' I growl.

Amara, Sally and Nathan's daughter, also my age, skips into the room gingerly, humming with a bright smile as if she was skipping through a field of daisies. She halts when all eyes land on her.

Amara holds her hands up, 'I didn't mean to break it, I swear. I'll replace it, I promise,' she says.

'What did you break this time, Amara?' my father asks.

'Oh, um, is this about something else?' she says nervously, fiddling with her fingers.

'Why did you tell my brothers that Micah and I are crushing on each other at school?' I ask her.

'Oh, because it's obvious,' she shrugs.

'It is not!'

'Yes, it is. Everyone sees how you look at each other and how you flutter your eyes at Micah like this,' she says, exaggerating the action of eye fluttering.

My brothers burst into laughter.

'Amara!' I say and chase after her.

'I shall better be going now, Alpha Maximus. I will keep you informed if there are any changes in the case,' Alpha Greg says.

'Thank you, Alpha Greg. I will talk to you later then,' my Dad says and walks him out the door.

Beth enters the room while holding a freshly cooked apple pie.

'So, who's hungry?' she smiles.

We all stop what we are doing and race to the dining table.

'Apple pie, my favourite!' Dad says, rubbing his hands together.

Beth potters around, serving a slice onto a plate for everyone.

'Lylah, you will have to tell me what kind of cake you want me to bake for your eighteenth?' she says.

'Sure, just chocolate will be fine,' I smile.

'Very well then, chocolate it is.'

There's a knock at the door. I jump out of my seat with excitement and run to answer it. I already know who it is.

Micah smiles, his sable brown eyes twinkling as we exchange glances. I want to reach my hand out and caress his face. His dense blonde hair shines in the sunlight. His shirt is tight and shows off his fit physique. His eyes lower, and he stares at my lips. My smile widens, and we remain silent, admiring each other until my Dad clears his throat behind me.

Chapter 2

'Alpha Maximus,' Micah says, graciously bowing his head.

'Micah, we were just talking about you,' Alpha Maximus says.

'Oh really? Good things, I hope?' he says and smiles at me endearingly.

I blush, 'Come on, Dad, move out of the way so Micah can come inside. You take up the whole doorframe, you know?'

'I'm a Lycan. I can't help being this big,' he shrugs, steps away from the door, and returns to the dining table.

Micah sits next to me. Our pinky fingers touch discreetly under the table. Micah hooks his finger around mine. We remain that way with coy smiles. The attraction between us is obvious to everyone in the room.

'Micah, I hear you will soon take over as Alpha of Storm Glenn?' Theo asks.

'Yes, my father is thinking when I graduate next month that I would be ready to be Alpha,' he replies.

'I've heard you're one of the best fighters around?' Alpha Maximus asks, joining the conversation.

'Well, I don't know about that,' he says, giving me a wink.

My finger tightens around his, and Micah clears his throat.

'If it's okay with you, Alpha Maximus. I was hoping to take Lylah out for a run this evening?'

My parents smile and nod in approval.

The first day Micah and I met, we had instant electricity. Micah transferred here from Storm Glenn a few years ago, residing with his Aunty. His Dad wanted him to have a good education and form a good rapport with us since we are the closest town to his. We are known for having the best education system in the state. Micah had grown up learning wrestling and boxing and continued it here. I love how seriously he takes it, and when he found me training myself in the woods, he offered to train me himself.

Of course, I said yes. Sometimes we train at school during lunch or after school at the gym or meet in the woods on the weekends and train there.

Everyone knows Micah has been training me for three years, but no one knows how good I truly am. They only see little bits and pieces, such as when I lose my temper at one or both of my brothers.

At school, we sit together in every class we share. At lunchtime, we train together. Afterwards, I sit on Micah's lap and eat my lunch. We haven't shared our first kiss yet, but our feelings have grown stronger each day as I approach my eighteenth birthday. I'm sure Micah is my fated mate. Even though I'm not supposed to feel the mate bond until I'm eighteen, my stomach flutters whenever he looks at me. I feel a tiny spark when we touch. I always want to be around him. Micah is the only guy I think about. I receive a lot of glares from all the girls at school. They call me a 'Freak,' or I should leave the pack and join the humans because they think I don't have a wolf or magic abilities like my mother. Unfortunately, they could be right. My father said it's rare, but some people have been born purely human, having the wolf or magic gene skip them and, in my case, altogether. My mother believes that my wolf or magic will awaken eventually, that I'm just a late bloomer like she was with magic. I guess time will tell.

Micah grabs my hand, sending a small spark up my arm, distracting me from my thoughts.

'Ready to go for a run?' he smiles.

I nod, and we leave the pack house.

Micah removes his shirt, and I goggle his six-pack and masculine arms.

Next, he removes the lower half of his clothing. My smile widens, and so does his.

I've seen him naked many times, as I've seen him shift frequently. I don't think I could ever grow bored watching him strip.

He shifts into his large dark wolf, which emits a great power. Micah lowers himself so that I can climb on. Then, holding on, he breaks out into a sprint. My platinum blonde hair whips violently behind me as Micah sprints vigorously ahead. An hour later, we arrive at our favourite destination by the waterfall. He shifts back to his human form, and I pass his clothes. Once dressed, he sits on the grass and pats his leg. I lay on my back, resting my head on his lap. Micah strokes his fingers through my hair while we gaze into each other's eyes. I can hardly keep my focus as I become lost in his eyes, and it's at this moment that I realise I love him. I'm deeply and truly in love with Micah.

'Lylah,' he says.

The way he says my name in a deep and husky tone sends my heart racing. At one point, I think my heart is about to grow wings and fly out from my chest.

My hand lifts on its own accord and cups his cheek. Micah presses his face into the palm of my hand, and then his beautiful sable eyes return to mine.

'Lylah, you are my world, my moon, everything to me,' he whispers.

'Micah,' I say, pulling his face to mine.

At first, Micah's lips touch mine, lightly, delicately, like butterfly wings, just long enough for me to absorb his minty breath and feel the warmth of his skin. Then, in response to our kiss's increasing heat and intensity, I feel myself sitting up and pressing in closer. Then, finally, our tongues meet. Both of us are jolted by our passionate kiss as we continue to lock lips. Micah's eyes open to find mine shining brilliantly in the moonlight at his, and he smiles.

'I've wanted to do that for a very long time,' he says.

'Oh? And how long is a very long time?' I smile.

'Since the day I met you. Three years ago,' he replies.

I blush and break eye contact looking away. Micah gently holds my chin and looks into my eyes. He begins to peck my lips between each word.

'Since. When. Did. You. Become. Shy. Around. Me?' He says between each kiss.

My blush deepens, 'Gee, I don't know. Perhaps since you kissed me, making me feel even giddier than I thought I could ever be?' I say in a playful tone.

Micah grabs my waist, pulls me in closer, and rolls us through the grass. I giggle as he laughs, and we end up lying next to each other, holding hands and gazing up at the moon.

'Do you think we are fated mates?' I ask.

'Of course. You can't tell me you haven't felt the minor sparks and chemistry between us?'

'Oh, I have. Since the moment we met,' I reply.

'I know,' he smiles, 'I remember when we first met, and we brushed past each other we both jolted from the one little spark,' he smiles.

Micah pulls me onto his lap, holding my back up against his chest and wrapping his arms around my waist. He nuzzles his lips against my neck and places a kiss.

'It's all perfect timing. You will be eighteen soon, and we can announce to everyone we are fated mates. Instead of me returning home to become Alpha of Storm Glenn, you will come with me as the future Luna of Storm Glenn,' Micah squeezes me with delight.

I look up at the stars, then focus on the moon and let out a heavy sigh.

'What's wrong?' Micah asks with concern, 'You don't want to be Luna and rule by my side?'

'It's not that, Micah, trust me. I want to go to Storm Glenn with you. I want to be by your side and take care of Storm Glenn with you. But what if no one likes me? What if I never get my wolf or my magic? What if I'm just human? Will everyone think of me as a weak Luna or worse, not want me as their Luna?'

'Oh, Lylah, I don't care what they think, or anyone thinks. You will always be my true love and my Luna in my eyes. Nothing in this world will ever change how I feel for you,' Micah turns me around, wraps my legs around his waist, and gives me a stern look, 'And for your information, Lylah, you are not weak. You were trained by yours truly, who happens to be the best fighter around, and you are the only one who has been able to keep up with me. I've trained men as big as me that couldn't even fight at your level,' he says.

'You're just saying that to make me feel better,' I say, returning the stern look.

'I am stating this because it's true, but if it made you feel better, I would whisper every sweet thing in the world to you if I had to.'

Micah cups my face delicately as if I were a porcelain doll that could break. The look on his face becomes serious, 'Lylah, I love you so much, I would die for you,' he says, and I believe him, every single word.

'I love you too,' I say, as my eyes well with happiness.

We kiss with such desperation and profound yearning for one another. Then, we break the kiss with heavy breaths.

'I will never let you go,' Micah says quietly.

'Then don't let me go. Promise me you'll always be with me,' I whisper.

'I promise,' he says and gives me a final sweet kiss before returning me home.

Chapter 3

Micah walks with me to the front door, 'We should go camping for your eighteenth birthday?' he says.

'That sounds amazing. Just you and me?' I ask.

'Just you and me,' he winks.

'Did someone say camping?' My father, Alpha Maximus, asks behind me.

'Micah is going to take me camping for my birthday,' I smile.

'What a wonderful idea! I'll let your mother know we will all be going camping,' he says and walks back into the house.

My shoulders slump, and I give Micah an apologetic look.

'Don't worry about it. The more, the merrier, right?' Micah says.

'Sure,' I sigh.

'Plus, we can always go camping together alone another time,' he smiles.

'That's true,' I say, perking up at the idea.

Micah leans in and places a gentle kiss on my cheek.

'Goodnight, Princess,' he says quietly.

'Goodnight, Micah,' I wave.

I stay lingering in the large doorway until I can no longer see Micah. My hand caresses the spot on my cheek where he left a kiss. As I close the door and turn around, I bump into my twin brothers, who have their arms crossed and the biggest smirks on their faces.

'What do you two buffoons want?' I ask.

Theo holds his hand to his heart and pretends to be upset, 'That hurts, Lylah,' he pouts.

'I'm sure,' I say sarcastically.

'Now move out of my way, or I'll give you some real pain to cry about,' I say, holding my clenched fists up in a fighting stance.

They roll their eyes and step apart, letting me through but proceed to follow me to the kitchen.

'We saw lover boy give you a smooch on the cheek,' Leo says.

'Yeah, and?' I say, making myself a cup of tea.

'Micah kissed you?' my mother asks, entering the kitchen.

I nod and blush.

'Lylah! He is such a sweet man. I'm so happy for you and pray to the Moon Goddess he will be your fated mate,' she says, embracing me.

'Thanks, Mum,' I smile.

'At least when you become Luna of Storm Glenn, you won't be too far away from us,' my mother beams.

I smile and sip my tea.

'Your father tells me we are going camping for your birthday?' she asks.

I nod.

Nathan enters the kitchen in a panic and exits through another doorway, paying no attention to us. Moments later, Sally enters, looking around, clearly on a mission. Her eyes brighten as she looks at a frying pan and picks it up.

'I'd like to see Nathan say humans are weaklings now!' she says with a manic laugh, flourishing the frying pan in hand and bolting through the same door Nathan fled.

'Are we all going camping?' Theo asks.

'Sure, the whole packhouse can come,' I say as I exit the kitchen and walk through the long corridors. I stop by the spell room and collect the spell book that my mother gave me, walk up the steps of the North tower and step out onto the open terrace once I reach the top.

Sitting on the stone ground, I place my cup of tea down. It's now cold. I flip through the pages of the spell book and read the odd incantation.

I have practised these spells thousands of times, and never once has it worked. The only reason I keep trying is because my mother and grandmother want me to.

There are different types of spells. The ones where you say the words aloud usually work better with a wand but are not always necessary. The very experienced and strongest witches who have full control of their powers can cast these spells without a wand. Then, there are the spells where you use your hands to touch or hover over the object or person and concentrate using your mind. This technique is best used for healing wounds, which happens to be what my mother and grandmother are best at. Using your mind can also be used to change or move objects.

I focus on studying the fire spell. Once I've read everything the fire spell can do, I reach for my cold cup of tea and place it in front of me. Concentrating, I place both hands on either side of the mug and repeat the words 'Inferno Flamo' in my mind.

Minutes pass, and nothing happens, so I slump myself back with a heavy sigh and lay on the ground, giving up. The moon is shining above me, and the smiling face on the moon is more prominent than usual. I can't help but feel the moon is laughing at me.

Before I know it, I find myself fantasising about Micah. His soft, full lips and the taste of mint. His sable eyes that bore into mine as if our souls were dancing together. His touch that sends a ripple of waves through my body. I smile at the thought that I'll spend the rest of my life with Micah. Even though I have no wolf and no magic, I'd give it all away if it meant being with him.

I should probably stop daydreaming about Micah and keep practising magic. I look around and see a small pot with a half-dead plant. Reaching out, I take it and place it in front of me.

'Revito Sprouto,' I say, flicking my hands towards the pot plant.

A gust of wind goes by, and crickets become louder.

'Revito Sprouto,' I repeat, narrowing my eyes on the plant.

As expected, nothing happens. So, I cast the spell again, but this time in my mind as my hands hover over it.

After a moment, I shove the pot plant away, sliding it back towards the open terrace door. Then, looking back at my cold cup of tea, I scoot myself over and hover my hands over it.

'Come on, Lylah. You can do this!' I tell myself.

Once again, I narrow my eyes and concentrate on the words 'Inferno Flamo,' repeating over in my mind. Minutes go by, but I keep pushing myself to keep going this time. Half an hour has passed, and beads of sweat have formed across my forehead as I keep as still as a statue focusing on the cold tea. An owl lands on the stone rail and hoots, startling me. I turn and glare at the brown owl.

'Thanks for that,' I say sarcastically.

The owl hoots again and flies off the terrace and towards the distant woods. Getting myself up off the ground, I pat the dust off myself and walk down the tower stairs. Tired and defeated, I make my way to my chambers.

Unbeknownst to me, steam begins to rise from my mug moments after leaving the terrace.

The castle is quiet, and everyone is asleep. The only sound is coming from my footsteps. I walk through the maze of corridors and slump my back against my chamber door with the dreariest enthusiasm, pushing my door open. Trudging my feet, I stand in front of my floor-length mirror and stare at myself. Unlike all the girls and women, I don't wear dresses. It's much easier to train and fight in black slacks, which my wardrobe consists of many. My boots are solid and perfect for hiding small daggers on either side. My long-sleeved shirt is brown and tucked inside my pants, along with extra concealed daggers. My shirt's arms are baggy, allowing me to move more freely. I take off my boots, then my pants, and reach for my nightgown. I pull it over my head and look in the mirror. My blue eyes have darkened in colour as they do when I become tired, fatigued or angry. They are a bright sparkly blue when I'm in a good cheery mood or feeling content. My mother pointed out that when I was little, my eyes changed to different shades of blue, which showed what mood I was in at the time. She said it's strange because her eyes and my grandmother's eyes never change shades.

I untie my ponytail, freeing my white hair, and brush it out before going to bed. As I'm about to lift my bed cover to hop in, something underneath it moves. I gasp and take a step back. It moves again. I step closer, mentally preparing myself to be brave. I fling the cover back to find a frog in my bed.

'Leo!' I yell and scoop the frog up.

The frog croaks in my hand as I approach my window and place it on the stone ledge. Then, with another croak, it leaps from the window into the garden.

Chapter 4

Excited to spend the day with Micah, I wake up early and run to my bathroom. Unfortunately, the packhouse being an old castle, has not yet been modernised. I've complained to my Mum and Dad about it, but they say the castle is perfect the way it is and that what is good for the gander is good for the goose. So, it's apparently good to put more effort into things such as pumping the water ourselves instead of simply turning on a tap. So, I begrudgingly pump the water into the large, round wooden tub. Once it's full, I reach for the bowl of rose petals and scatter a handful into the water. Steam rises above the water, along with the aroma of the petals. I pull off my nighty, toss it aside, and step into the water. Slowly submerging myself in the tub, I hold my breath for as long as possible. I fantasise I'm in the ocean, and Micah is swimming toward me. His hand reaches out towards mine. My hand, in return, reaches out to his. Our fingers touch, and we clasp our fingers together. Micah's free hand cups my face, and he slowly pulls me in for a kiss. Moments after our lips touch, his tongue enters my mouth. He works his tongue with fiery passion against mine while his hand moves slowly up my thigh. His fingers are about to caress the most sensitive area between my legs when I'm suddenly feeling light-headed. I abruptly sit up in the tub and gasp for air. I shuffle to the side and hang my head over it whilst holding the ledge for support.

'What in the wands was that?' I say, gasping for air.

I can't believe I almost passed out in the water, fantasising about an intense and very hot moment with Micah. I fan my flustered face with my hand.

Not wanting to stay in the water any longer, I quickly scrub myself with the soap and step out of the tub.

I wear a fresh pair of black leggings, a dark grey shirt, and a grey hoodie, put my boots on, and then sit at my dresser. Looking in the mirror, I put my hair up in a ponytail and notice my eyes are dark blue. So, I close my eyes and relive the moment Micah, and I passionately kissed. A warmth spreads through me as I imagine his lips kissing me tenderly again, and I open my eyes to see they are bright sparkly blue. I nod at myself in approval and smile.

Even though I am fully clothed, I feel completely naked and vulnerable without my daggers. You can't blame a girl for relying on weapons to use when she has no wolf or magic to protect themselves in this world. I walk over to my collection and ponder on which ones to stash in my boots and the ones to tuck into the waist of my leggings. They mostly look the same, so I grab two randomly and tuck them in each boot, and another two I tuck under my shirt in the back of my leggings. Satisfied, I leave my chambers and join my family for breakfast.

A smirk appears on my face as I see the back of Leo whilst he stuffs his face with cereal. I approach casually as he leans over his bowl to scoop the cereal with his spoon. I place my hand on the back of his head and push his face into the bowl. Theo bursts into laughter as Leo flings his head back and gasps for air.

'What was that for?' he growls.

'That is for putting a frog in my bed in an attempt to scare me, which it didn't, mind you,' I scowl.

'Oh...,' he says, looking away.

'You get what you sow, brother,' Theo laughs, 'Even I'm not silly enough to dare prank Lylah.'

I sit at the table as Mum and Dad enter the dining room to join us.

'Theo, why do you have milk all over your face?' my mother, Hope, asks.

'Because he wasn't wearing his bib,' Theo says, bursting into laughter again.

Leo flicks cereal from his spoon across the table, hitting Theo right in the cheek.

Now it's Dad and me laughing as Theo glares at Leo whilst wiping the cereal from his face.

'Oh dear,' Mother sighs, then looks at me. 'What are your plans for the weekend?'

'I'm spending it with Micah, just like I do every other weekend,' I smile.

'Of course,' she smiles. 'Do you think you will move to Storm Glenn as soon as it's confirmed that you and Micah are mates, or do you plan on waiting until he becomes Alpha in the next month or so?'

I shrug my shoulders, 'I'm not sure. I'm not phased either way, though. As long as I'm with Micah, then I'm happy,' I reply.

Mother nods. As I'm about to finish my breakfast, there is a loud knock at the door. Theo, Leo and I stand at the same time. We all know it's Micah at the door.

'I'll get it,' I say excitedly. I jump onto the dining table, run across, and jump back down on the other side.

Theo and Leo look to our parents, expecting them to growl at my unladylike behaviour, but instead, they shrug and resume eating.

I pull the door open and leap into Micah's arms. He holds me close, and we kiss tenderly as he carries me away from prying eyes. Micah places me down and removes his clothes. I watch as he shifts. I collect his clothes before climbing onto his back.

Instead of going to the waterfall, we run deep into the woods to the area we train. It's a small open area where the trees had been cut down years prior. As a result, the stumps are at different heights, making them perfect for practising high and low kicks, punches, and other moves.

Micah shifts into his human form. I pass him his clothes and begin practising my punching moves on the stumps as he dresses.

My movements are swift and elegant. I now move on to high kicks and spins. I fall back but land softly to roll and jump back on my feet in a fighting stance.

Micah claps his hands, applauding me as he walks over to me.

'You know, watching you fight is like watching you dance. Your moves are quick yet graceful. You hit with force but with passion. Your energy is immense, and your determination shines through,' he says as his fingers brush over my lips. I slowly lean into his hand as it glides up my cheek. His lips suddenly devour mine. His tongue thrusts hungrily against my tongue, just like I envisioned in the tub. Our hands explore each other's bodies. I pull myself even closer to him and grip his hair. Our heads slightly fall back as we gasp for air, then gaze lovingly into each other's eyes.

Micah places his hand on my chest and feels the warmth of my beating heart seeping into the palm of his hand, 'You have a heart of fire,' he says.

'It was you who ignited my heart of flames. It burns for you,' I whisper.

His smile widens, and he reaches into his back pocket and pulls something out wrapped in light material.

'I want to give you your birthday gift now if that's okay? I didn't want you to open it in front of your parents, in case they don't approve,' he explains.

He places the gift in the palm of my hands. I slowly and carefully unravel the material and become speechless as I look upon the magnificence and brilliance of a silver sheath. Finally, I pull the dagger from the sheath and watch it shine and glisten in the sunlight.

'It's so majestic,' I say.

The blade is made of moonstone, opalescent of blues and whites and then forms into steel. I gently glide my fingertip across the blade. It's the sharpest dagger I've ever held. Blood trickles from my finger. I gasp as Micah takes my hand and sucks the blood from my finger, causing my insides to burst into song. It's as if an entire choir and orchestra are performing inside me. Blushing as he gently releases my finger from his lips. I resume inspecting the beautiful dagger. The fuller that runs down the middle of the blade is diamond-shaped and has a stunning engraving that looks like an eye, a familiar eye at that, with a hint of sable. It shimmers as I tilt it. The spine and quillon are made of silver. The handle seems to be made from bone.

'Micah, I don't know what to say. I've never seen anything so incredibly beautiful as this. Where in the wands did you come by something so amazing?' I ask in utter awe.

Beaming proudly, Micah tilts himself back and forward from his tippy toes to his heels, 'Well, actually, I didn't come across it. I made it. It's taken me many months to forge. I wanted it to be perfect,' he smiles, 'I used the finest and rarest materials to make it. The sheath is made of silver, and the dagger is made from Moonstone and Silver. I engraved my eye into the fuller so you know I always have my eye on you,' he winks, 'And the hand of the dagger is made from dragon bone.'

'Dragon bone!?' I exclaim.

'Well, that's what the old man told me when I bought it off him. He said it was handed down through many generations and came from another dimension hundreds of years ago. He had no children to pass it on and decided it was time to move it on to someone else. Most likely, it's just an old animal bone,' he shrugs.

I fling my arms around Micah's neck and cover him in kisses.

'This is the most precious, most amazing present anyone has ever given me,' I say.

'What else could I give my princess who has given me her heart of flames,' he says.

Chapter 5

I place the dagger back into its sheath and tuck it into my belt. Then I take fifteen steps back from the tallest tree stump. A couple of years ago, Micah and I spent time carving silly faces into all the stumps we use as targets. I halt once I'm far enough away from the stumps and take the two old daggers tucked into the waist of my belt. Then, flourishing them in my hand, I aim and throw them at the tallest target. They spin through the air and hit the target but land an inch off where I had aimed.

'Try it with your new dagger,' Micah says.

'I don't want to damage it, though,'

'You won't,' he laughs, 'Trust me. It's indestructible,' he smirks.

His crooked smile makes me giddy and puts me in a trance. I nod in response.

With my new dagger in hand, I narrow my eyes at the target and throw.

The dagger struck right between the eyes of the target.

'Bullseye!' I squeal.

Micah lifts me and hugs me, 'I knew you could do it,' he says and then walks over to the stump and pulls the daggers out.

'I wonder why I could never get the other daggers to hit the same spot? I didn't do anything differently,' I say.

Micah stands behind me and drapes his arms over my shoulders. 'See here,' he says, holding one of the older daggers. If you look at it from this angle, you can see the blade is slightly bent. This one is also a little warped,' he points out. 'Also, you haven't been taking note of the wind and which direction it's going. Think like an archer. When you release the arrow, the wind can affect where it lands.'

'Oh, you're right. What would I do without you, Micah?' I say playfully and turn around to face him. He pulls me closer, and our lips caress each other's mouths for a few moments before we kiss. We break the kiss, and I step back with a hand on my chest. The thought of not being with Micah sends a horrible ache to my heart.

'What's wrong?' Micah asks with concern.

'I love you so much that it hurts,' I say truthfully.

Micah steps toward me, closing the gap between us and gently holds my chin and tilts my head to look him in the eyes.

'Lylah, you are the best thing that has ever happened to me. We will have the best future together and the most beautiful pups. Everyone will be envious of us,' he smiles.

I blush at the thought of having pups with him and his sweet words.

'Once I'm eighteen and it's confirmed we are fated mates, will I be going straight to Storm Glenn with you, or will we wait until you are made the official Alpha?' I ask.

'I was actually going to talk to my father and see if I can hold off being an Alpha until I'm nineteen.'

'Why, is something wrong?' I ask in a worried tone.

'No, I was hoping to have you all to myself for at least a year. I figured maybe we could travel. All I want to do is climb mountains with you, swim the oceans and count the stars on the darkest nights with you. I want to do everything with you before we commit ourselves as Alpha and Luna of Storm Glenn,' he says.

'Micah,' I whisper, 'How lucky and blessed I am to have you.'

'You are everything to me, Lylah,' he says, cupping my cheek. He pulls my face closer, and we kiss slowly, absorbing and enjoying the moment.

My stomach grumbles, breaking the kiss.

Micah laughs, 'I guess this means it's dinner time?'

'Yeah, but I don't want to return home just yet. I want to stay here a bit longer,' I say.

'Okay, well, let's hunt a rabbit and make a fire then,' he says.

I nod, take his clothes as he strips, and place them in a neat pile. As soon as he shifts, I climb onto his back. He runs for a few minutes, slows down, and begins sniffing the air. Because I don't have my wolf, I can't smell as well as Micah can. Instead, I climb down from his back and stealthily walk around and listen for any sounds of wildlife. I have my dagger in a firm hold, ready to strike my dinner at any moment.

Half an hour goes by, and there is a rustle in a nearby bush, but before I can throw my dagger, Micah leaps out from the shadows and pounces on his prey. He prances towards me with the rabbit hanging from his mouth and drops it at my feet.

'If you waited for a second, I could have caught it myself, you know?' I smirk at him.

He playfully nudges his head across my chest and almost knocks me over. I pick the rabbit up and climb onto his back.

Once we have returned to our training area, he shifts back and dresses as I collect sticks for the fire.

'Do you want me to skin the rabbit, or do you want to do it?' Micah asks.

'You can get the rabbit ready. I'll get the fire started,' I smile.

He nods, picks up the dead rabbit and swiftly takes a cruddy knife from my boot.

'Hey!' I say.

Micah shrugs, 'Well, I'm not going to skin it with my teeth, am I?'

I laugh, 'Yeah, okay, okay.'

I continue to collect sticks, twigs and dry leaves, then find a couple of old dry small logs. I place them in a pile, collect rocks and place them in a circle to create a ring. Then, looking at the sticks, I choose one with a long groove and pick out another. With my knife, I shave the tip making it sharp and pointy. Next, I take a pile of dried leaves and place it on the end of the stick with the groove and with the other stick, I begin rubbing it repetitively on the groove. Once the leaves begin to smoke, I tip them onto the sticks with added dry leaves and blow the smoke. The sticks catch fire, and I place the old dried logs on top and smile proudly at myself.

'Nice work, princess,' Micah says as he finishes removing the skin from the rabbit.

I walk over and watch him gut it. I had never prepared a rabbit before, so I preferred to get the fire going. I watch how he prepares it. Micah then pierces a stick through the rabbit and walks to the fire. I follow and sit next to him.

We take turns holding the stick and slowly rotating the rabbit.

'Do you think you will be okay when you turn eighteen and still don't have a wolf or magic?' he asks.

'I hope it doesn't bother me. I've been telling myself I probably won't have a wolf or magic, so I'd like to think I'm mentally prepared for it. I guess I won't know until then. But they would still be the least of my problems. As long as I'm with you and you don't mind that I remain human, then that's all that matters to me.'

'Well, you already know I think you're perfect the way you are,' he smiles.

I lean my head on his shoulder, and we watch the fire in a content silence unless the rabbit is cooked. Micah passes the stick to me so I can eat first. I manage to eat a quarter of it and pass it back to him to finish.

Micah bites into the flesh, clearly hungry but stops and looks around.

'What is it?' I ask.

He sniffs the air, 'We have company.'

Billy, Amara, Theo and Leo step out into the clearing.

'So this is where you two canoodle?' Amara smiles.

'What are you all doing here?' I say.

'Well, Mum and Dad were becoming worried as it's getting late, and because you don't have a wolf, we couldn't mind-link you to see where you were,' Theo explains.

'I can take care of myself. Mum and Dad know that and know I'm with Micah anyway. So they have nothing to worry about,' I say, clearly annoyed.

'I'll mind-link them now and let them know you are okay,' Leo says.

They all join us and sit around the fire. Billy leans over, takes Micah's stick, and begins eating the rabbit.

'Billy, get your own rabbit,' Micah growls, snatching the stick back and resuming eating.

Once Micah is finished eating, I rest my head on his shoulder. He wraps his arm around my back and pulls me close.

Chapter 6

Everyone admires the love and affection Micah and I are showing each other. Micah tucks my hair behind my ear and sweetly pecks my cheek. I snuggle closer to him and rest my head on his chest as his fingers caress my back. Then, I take his free hand and hold it tenderly on my lap.

Leo wiggles his eyebrows at me, 'What?' I ask, giving him a look.

'If you two continue to be so damn cute together, my heart might spontaneously combust with happiness for you two,' he smiles.

Micah wraps his arms around me as we laugh, pulls me onto his lap, and I cup his face with both hands, and we share a passionate kiss.

As soon as we finish our kiss, I turn to Leo, 'So, did your heart explode?' I ask him with a big grin.

Leo clutches his chest pretending to be in pain, and falls back from the log he is sitting on, 'My heart, it's about too… boom!' He says, tossing a handful of dry leaves in the air to imitate an explosion.

We all burst into laughter as the leaves float back down to the ground.

'I hope one day I meet a man just as sweet and loving as Micah,' Amara says, staring dreamily at us.

'You will,' I say to her.

'I highly doubt it. I'm so clumsy it would put any man off,' she pouts.

'That's not true... well, you being clumsy is true, but when someone truly loves you, Amara, they will think you are perfect, no matter how clumsy you are,' I assure her.

'Lylah, that is the sweetest thing you have ever said to me,' she squeals, holding her hands to her heart, and jumps up to run towards me but instead falls over flat on her face in the dirt.

Billy immediately helps her up.

'Thanks,' she says, blushing.

'No problem. Are you hurt?' he asks.

'I'll probably end up with bruised knees, but I'll be fine,' she says, smiling appreciatively at Billy.

Billy gestures for her to sit by him. Amara's face lights up, and she takes up the offer and nestles beside him.

I gaze above the fire that sends a silver line of smoke towards the sky and stare at the infinite mass of stars. A smile spreads across my face as I remember what Micah said about wanting to count the stars with me.

Suddenly memories from school flash through my mind sending a sense of dread throughout my body. The constant bullying from Vicky and Tamara calling me a freak. Informing me that I'm so ugly, not even my wolf wants to be with me. Amongst many other horrible things, they say. Although I keep a blank face and don't respond, seeing me upset will only encourage them to bully me more. Hearing these things makes me doubt that I'm not good enough for Micah or to be Luna of his pack. I know Micah loves me and assures me I am good enough, but when you're constantly put down, you can't help but think these things.

Micah caresses my wrists, sending a subtle tingle of sparks along my arms, and my heart quickens. I solemnly stare into his eyes. He can sense something is wrong.

'You seem lost in thought?' he says, then, feeling my strong heartbeat, withdraws his hands from my wrists and instead holds my two hands in his.

'What are you thinking about?' he asks with worry.

'Those girls at school,' I sigh sadly.

Micah grips me tightly and gazes into my eyes, 'Listen, Lylah. I'll trade my might and breath to make you happy. Vicky and Tamara won't ever amount to anything with their attitudes. But you, you are going to be my fated mate. I just know it. You will be a Luna, while Vicky and Tamara will live on envious of you. You are my perfect mate, and you will be the perfect Luna,' he smiles and kisses my lips.

His words send a warmth at the thought that his love for me is as strong as my love for him. I become lost in his gleaming eyes and return the kiss.

'We better return home now,' Theo says.

Everyone shifts. I climb onto Micah's back and race through the woods.

Clutching Micah's soft fur in a tight grip to not fall, I can't help but wonder what it would feel like to be a wolf.

We arrive home. I don't want to let go of Micah's hand. I want him to stay with me.

Leo and Theo can sense my sad aura from having to say goodbye to Micah.

'We should let our parents know we are home,' Leo says to Theo.

Theo nods and walks into the packhouse. Amara and Billy also give us privacy and follow the twins inside.

Micah steps closer, closing the gap between us and cups my cheeks with his hands.

'Very soon, we will be living together and won't have to bid each other goodbye each night. Sweet dreams, my princess,' he says and kisses me tenderly, 'I love you,' he says, retracting back.

'I love you too!' I say as I watch him disappear in the distance.

Entering the packhouse, I make my way to the large open lounge room where everyone is watching the news on the television. Everyone looks worried.

'What is it?' I ask, joining them.

'Two more humans were found drained of blood today,' Leo says.

My insides churn. Those poor people. How horrific to suffer such a fate.

The journalist continues to talk, 'The bodies of the deceased have been killed in the same tragic way the group of people had been earlier in the week. Although people reported wild wolves lurking near the scene of the first group of deaths. The coroner has been unable to match the bite bites with any know wolf or dog. Making this case more unusual and suspicious.'

Dad turns off the television, 'We have to hope that the humans don't find leads in the case, exposing that we werewolves and Lycans exist. The vampires must be doing this on purpose, but why?' my Dad says, pacing the lounge room, 'We only live peacefully in the world amongst humans because they don't know about us. We would be hunted if they ever found out about us.'

'Are we sure that these killings are by vampires?' I ask.

Dad stops pacing the floor and nods at Nathan, who approaches me and hands me an envelope.

The twins, Amara and Billy, hover around me to see as well. I open the envelope and pull out the photos. A young girl around my age is dismembered. Her skin is grey. Amara dry reaches and walks away, not able to see anymore. Billy follows her and gets her some water. The next photo shows two small circles close together. It's a bite mark. The next photo shows two men with the same injuries. Then an image of an older woman. I inspect the photos closely. They all seem to have the same injuries except for the older woman. I see long marks on her thigh. The same claw marks my family leave when they go hunting in their wolf or Lycan form on the deer they hunt. But the puncture marks and the fact they have been drained of blood would mean their deaths must be by vampires, right? I pass the photos back to Nathan, agreeing with my Dad that only vampires could have caused these killings.

The next morning Alpha Greg arrives.

'Alpha Maximus, I think we need to send more warriors out to the human territory. The amount we have is not enough, seeing as two more people were killed yesterday. These vile vampires must be captured and killed before the humans figure out the deaths are not caused by wild wolves. The last thing we need is for humans to discover supernaturals exist.'

'I agree, Alpha Greg. I will send a dozen more today. We must find the vampires and stop these killings before the humans discover us.'

'I will also organise a dozen more warriors from my pack to join yours.'

Dad and Alpha Greg walk outside, but their deep voice makes it clear that they are still discussing the situation.

'Coming to have breakfast with us?' Amara asks.

'Sure,' I reply and walk with her to the dining room.

My mother makes eye contact with me. She is so beautiful with her white hair and blue eyes.

'Make sure you practice your magic today, Lylah. You have barely been practising lately. I want to practice before you at least spend the rest of the day with Micah,' she says.

With a heavy sigh, I reply, 'I'll practice right now then,' I huff.

'Lifto Levitatious,' I say, annoyed, waving my hand toward a teaspoon.

My brothers and Billy laugh until my mother glares at them, and they stop.

'There, I practised, and like always, nothing happens,' I frown.

'Lylah, you need to believe in yourself. There's magic in you. I'm sure of it. Practising will help you connect with your magic. You are my precious daughter, and I believe wholeheartedly you can do this.'

Her face shows her concern. I drop my head in dismay, knowing she wants to see me awaken my magic. I leave the dining room without saying a word. I'm worried that as time passes, she will be disappointed to see that I do not possess any magic abilities like her.

Chapter 7

Returning to my room, my eyes rest silently on my collection of odd daggers. Most are blunt, and only a few have a subtle shine. Yet, no matter how old or blunt they are, I wouldn't get rid of them. They each represent a certain phase of me. Each tells a tale of how I had grown to become the skilled fighter I am today. I want to be a pack warrior one day, even if I'm also a Luna.

Staring at my dull collection taunts the warrior in me. My hands flinch as they urge to hold and flourish the daggers. I take my new dagger from my belt and run my fingers over the sheath.

I'm grateful Micah taught me all I know about fighting. The only downfall is that I cannot use my fighting skills against Tamara ad Vicky. It would affect my role and reputation at Storm Glenn when I am to become Luna if I fight them. Not only that, I don't want it to cause any trouble for Micah. I'm certain his father already dislikes me, although I've only met him once. His father, Alpha Varan, came to visit Micah last summer. He seemed to like me at first but then became short with words and withdrawn from the conversation when he learnt that I was still waiting for my wolf.

I'm craving Micah's company, but I know I must practise spells before seeing him. I place the book of spells and a candle on the ground. I light the candle and hover my hands on either side of the candle, 'Dimulous,' I say. The candle casually flickers but stays alight.

I repeat the word many times, flicking my hands towards the candle, even standing and spinning myself at the candle. The gust of air I made from twirling towards it wouldn't even extinguish the flame.

'This sucks!' I say, falling back onto my bed.

A knock on the door rudely interrupts my moment of frustration.

My mother, Hope, pokes her head in and smiles when she sees the spell book and candle on the floor, 'You've been practising, I see?'

'Yup, and as usual, I'm nailing it,' I say sarcastically, not even budging from my strewn position on the bed.

My mother approaches, flings herself onto my bed, looks up, and squints. Then, after a moment, she asks, 'I want to know what is so interesting about your ceiling?'

My bad mood begins to dissipate as I grin and turn my face to look at her, 'Nothing, Mum, I'm just frustrated that magic wants to be difficult for me,'

'I see,' She sits up properly and looks down at me. 'I was going to wait until your birthday through the week, but I feel you should have it now,' she says.

I sit up and raise my eyebrow in curiosity. Another early birthday present. 'Mum, you don't have to get me anything. You being my mum is a present in itself,' I say.

'Oh, sweetheart. What have I done to be blessed with such a sweet daughter?' she says, wrapping her arms around me for a hug.

Mum breaks the hug and holds her hands out, 'Materialise,' she says, and a slim box appears across the palm of her hands.

I take the box from her hand, 'Are you sure you want me to open it now?'

'Yes, Lylah, I want you to open it now,' she smiles.

I slowly lift the lid to see a brown wooden wand. The handle has intricate patterns carved into it, 'Is this a wand?' I ask in awe.

Mother nods her head.

I take the wand from the box, hold it to the light, inspect it, and nod.

'Thanks, Mum, I love it,' I say and hug her.

'Let's try it out,' she says and sits next to the spellbook and candle next to the floor. I sit back in front of the candle. Instead of using the spell to dim the flame, I try the opposite spell to make the small flame light up my whole chamber, 'Illumini,' I say, slowly waving the wand over it.

My mother watches the candle nervously, 'Keep trying, sweetheart,' she says.

'Illumini,' I repeat a few times.

'Try another spell,' she says encouragingly.

'Dimulous,' I say, flicking my wand towards the candle. Nothing happens.

'Dimulous,' I say again and tap the candle with the wand's tip. Again, nothing.

'You just keep trying no matter what, okay, sweety?' Mum says.

'Okay,' I sigh.

My mother takes in my frown and then smiles. 'How about you go see Micah now since you have been practising magic all morning?' she suggests.

My frown turns into a smile, 'Thanks, Mum!'

I quickly run to my mirror, neaten my clothes and kiss my mum on the cheek before running out the door. I unzip my hoodie and place the wand into the hidden pocket whilst I race through the large hallways and down the stairs to the heavy front door.

I jog towards Micah's house and find him along the walking track heading to my place. He opens his arms as I run towards him and leap up. He catches me and spins around, and falls back onto the ground. We kiss and laugh between kisses and cuddles and playfully roll again, so I'm on top of Micah.

'You won't believe what my mother gave me for my birthday,' I smile.

'Oh, aren't you a spoilt one? Another early present,' he smirks.

'Yup, I can't help it. I'm just so cute and adorable, you know?' I say playfully.

Micah rolls and pins my hands above my head and begins a trail of kisses from my neck to my lips. My back arches from the pleasant sensations.

'Cute, adorable, beautiful, smart. You are everything, Lylah,' he says.

He releases my wrists. I instantly pull his face to mine. I kiss him, and I take control of the kiss this time. His lips are warm and soft. They part slowly, allowing my tongue to slip inside. My tongue dominates his. I hear and feel his wolf growl through his chest in satisfaction.

We part and remain gazing into each other's eyes for a few moments.

His eyes are black from his wolf and full of lust.

'So, what is this gift your mother gave you?' he asks, placing a kiss on my forehead. His eyes return to sable as he subtly takes back control of his wolf.

I smile and sit up, 'Let's go by the waterfall, and I'll show you.'

Micah nods and undresses to shift. He lowers as I climb up on his back and hold on to his clothes. Micah races through the woods until we arrive at the waterfall. I climb down, and he shifts. As he dresses, I unzip my hoodie and pull my wand out, waiting to show him.

Micah turns around and smiles, 'A wand?' he asks.

'Yep.'

'That's pretty cool,' he says, stepping closer. I hand him the wand for him to inspect.

'Hand carved. I like it,' he says, handing it back.

'Wands are supposed to help with magic. I think Mum is hoping it will help awaken mine.'

'Your mother doesn't have a wand, though?' Micah says, confused.

'Nor does my grandmother, but that's because they are in full control of their magic and highly experienced. Wands are optional when you become as magically strong as they are,' I explain.

'Do you want to practise some magic with it now?' Micah asks.

'I suppose I could,' I reply, looking for something to practise magic on.

I watch the water come crashing down from the waterfall onto the rocks and flow down the river.

'Maybe I'll try a water spell?' I say.

Micah smiles and nods.

I pull my sleeves up, tilt my chin higher and clear my throat, 'Aqua Bedew,' I say.

I manoeuvre the wand differently as I repeat the words flicking, flourishing, twirling, and nothing happens.

Micah can see I'm becoming frustrated, 'Hey, you did well. How about we practice throwing your rusted daggers at some trees?' he smiles.

'A man that knows the very words to my heart,' I say, clutching my chest.

Micah laughs and playfully lifts me over his shoulder. I squeal as he runs through the woods until we arrive at our training spot.

Chapter 8

Micah places me down. I pull half a dozen old daggers out from different areas of my clothing and begin to aim and toss them one by one at the trees.

As usual, each blade lands an inch away from where I wanted it to go. I pull the daggers out and hand them to Micah so that he can have his turn. Each time he throws, they land an inch on the opposite side to where mine landed. Micah shrugs.

I giggle. Micah turns and pulls me close against his body. He gives me a mischievous look and begins to waltz. Micah is an amazing dancer. He is good at everything, to be honest. Fighting, schooling, especially maths and science, dancing, cooking. He is perfect at everything he does and perfect in every way. His kind, sweet personality. His face that the Gods must have chiselled themselves. His sable brown eyes which remind me of Autumn. His scent, oh Gods, his scent sends the cauldron inside me bubbling.

I continue to follow his lead. Our feet move swiftly together and our eyes glimmer, gazing at one another. Micah twirls me around, and we sway, step, and weave in and out. Micah suddenly stops dancing and presses me as close as possible against his body. His eyes linger on me seductively, and his lips crash against mine. Our tongues make love while my hands creep up his shirt and feel his masculine pecs. His hands also find their way under my shirt, one hand grips my waist tight, and his other hand caresses my back.

We part, breaking the kiss, only to avoid passing out due to lack of air. Otherwise, we would probably stay like this forever and never break the kiss.

'Lylah, I love you so much,' he whispers, keeping eye contact.

My body wants to melt further into his arms, but because I physically can't, I respond by caressing his cheek and softly rubbing the tip of my nose against his, 'I love you too, Micah,' I say endearingly.

We kiss again, but slower. As we part, Micah winks, walks over to the tree, pulls the daggers out, and returns to stand in front of me.

'Lylah, you're a born fighter, and I've always admired your passion to become a warrior for your pack. These,' he holds the daggers against my chest and swiftly withdraws the dagger he made for me from my leather baldric and stares at it. 'These are your best friends. Keep them close to you at all times,' he says in a serious tone.

'You know I always have them with me,' I say, reaching out and taking the dagger he made me. I flourish the dagger with my fingers and swiftly insert it back into its sheath and place it back into my baldric.

'Without your wolf and magic and if your family or I'm not nearby. You only have your fighting skill and these daggers to defend yourself and keep safe. I could never live with myself if any harm ever came to you,' he says.

I give Micah a solemn look and decide to show off my fighting skills to reassure him that no one could ever physically harm me. I move slowly away from him, shift my right leg forward from my left in a fighting stance, and swing the dagger to my right and back to my left, repetitively with speed. Then, as quick as lightning, I throw it up in the air and tumble forward, landing steadily in a crouching position. I hold my right hand up, catching my dagger that returns from the air. I place it back in my baldric and do a backflip. I land steadily on both feet, pull my old daggers from my boots, and throw them towards Micah, who doesn't flinch. They fly past either side of his head, missing his ears by an inch and strike the tree behind him. Reaching for my good dagger again, I dart towards a tree with haste.

A flashback suddenly consumes me. Within a moment, the tree splits into two and forms into Vicky and Tamara. They stand in front of other school students who also like to taunt me with constant bullying.

They all turn and point their fingers at me.

'Freak, freak,' The words echo through my mind. My legs stop in their tracks. I can't move.

'She's a freak. She's not a wolf,' a voice sounds behind me. I look back to see other students standing in pairs, whispering to each other.

'You don't belong here. You're not one of us.'

'Freak.'

'She needs to leave and live amongst the humans where she belongs.'

'Show us your wolf, Lylah! Oh wait, that's right, you don't have one!' Vicky laughs.

Tamara stands before me and glares, 'Being so weak that you have no wolf and cannot even cast a simple spell like your mother. Your family must be so disappointed and ashamed of you,' Tamara smirks.

My mind spirals as the taunts continue all around me. I steel myself refusing to give them the satisfaction of one single tear.

'She's supposed to be the daughter of Alpha Maximus, a powerful Lycan and Alpha,' a voice echoes.

'Yet, he created a worthless freak! He mustn't be as powerful as they say he is,' another says.

A slow but intense moment of pain and shame continues as I hold on to my anger. My fists clench, and I shake. I could easily break their arms or force them to the ground with one blow to the face. But doing so would make things worse for me. I can't risk hurting them and affecting Micah's reputation and my position as his Luna. Other than joining the warriors in his pack and becoming Luna. Being by his side for the rest of my life is all that matters to me.

A loud growl erupts, silencing everyone as Micah walks up behind me.

'Get away from Lylah now! Before I rip your heads off,' he growls. Everyone begins to back away and dissipate into the main building.

'Lylah, Lylah. Are you okay?' he says, gently shaking my shoulders. 'Lylah!' he yells louder.

I'm Instantly back in reality and realise I had a flashback. I look up at Micah with a sad look.

'You completely zoned out. You were calling yourself a freak and that you don't belong here, amongst many other things,' Micah frowns. 'You're not a freak,' he adds softly. 'You are my whole world Lylah,' he says and wraps his arms around me.

'I'm sorry, I don't know what happened. I suddenly had a flashback to that day I was bullied outside the front building at school,' I explain.

'One day, when I am Alpha, I will make them all pay for how they treated you,' he says.

'I don't want it causing you trouble, Micah. It's best you just leave it.'

'I don't care what trouble it brings me, Lylah. You are suffering as we speak from the effects of the bullying. I will personally deal with Vicky and Tamara myself,' he says.

My heart flutters that Micah wants to help give me closure and deal with my bullies personally.

We climb the large boulders to sit on a tall ledge. Once we reach the top, we lean into each other and hold hands. Micah and I watch the sunset.

'Tell me about Storm Glenn. What does it look like?' I ask.

'It's very different compared to here. It's quiet, serene and lush here. We are surrounded by nature, birds, deer, pigs, and other animals. It's so beautiful. It's village-like with its vast fields and forests, whereas Storm Glenn is very loud and busy in a modern environment. There are people everywhere who always seem to be in a rush. It's full of modern houses and roads with small gardens. Large stores and many to shop in. It's no different to a human town. I swear my pack acts more human than they do wolf,' he sighs.

'You don't like Storm Glenn?'

'I do, but if I was, to be honest, I much prefer it here,' he smiles at me, 'But perhaps it's because I'm with you,' he winks.

'I worry your pack won't like me,' I say, fiddling with my fingers.

'Of course, they will. Everyone in Storm Glenn will love you, Lylah.'

'But, your father?' I say and look at him with sadness.

'Don't worry about my father. He will come to his senses eventually.'

'If you say so,' I reply, unconvinced.

Micah immediately notices my eyes change to a dark blue. He holds my chin delicately with his fingers.

'I promise you, Lylah. One day my father with have the utmost honour and respect for you.'

I curl my fingers through his, and my eyes are now light blue again.

Chapter 9

Dark clouds fill the night sky, and it begins to rain heavily on us.

I look down the slope of rocks and frown, 'Be careful when you climb down, Micah. It's slippery,' I caution him.

'I'll be fine,' he smiles. 'Can you see anywhere we can take cover?' he asks.

I look around, but the moonlight is shrouded by the dark clouds blocking any light. As a result, it's pitch black all around me.

'I can't see anything, no wolf remember?'

'Oh, yeah. Sorry, I sometimes forget you can't see like the rest of us in the darkness.'

Micah takes my hand, leading me to the ledge. He slides down onto the first boulder and reaches out to lift me down. Once we reach the third boulder, he sets me down. A loud crack of thunder strikes nearby. I scream, slip and fall.

'Lylah!' Micah yells and reaches out to grab my arm, but it's too late. I fall into darkness, slamming into boulders on my way down. When I'm finally still, I feel my entire body ache, stinging with pain.

I groan in agony. A warm liquid trickles down my face, and there is a metallic taste in my mouth.

'Lylah, oh Goddess, Lylah!' Micah says, falling to his knees beside me.

The rain becomes more ferocious. Each drop feels like a prick of a needle. Micah hovers over me to help protect me from the weather. I groan in pain again as he carefully lifts me and holds me against his chest. He then runs towards an alcove in the trunk of a gigantic tree.

It only provides some protection, but it's the only form of shelter that is nearby. Micah faces me. His back is taking the brunt of the weather, shielding me from the rain and strong wind.

'Lylah, is anything broken?' he asks as he scans my body for injuries.

The wind is howling ferociously. I can barely hear what Micah is saying. It's times like this I'm annoyed that I don't have a wolf. I'd be able to hear what he is saying. My head is pounding, and although I can't see anything, everything is becoming darker. I black out, falling limp against Micah.

As I wake, I feel something slimy tracing along my forehead. My hands instinctively try to push whatever it is away. I feel fur between my fingers and heavy breathing as drops of slime dribble down my face. Finally, my eyes open to see Micah in his wolf form licking my face with his huge slobbery tongue. The storm has passed, and the sun is shining on us.

'Argh! Gross Micah, stop!' I say, shoving him away. He whimpers and sits like a good obedient dog. I look down to find I'm only wearing a bra and undies. I blush and quickly cross my arms to cover myself. 'Micah! Where are my clothes, and why am I covered in drool?' I growl.

He whimpers again and shifts into his human form. I glare at Micah for the first time in history.

'Lylah, don't look at me like that,' he sulks. 'I'm sorry, but I had to remove your clothes to help mend all your wounds,' he says.

In saying that, I realise I'm nowhere near as much in pain as I was during the storm. My eyes scan my arms and legs, and then I feel my head to find most of the wounds have healed or at least half healed. I give Micah a confused look.

'Werewolf saliva is meant to help heal wounds,' he shrugs. 'Now, let me shift back into my wolf and finish licking those wounds for you,' he says as he is about to shift.

'No!' I shout, 'I mean, no, thank you. I think I'm at my limit of your saliva for the day,' I say, flicking a handful of it from my face onto the ground.

Micah grins, shuffles over to me, pulls me onto his lap, saliva and all and begins to stroke his fingers through my hair.

'You had me so worried. As soon as you blacked out, you wouldn't wake up no matter what I tried. So, I stayed awake all night until the storm passed. Which, of course, was right before the sun started to rise.'

My body stiffens, 'We've been out all night! My parents will be so worried!' I panic.

'I would have mind-linked them, but I couldn't because I'm not part of this pack.'

'It's okay. My parents will understand. The main thing is we are both okay,' I smile.

Micah cups my face, placing the most delicate sweet kiss on my lips.

'Lylah,' he says.

'Micah,' I reply.

We share a moment of silence, holding each other.

'I better get you back home to your parents,' Micah says.

'You're right. We better get going now.'

Micah helps me to stand, but my knees buckle with pain. He catches me before I fall.

'If you let me finish licking the rest of those wounds, you'd be able to walk by yourself,' he says.

I roll my eyes, 'And what, drown in dog slobber?' I huff. 'I think not!' I smirk.

Micah gives me a look of shock and horror, 'Dog slobber? I'm not a domesticated dog. I'm a werewolf,' he says, puffing his chest out. We both burst into laughter, and Micah begins to carry me home.

Halfway home in the middle of the woods, a search party finds us.

'Lylah!' Amara shouts, racing towards me. I can see her parents, Sally and Nathan, following behind her. 'Are you okay? What happened? Your parents are beside themselves with worry. They half the whole pack searching everywhere for you,' she says.

'I'll mind-link them and let them know we have found you,' Nathan says.

Micah nods.

'I slipped and fell off a small cliff during the storm. So, we had to stay put until the storm passed,' I explain.

'That storm was pretty crazy. I couldn't sleep, so Billy stayed with me by the fire, and we drank hot chocolate all night. Until your frantic parents made everyone start searching for you,' she laughs.

'Sorry,' I say, feeling bad I interrupted her night with Billy.

'It's okay. I'm just glad you're safe,' Amara smiles and leans in to hug me.

Theo and Billy come running towards us.

'Lylah, you're okay?' Theo says, relieved to see me.

'Yeah, I'm okay. I slipped, fell, and we were stuck in the storm.'

'Let's get you home then,' he says.

We are almost home, and Amara begins to twirl around in circles, humming to herself. She suddenly slips and yelps in pain.

'Amara!' Billy says and drops to his knees in front of her. Sally and Nathan also run to her aid.

'My ankle,' she says.

Billy holds her foot up to see her swollen ankle and frowns, 'I think it's sprained, but since you're a werewolf, it should be fully healed by tonight,' he says and lifts Amara to carry her home.

'Oh, thank you, Billy,' she grins, all giddy and happily wraps her arms around Billy's neck.

Everyone around tries not to smirk. The chemistry between Amara and Billy is just as obvious as the chemistry between Micah and me.

As we arrive home, my father barges out the front door, sending it flying across the nearby garden bed. My mother steps out behind him with her hands on her hips, looking at the heavy door in her garden. But when she sees me, the door is no longer a problem. They run towards me, and my Dad takes me from Micah's arms and hugs me very tight.

'My baby girl! We were so worried!' he says, squeezing me.

'Dad, I can't breathe, and I'm not a baby,' I say,

'Even when you are forty, you will still be my baby girl,' he says, lessening his grip. 'What happened? Were you hurt? Is that why your clothes are covered in blood? And why are you so slimy?' my dad asks.

Micah scratches the back of his head nervously. It's obvious he doesn't want to help me answer these questions. I don't blame him, though. My Dad is a Lycan, after all.

Chapter 10

When I explained to my dad that I was covered in Mica's slobber to help my wounds heal, the look on my Dad's face was classic. Except for the part where he dropped me when he realised he was touching Micah's saliva. Thankfully with Micah's swift movements, he was able to catch me. My mother was so mad at Dad that she even asked Sally to fetch her the frying pan. My Dad retreated quick-smart. My mother is the only person I have ever seen my father fear. Seeing him bolt inside the packhouse was hilarious.

Micah carries me to my room and into the bathroom. My mother follows.

'I'll come back later to check on you,' Micah says and places a kiss on my forehead.

'Okay,' I smile, happy knowing I will see him again today.

Sally enters my room and prepares my bed and a fresh nighty, while Bella brings up a bowl of hot soup and buttered bread for me to eat.

My mother helps me and unzips my hoodie. She frowns at the baldric I'm wearing and the shiny silver sheath inserted into it.

'Lylah, where did you get this baldric? And is that a new knife?' she asks, not surprised.

Knowing I can't hide it from her any longer, I take the sheath out of the baldric, withdraw the dagger, and flourish it with my fingers.

'It's my birthday gift from Micah,' I say proudly. 'The baldric, I found whilst exploring some of the many rooms we never use.'

I place the dagger in my mother's hands. She glides her fingers over it, 'Is this part silver?' she asks. 'You know Silver is deadly to werewolves, Lylah? Wounds from silver won't heal quickly and only at a human rate which increases the chance of killing werewolves. As beautiful as it is, I'm not sure your father would approve of you having such a weapon.'

'I think Micah made it for me to protect myself from all beings, including werewolves. Rogues do exist, you know, Mum?' I retort.

'Lylah, just don't show it to other pack members. It might cause some trouble in the pack if they know you are carrying a weapon that consists of silver.'

'You mean you aren't going to take it from me?' I say, surprised.

'Lylah, I must have taken a dozen daggers from you over the years only for you to somehow end up with an even bigger collection,' she says and pulls my shirt up over my head.

She sighs as she sees three old daggers and my wand tucked into the waist of my leggings.

I bite my lip with guilt as I pull them out and place them beside the bathroom sink. I then grin at my mother as I withdraw the rest of my daggers from my boots.

She narrows her eyes at me and places her hands on her hips, giving me a silent look that says it all.

'Mother of wands,' she says and helps me into the large wooden tub.

She helps to scrub all the dirt and dried blood from my body and, of course, to her dismay, Micah's saliva.

Now washed and dried, she pulls the nighty over my head, helps me to bed, and brings the tray of soup and bread to me.

'Thanks, Mum. I'm sorry that I worried you so much last night.'

'I know, sweety. I'm just relieved you are okay and had Micah with you. Now eat your soup and have a rest,' she says and leaves my chamber.

I guzzle the soup and bread up, roll over and instantly fall asleep. As I wake, I feel my head on something warm that slowly rises and falls. My arm is draped over as well, hugging it tightly. My eyes flutter open, and I tilt my head to see Micah's sable eyes and his dimpled smile.

'I hope my princess is feeling better?' he asks.

I stretch my arms and sit up, 'I'm feeling much better. I think all my wounds are healed. I don't feel any more pain,' I say, inspecting myself only to find small bruises around my knees but feel no pain.

'You slept all day and night,' Micah smiles and sits up.

'Is it really the next day?'

'Yup,' he says.

'Wands!' I say and jump out of bed.

'That means tomorrow is my birthday!' I say, throwing my fist into the air. I turn to face Micah, who is smiling. I leap onto the bed, straddle him, and cup his face, 'Tomorrow, Micah! Tomorrow is the day we will officially be mates. I just know it!' I beam.

Laughing happily, Micah hugs me, and with our outburst of excitement, we fall off the bed together. I land on Micah, and we only laugh further, then roll across the floor, kissing each other.

A knock on the door interrupts us. Leo and Theo enter and smirk as we get up from the floor on the other side of the bed and straighten ourselves up.

'Mum and Dad told us to make sure you are up, to join us for some family breakfast,' Theo says.

'I'm up,' I blush, brushing my messy bed hair with my fingers.

'So we see,' Leo laughs.

'We will see you downstairs shortly then,' Leo and Theo say in unison and leave the room.

I run over to my wardrobe while Micah puts his shirt on. I rummage through my clothes and grab fresh undergarments, leggings, a shirt and a hoodie. Then, I race into the bathroom and change. Once I'm ready, I find Micah waiting in the hallway outside my chamber for me. He pats his shoulder and smiles. I leap onto his back, and he piggybacks me all the way downstairs.

Laughing, we enter the dining room, and Micah helps me down.

'How are you feeling, baby girl?' my father says.

'Thanks to Micah and some rest. I'm feeling great,' I say, kissing my dad on the cheek.

I look down at the newspaper on the table before him and take it.

'Serial Killer or Feral Wolves? Investigation continues over the two incidents that saw an entire family killed at a gathering and the couple killed who had gone on their regular nightly walk,' I read out loud and lean over to take a slice of toast on my Dad's plate and bite into it. 'So, does that mean there haven't been any more killings since the second one?' I ask with a mouthful of toast.

My Dad crosses his arms and narrows his eyes at the toast I'm eating, 'Thankfully, no, and Alpha Greg and the warriors have been discreetly patrolling the areas where they were killed and the outskirts of that town. Whoever was responsible seems to have moved on.'

'That's good, then,' I reply.

'As long as they don't go killing humans elsewhere, that's when it will be fine,' he says. It's clear he is still very concerned about the perpetrator.

My mother clears her throat, 'So, changing the subject to something more pleasant. Your eighteenth birthday is tomorrow,' she says with a smile and looks between Micah and me.

'I'm so excited!' I say.

'We're all excited,' Amara says, 'I've even packed my bag, ready for camping tomorrow,' she laughs.

'Whereabouts are we camping?' Leo asks.

'By the waterfall, I was thinking,' Micah says.

Everyone nods and agrees.

Chapter 11

Once we finish breakfast, I take Micah's hand and walk through the corridors and up the vast amount of steps until we reach the open terrace at the top of the North Tower.

'Practising spells?' Micah guesses.

'Yep,' I say.

We sit together on the stone bench. Micah holds the book for me while I wave my wand repeating incantations and spells.

'Visionous Memorious!' I say firmly, holding my wand.

'Tremendous Nebulus!' I say, flicking the wand.

Nothing but a natural cool breeze blows past my face.

'Focus, Lylah,' I say.

I face the small pot plant, pull my sleeves up, and wave my wand, 'Lifto Levitatous,' I repeat a few times in different tones.

After an hour of failed attempts at casting spells, I sigh and turn to Micah, 'Let's do something else,' I suggest.

'What do you want to do?'

I tap my foot and look around in thought and an idea springs to life, 'Catch me,' I smile.

'Catch you?' Micah says, confused.

I shake my head yes, race from the open terrace back into the tower, and run down the stairs. I hear Micah running behind me. I skid across the foyer at the bottom of the steps and head through a corridor. My hair bounces around, falling loose from its ponytail. I turn my head as I continue to run to see Micah a few metres behind me. Leo and Theo are down the opposite end of the corridor talking. They stiffen and quickly part against the wall as they see me racing towards them with no sign of slowing down. I giggle and laugh, and Micah almost manages to snatch me a few times but misses. Making it to the kitchen, I bump into Beth, who spills the bowl of flour on herself.

'Sorry!' I say, trying not to laugh and using the huge kitchen island to keep distance between Micah and me. But, as soon as I go left, he goes right to catch me. So I pretend to go right but sneak under the island and race out of the kitchen through the large hall.

'Sneaky move,' Micah shouts behind me.

I turn and poke my tongue out, then continue running. I enter the round study, where my father, Nathan and Alex sit, nonchalantly drinking scotch, paying no attention to me jumping over my Dad's chair and climbing onto the window ledge, laughing. They are used to my rambunctious personality and shenanigans. I push the stained glass window open and turn to see Micah jump over my father. I squeal, turn and jump out the window, landing softly on the grass only a foot from the ledge. I hear Micah land behind me, so I run to the stable. A moment after, I enter. Micah catches me, and we fall onto the hay laughing, which leads to us kissing for a moment.

Puffed out, we lay on our backs in the hay and try to catch our breaths. We turn our heads to look at each other and laugh.

'Did you see the bowl of flour go flying and land all over Beth?' I ask.

'I think Beth was going to use that to make your birthday cake,' Micah chuckles.

'Oops,' I giggle.

We return to the packhouse, and we help Beth clean up the flour and apologise.

'Young love,' Beth huffs. 'It makes you crazy, I always say, but no one even listens to me,' she says, pottering around the kitchen and taking a mixing bowl.

'So, you're not mad at me, Beth?' I ask her.

'Mad at you, Lylah? Never,' she smiles, potters over to Micah, and pinches his cheek. 'How is my handsome lad going these days?'

Micah rubs his pinched cheek, 'I'm always good, especially when I'm around Lylah,' he says.

'Good answer,' Beth says and resumes to the island and stirs a mixture in the bowl.

***

Micah wraps his arms around me and pulls me into his chest, 'I'll be back first thing in the morning, Lylah. As soon as the sun rises, I shall be here,' he says tenderly and places a kiss on my lips.

'I don't know how I am supposed to sleep tonight, knowing we are going to be fated mates tomorrow?' I say as soon as we break the kiss.

'I know. I'm excited as well. I can't wait to shout from the rooftops that you are officially mine,' Micah laughs.

'Micah, you wouldn't?' I laugh.

Micah bites his lip, gives me a mischievous look, and winks, walking backwards. I lean in the doorframe of the packhouse door with my arms crossed, each hand holding either elbow. Micah is now out of sight, but I remain and look at the moon for a while.

'Please, Moon Goddess, if you can hear me, please let Micah be my fated mate,' I say, and a tiny shooting star instantly soars through the sky, ever so quickly near the moon.

Any unease I was feeling has now gone. I smile, close my eyes and take in a deep breath of the night's cool air. Relaxed, I close the packhouse door, gingerly hum, and skip all the way along the corridors and up the stairs to my chamber.

As I enter my room, I hug the dagger Micah gave me before I set it down on my dresser. I'm probably the only girl who has daggers in place of hair brushes, fancy pins and perfumes. I laugh at the thought but then stop as I stare at myself and wonder how I would even look in a dress. It's been so many years since I wore one. I must have been around seven years old. It's the only time I can remember wearing one. It was yellow with white daisies, to my disgust. Afterwards, I would sneak into Theo and Leo's room and 'borrow' their trousers. My Dad couldn't stop laughing when I came stomping down the stairs with pants that were pulled up to my chest and wore a pillow case I put holes in and wore as a shirt. It was tucked into the pants, and I had tied a rope around my waist.

Everyone thought it was to keep my pants from falling, but I wore it, pretending it was a belt, and I would tuck sticks in there and pretend they were daggers.

Mother was never able to get me into a dress since that day. She had no choice but to buy me slacks and shirts as I refused to dress at all. I would run nude throughout the packhouse whilst she chased me down.

Removing my clothes, I stand sideways and take in my body, which has changed since I was a child. My hips and thighs are slightly curvy, my waist is small, and my bust is more noticeable. I could probably fit into some of my mother's dresses that would modestly show I'm far from a child but a woman now. The look on everyone's face if I wore a dress would be priceless. I shake my head of the thoughts, place my long-sleeved baggy white cotton nighty on, which is the closest thing to a dress I own and enter my bathroom to wash my face and brush my teeth.

Excitement once again overtakes me at the thought of finding out in a matter of hours that Micah and I are mates. I happily dance out of my bathroom, spinning and twirling in my room until I become too dizzy and land on my bed. Laughing and hugging myself, I squeal. Then I crawl up my bed and hop under the covers and face my terrace so I can watch the stars. The lace curtain flows up, and the wind caresses my skin.

The stars continue to flicker, and the moon watches over me until I fall asleep.

Chapter 12

'Lylah,' Micah calls out.

I wake as my name is being called. An alluring smell of Thyme and cedarwood drifts through my terrace and into my room. An overwhelming urge takes over my senses. I find myself subconsciously racing towards the terrace and clutching the stone rail. My body trembles with delight as I see Micah waiting eagerly below my balcony.

Our eyes instantly meet, 'Mate!' we say in unison. It feels as if we are the only two people that suddenly exist. Just when I thought I couldn't love Micah any more than I already do, my body explodes internally with vast feelings of overwhelming love. An urge to never be out of Micah's sight, an urge to always be by his side, an urge to touch him, an urge to make sweet love to him.

I feel a wholeness that I never knew needed filling. My heart beats rapidly as my eyes stare hungrily into Micah's. As Micah steps forward to climb up my balcony, my body has other plans and cannot wait for another second, longing for Micah's touch. I leap off the terrace, and Micah catches me with ease. Our bodies explode with tingles and heat from each other's touch. Our mouths crash against each other's lips, and the flame in my heart I always felt for Micah suddenly explodes into a furnace.

'Micah,' I moan as one of his hands finds its way up my thigh, and his other makes its way towards my breasts.

I jump up, wrapping my legs around his waist, and my fingers glide through his hair as we continue to kiss.

Suddenly I hear a commotion towards the front door of the packhouse. It's Leo and Theo shoving each other, trying to get outside.

They hi-five each other when they see us making out in the garden. Leo turns back to the door and yells up the corridor, 'Mum, Dad, they are definitely mates!'

Moments later, my parents and the entire packhouse, including Beth, run outside. Micah and I part and blush, embarrassed that everyone has come outside to find us making out.

My mother smiles, 'So, it's true? You are fated mates?' she asks.

Micah holds his finger up, signalling for them to wait a moment. He then lifts me bridal style and runs, carrying me inside the packhouse, up the stairs of the closest tower.

'What are you doing?' I giggle as he gently puts me down on the terrace. Micah replies with a grin, jumps onto the stone railing, and climbs the thick vines onto the roof.

'Micah!' I shout, worried he may fall.

Standing proudly on the rooftop, Micah takes a deep breath before shouting, 'The Moon Goddess has blessed me with the greatest gift in the world. She has given me Lylah as my true fated mate.'

Everyone cheers at Micah.

'Okay, Micah, now that you have shouted from the rooftops just like you said you would, I need you to come down to me where it's safe and maybe... kiss me,' I laugh.

Micah smiles and carefully climbs down. He grabs my waist and tilts me backwards, kissing me.

Holding hands, we run downstairs to rejoin everyone. My mother hugs me while my Dad shakes hands with Micah. Sally, Bella, Beth then Amara pull me in for a group hug and squeal in delight.

'I knew it, I knew it,' Amara says, squeezing me.

'I'm so happy for you,' Bella says.

'This is the best news!' Sally says.

'Happy eighteenth, Lylah! We are so happy Micah is your fated mate.' Leo and Theo say in unison.

My Dad mind-links the pack with the good news and for everyone to join us in the pack's hall for lunch.

Alex and Nathan pat Micah on the bad and congratulate him.

Pack members come running from their houses to the pack house to congratulate Micah and me and to celebrate in the hall.

I'm having the time of my life until I see Vicky and Tamara approaching. Their parents are not far behind them and look annoyed to be here. Their arms are crossed, and they walk like misbehaved children stomping their feet. I assume their parents have forced them to come since my Dad has mind-linked the entire pack to attend and celebrate.

Their parents glare at them. I can tell they are being scolded through a mind-link by the unimpressed looks on their faces.

Vicky stands in front of me with a glare and then purposely puts on her biggest fakest smile, 'Lylah, how nice that Micah is your mate. Congratulations,' she says through gritted teeth and storms off to the other side of the hall.

Tamara doesn't even make eye contact. Instead, her chin tilts up high, and she speaks sarcastically,
'Congratulations, Lylah. How wonderful,' she says, then stomps away to rejoin Vicky.

Their parents hug me and seem genuinely happy for me.

I'm suddenly overwhelmed by half a dozen other girls around my age,

'Has he marked you yet?'

'I bet he is a good kisser with those lips?'

'What does his scent smell like?'

'He is so handsome! He doesn't happen to have a brother by any chance?'

They all giggle and act as if they are best friends of mine when they have never really paid attention to me before. Micah can sense that I'm uncomfortable and approaches.

'Lylah, my princess,' he says and holds his hand out.
'Will you dance with me?' he asks.

I nod, taking his hand, and we begin to waltz around the hall. Everyone watches us as we gaze into each other's eyes. His hand on my waist is sending sparks throughout my body.

'My heart is beating so fast,' I say.

'Mine too,' Micah says, twirling me around, weaving me out, and then back in so my back is against his front. We sway for a few moments, and he twirls me around again and pulls me close to his chest again but this time facing him.

'I feel like I'm in a fairytale. You know, like the ones where the princess ends up with her knight in shining armour?'

'Hmm, I suppose you're right because I have ended up with my princess,' he smirks.

Micah leans in, kisses me passionately, and then whispers in my ear, 'I don't think I could ever get enough of you, my sweet Lylah.'

I blush and lean against his chest as we slowly sway for the rest of the song.

Everyone applauds, and we sit and gather at the long tables. Beth has cooked up a storm. Not an inch of the table is bare. The whole table is covered with platters and trays full of food.

'Micah,' my Dad says,

'Alpha Maximus,' he replies respectfully.

My Dad stands, and the hall becomes quiet, 'The last few years since you came into my daughter's life have been the happiest I have ever seen Lylah, and because of the immense happiness that you have given her. I am honoured that you are fated mates and that Lylah's dreams and prayers have been answered. I know you will make so many happy memories together,' he holds his cup high. 'To Micah and Lylah, fated mates, and to the Moon Goddess for making this possible!' he shouts proudly—everyone cheers, shouts and applauds.

We all eat, drink and dance until Beth enters the hall, pushing a serving trolley with a beautiful large purple three-tiered cake on top, covered in butterflies made from fondue. Micah stands behind me and wraps his arms around my waist as everyone sings Happy Birthday. I blow out the candles, 'Make a wish,' Micah whispers in my ear.

'Why make a wish when I have everything I could ever wish for right here?' I smile.

Micah kisses my cheek, and I cut the cake. We take a slice each and playfully take a bite from each other's slice.

'There's only one thing that tastes better than this chocolate cake,' Micah says.

'Oh? And what would that be?' I ask.

Micah places his slice of cake down, 'Your lips,' he says and pulls me into his chest and kisses me.

Chapter 13

Micah lays on my bed and watches me as I pack my bag, placing a change of clothes and a torch on top. Then, noticing cake smeared on my hoodie, I laugh, pull it off, and toss it aside before grabbing a fresh one from my wardrobe and putting it on.

'Ready to go camping? It's going to be nightfall soon, and we haven't even left yet,' Micah laughs.

'Yeah, well, it's not my fault Dad had my party drag out all afternoon,' I reply.

'Alpha Maximus was just so excited for you, for us, that we are fated mates. He was definitely making the most of it and was very proud to show us off. It was also a great party,' Micah laughs.

'Yeah, I'll admit it was lots of fun,' I say, swinging the bag over my shoulder, 'Ready?' I ask.

'I'll carry your sleeping bag. Do you want me to carry that bag too?' Micah asks, pointing to the bag over my shoulder.

'Nah, I'm a big girl. I can carry this myself,' I say and kiss his cheek.

Micah smiles and nods, then follows me downstairs to where we find everyone waiting. No one but Sally and Amara has packed a bag.

'Are you not bringing any supplies?' I ask my Dad and brothers.

'We were just going to sleep in our Lycan forms to keep warm and hunt down a rabbit if we get hungry,' Leo says.

'Of course,' I say, rolling my eyes.

'What about you, Mum, and Bella?'

'We were just going to shift into our wolves, and I can use magic to start a fire, so I don't need supplies,' Mother shrugs.

'I was going to go wolf mode too,' Bella laughs nervously.

Sally walks over to me and drapes her arm over my shoulder, 'It's okay, Lylah. I packed a human survival pack to get us through the night since I don't have a wolf either, nor do I wield amazing, magical powers like your mother. Us humans have got to stick together, you know?' she laughs and unzips her bag. 'But don't fret, my dear Lylah, I have lighters, torches, rope, duct tape, tarp, whistles, glow sticks, batteries, wire, cable ties-'

'Um, Sally, my sweetheart. We are only camping for one night, and you have packed the essentials of what a serial killer would bring,' Nathan points out.

'What can I say? I'm human. Better to be safe than sorry?' Sally laughs.

I turn to Amara, 'Why have you packed a bag then? Are you not going to sleep in your wolf form?' I ask her.

'Oh, um,' Amara unzips her bag to show nothing but snacks, popcorn, marshmallows, chips, biscuits, you name it. 'Someone had to pack the essentials,' she laughs.

I shake my head, smiling at her, 'Okay, let's get out of here then.'

Micah shifts, I climb on his back, and he bolts into the distance. My white hair bounces in the wind. I can hear the scurry of the others in their Lycan or wolf form racing along with us. They are too fast for me to see them.

We arrive near the waterfall before nightfall, giving us time to collect sticks for a fire.

'Inferno Flamo,' my mother says, starting the fire.

Micah sits on my left, and Amara sits on my right and hands me some long sticks and a bag of marshmallows.

'Thanks!' I say to Amara and pass Micah a stick.

'You're welcome,' she hums and gives a stick to Billy as soon as he sits next to her.

We poke the marshmallows on the end of the sticks and hover them over the fire.

'We should tell stories?' Theo suggests sitting on the opposite side of the fire to me.

'Maybe Dad could tell us his story of how he met our mother?' Leo says.

'Oh, boy,' Nathan says nervously, scratching the back of his head and giving Alpha Maximus and Alex a glance.

'I'm not sure if you should know in detail how we met. It might be too upsetting?' Dad says.

'But you and Mum are here now, together,' I say. 'So we know you at least have a happy ending,' I smile.

'That's very true. If your father wants to share the more in-depth details of us finding each other, then I'm okay with that,' she smiles and nods at my Dad.

Dad tells us how he came from being mateless and shunned and the last Lycan to now being with his true my, my mother Hope, and no longer being the last Lycan as he now has twin sons and then me, his daughter.

I can't stop staring at Micah and holding his hands. He also seems to be struggling to keep his hands to himself. While everyone is talking and laughing amongst themselves. I pull Micah's hand and gesture to follow me into the woods.

Once clear, Micah halts. 'Hop on,' he says and shifts. I climb onto his back, and he races through the trees. The moon is mostly blocked by clouds, so I can only manage to see what is directly in front of me. The breeze is cool across my skin, and I feel the odd leaf and debris whip past my ears from Micah's speed. Finally, Micah slows down and shifts back.

'We should be far enough away that they shouldn't disturb us,' Micah smiles.

I smile too, and notice he isn't redressing himself. We both have a look of hunger and desire in our eyes. I'm a few metres away from Micah. I slowly look him up and down, taking in every inch, every muscle on his body, along with his member standing very firm and salute. I stride slowly towards him. Once our faces are near, I remove my hoodie, pull my black tank top over my head and kick off my shoes.

Our lips are so close as our breathing heavys as I now remove the rest of my clothes, along with my many daggers. Micah's eyes turn black with hunger as he looks me up and down. We stay like this for as long as we can control ourselves.

Micah's hand caresses my arm, he leans in, and our lips brush a few times before our mouths devour each other. I grab his phallus, making him moan. Micah's fingers find their way between my legs and to my core. We moan as we touch and stroke each other for a while, taking in the moment and making it last. The moment we have been waiting years for, and a moment we never want to end. We both explode our moans echo, sending birds flying from the nearby trees. Micah lifts me, and I wrap my legs around his waist. My hands explore his muscular chest as he leans against a tree. Micah lays me down on the soft ground, strewn with leaves that have not long fallen.

We gaze into each other's eyes, 'I love you, Micah,' I whisper.

'I love you more than you'll ever know, Lylah,' whispers, and his length slowly enters between my legs.

I let out a gasp in pain and pleasure. Once Micah can sense the pain subside, he thrusts faster and harder. As we are about to climax, I see his teeth elongate. He is about to mark me. I tilt my head showing I've submitted to him and for him to mark me. Generally, the she-wolf would mark the other as well, but I can't as I don't have a wolf.

As I feel waves of pleasure ripple throughout my body, Micah bites down on my nape. The pleasure triples instantly. It's incredibly euphoric. I can feel Micah's warmth filling me, and we both moan again, this time sending any nearby deer and rabbits running from any bushes.

Micah rolls onto his back breathing heavily, 'That was amazing,' he says and takes my hand. He kisses it and places my hand on his chest.

I lean on my side, 'That was magical,' I smile, looking down into his sable eyes.

Micah gently pushes my hair over my ear and cups my cheek. I lean down, and we kiss passionately. I wince as he accidentally touches my mark, and we sit up.

'Here, let me help the pain,' he says, licking the mark.

It causes the heat between my legs to reignite, and the look on Micah's face says he knows it too.

'Micah?' I say, now touching my mark to find the pain is almost gone.

'Yes, my princess?' he asks.

'Does it bother you that I can't mark you?'

'No, and it will never bother me, Lylah. You know that,' he smiles.

'I love you, Micah,' I smile.

'I love you too, princess,' he replies and leans over me and kisses me across my collarbone and up my neck.

Micah suddenly pauses and sniffs the air. A concerned look appears on his face.

'What is it?' I ask.

'Get dressed. Something is coming our way. I can hear them and smell them. It's like nothing I've ever sensed before. It's dark and powerful, and there are many of them, whatever it is,' he says. 'Once you are dressed, jump on my back. We need to get back to the camp. There may be too many for us to take on.'

Dressed within seconds, I make sure my daggers are in reach. I climb onto Micah's wolf form, and we suddenly hear the sound of sticks snapping nearby and the cryptic sounds of creatures we have never heard before.

'M-Micah,' I stutter, sensing we're in trouble.

Chapter 14

The moon hides behind dark clouds. It's pitch black, whichever direction I look. I can't see anything. I can only feel Micah's soft fur I have clenched tightly in my hands.

'Micah,' I whisper as he gets down as low as possible. He looks around carefully and slowly as the creatures dash past us. Micah creeps backwards and begins to run in the opposite direction to the creatures. After a few minutes of running, we are further away from the campsite—Micah shifts and dresses.

'We will take the long way around, back to camp to avoid the creatures,' he says.

'What were they? What did you see?' I ask, panicked.

'I don't know what they were. There were at least a dozen of them, maybe more. They were dark and fast. Faster than any werewolf I have seen.'

'What do you think they want?' I ask.

'Death. That's all I could smell on them, old blood, fresh blood, the flesh of many,' Micah says. 'I thought I saw... never mind,' he says.

'Saw what? What did you see?' I ask.

Micah frowns as he makes eye contact with me, 'Red eyes,' he says.

'Red eyes? Werewolves and Lycans don't have red eyes. Not even rogues have them. So, what else could it be?' I ponder. Suddenly an overwhelming sense of fear takes over, and Micah places his hand on my shoulder and realises I have the same thoughts as him, 'Vampires?' I whisper to him.

Micah bites his lip and nods his head.

'We better get going, come on,' he says, gently pulling me behind him. We remain quiet, walking towards the camp being as stealthy as possible. I trip over a log, but Micah catches me.

'I can't see anything, Micah,' I whisper.

'It's okay, just keep hold of my hand and- '

Something bolts towards us and knocks Micah away from me. I can hear Micah struggling to fight the creature.

'Micah!' I say, withdrawing my dagger.

'Run, Lylah!' Micah yells.

'No! I won't leave you!' I yell, then gasp as I feel the creatures run past me. Towards Micah. 'No! Stay away from him! Get away!' I shout, swinging my dagger in the darkness.

I try to follow the sounds of Micah struggling and hear him shift. His wolf lets out a loud howl. He is calling for my father and the others for help. I can hear him snapping and snarling. Drops of blood spatter across my face as he bites a creature that lets out a hissing sound.

Micah whimpers in pain as he continues to fight. I'm close enough to Micah that I could feel him if I was to reach out. But I need to help fight. I kick and roll, and swing my dagger. I've injured a few of them, but I'm unsure if any are dead. I can't help but feel we are surrounded by even more. I stab one and then another. Then something or someone grabs my ankle and yanks me to the ground. My head hits a rock, but I ignore the searing pain and the blood trickling down my hair. I'm being dragged across the ground with speed. Sticks and rocks dig into me. Finally, I grab onto a tree trunk and yank myself from the creature's grip. I jump and land on my feet in a fighting stance. I can feel it, the creature breathing heavily in front of me, staring at me as if fascinated or intrigued by me.

'Why aren't you fighting me? What are you doing? What do you want?' I shout.

I hear Micah whimper from where I was earlier. I swing my dagger, piercing the creature in its arm. He hisses and steps back as I run back to Micah to help him. The creature I just stabbed now stands in front of me. I fall back, and as I try to stand, I scream as two red eyes look into mine. Its breath is rotten and sticky. I hear howls in the distance and know it's my family. I stab the creature in the neck and push it away, desperate to get to Micah.

I stand and run in the darkness towards him and trip. I cry out and grab my ankle, which is swelling. I bite down on a thick stick to help me through the pain as I stand and limp toward Micah and the creatures, stabbing as many creatures in my path. They begin to dissipate after a loud hiss is heard, and the clouds move just enough to let a little moonlight into the area. My eyes adjust. I can see blood everywhere but no bodies.

'Micah! Micah! Where are you?' I shout, looking everywhere. I halt as I see a tall shadowy figure with its back to me. It's wearing a black cape and is holding something against a tree. It's holding Micah up, but I'm not sure what it's doing to him. I drag myself towards them.

'Get away from him! Get away from Micah now!' I yell.

The vampire drops Micah to the ground and disappears further into the woods. Micah lays limp.

'Micah?' I say, lifting his head onto my lap and gasping when I see two puncture marks on his neck. He is deathly pale, and I realise the vampire has just been drinking Micah's blood.

Micah fights to keep his eyes open, and then with more Moonlight, I see his stomach has been shredded open. I burst into tears as I see his exposed organs. His left leg is barely attached, and he has bite wounds along his arms.

Micah makes some unsettling sounds and tries to take a deep breath.

I place my hands over his body, concentrate, and pray to the Moon Goddess to let me heal Micah. I can hear my parents' howl. They are almost here. I try holding my wand over Micah, sobbing profusely in hopes my wand will work. When I realised no magic would be coming to my aid, I burst into tears. Micah weakly takes my hand, squeezes it gently, and tries to talk. 'Shh, shh,' I say, crying. What feels like a myriad of tears, fall from my eyes onto Micah's face. 'You're going to be okay, Micah. You just need to save your energy, okay? My mother will be here any moment, and she will heal you,' I assure him and begin to hum while I comb my fingers through his hair.

'I'm dying,' Micah whispers and squeezes my hand.

'No, you're not, Micah!' I say sternly, shaking my head. 'You're not dying, you're not going anywhere, and you're not going to leave me. You are my fated mate. You are meant to stay with me forever. First, we're going to travel just like you wanted, then we will become Alpha and Luna of Storm Glenn and then,' I burst into tears even louder. 'And then we are going to have lots of babies. Beautiful babies. So, you can't die, even if you wanted to,' I cry.

'Don't cry, my sweet princess,' Micah whispers, 'I will always be here with you. I will always be by your side in spirit and have my happily ever after with you. But Lylah. Your life doesn't end here with me. More is waiting for you, and I want you to find it. You will go on adventures. I know you will find someone and fall in love all over again. I want you to find happiness. I want you to live again and know it's okay to be happy without me,' he whispers.

'Micah, I don't want anyone else. I only want you! I only love you! I will never love again, Micah. Only you can make me happy,' I cry.

I lean down, and we share a kiss. I wipe the tears from my face, and then I wipe the tears from Micah's face, and we spend the last moment gazing into each other's sombre eyes.

'Live and love again, my princess. I love you forever,' he says, and his head drops to the side.

'Micah?' I say and gently shake his shoulders. 'Micah!' I scream, but he doesn't move. He is dead.

I cradle my arms around him and rock as I scream and cry into him.

My parents and Theo, Leo, Nathan, Billy, Alex, and Amara, appear in their wolf and Lycan forms. Sally hops down from Nathan's back, and she is the first to run over to me as everyone else shifts back into human form.

Everyone approaches slowly, taking in the horrific scene. I look up to see my mother shaking her head at my father.

'Mother, please. Please heal him. There's still time!' I cry.

She looks at Micah's torn body and the puncture marks on his neck.

'I'm so sorry, Lylah, he has no blood left. His wounds… they….'

'You have to try!' I shout at her angrily.

My father places his hand on my mother's shoulder and nods for her to try even though he knows all the magic in the world could never bring Micah back.

Chapter 15

My mother hovers her hands over Micah, crying, while my father squats down to be eye level with me, and he grabs my face.

'Who did this to him? What happened?' he asks me. I can see the anger and heartbreak in his eyes.

'I couldn't see them at first. Even Micah struggled to see them. He said they were so fast. Faster than werewolves and smelt of death. There were so many of them, Dad. Their eyes…' I say, and my hands begin to tremble.

My Dad takes my hands in his and holds them firmly to cease the shaking.

'Keep talking, Lylah. We need to know,' he says,

'Their eyes were red like blood. I saw one. He was tall in a black cloak, and he was….' I take a few moments, feeling dizzy. 'He was drinking Micah's blood and only let him go when I heard your howls. The others with him had already fled before I could get a look at them. Vampires did this. They did this to my mate,' I say, bursting into tears again.

Billy and Leo are vomiting in the bushes from the gory sight of Micah's body. Nathan, Alex and Theo scan and search the area. At the same time, Amara and Sally comfort each other, crying.

My mother turns her attention to me and wipes the tears from her face, 'I'm sorry, Lylah. I'm so sorry,' she cries.

'No, your magic has to work. Micah has to be okay?' I tell her.

My parents somberly gaze at each other for a few moments before Dad kneels beside me. He tries to move Micah's head from my lap gently.

'No, what are you doing? He is my mate! You can't take him away from me. He is mine!' I yell.

'Sweety, your ankle might be broken. I need to move Micah so I can carry you home,' he explains.

'No! Don't touch me. Don't you dare touch me!' I say, punching his hands away from me. 'I'm not leaving Micah. You can't take him from me!' I shout, clinging onto his lifeless body as tight as possible.

Nathan approaches, 'Alpha Maximus, we've searched the perimeter. Other than blood, there are no bodies or sightings of any vampires. They have long gone. They must be fast to have gotten out of here this quickly,' he says.

'Thanks, Nathan. I need you to get Alpha Greg here straight away. Tell him the vampires are back and have killed Micah,' my Dad looks at me as I continue humming and rock Micah in my arms as if he is simply taking a nap. Dad takes a deep breath as he slowly looks over Micah's body and turns back to Nathan. His voice trembles, 'Tell Alpha Greg he will need to bring everything.'

'Yes, Alpha,' Nathan nods, shifts and runs to get Alpha Greg.

Theo brings me a bottle of water and wipes the tear from his cheek. He leans closer, waiting for me to take the water, but I hit it out of his hand, sending it flying a few metres away, and then I resume humming, looking down at Micah's peaceful face. Theo doesn't say anything. Instead, he quietly sits next to me and cries. Leo removes his shirt, places it over Micah's open stomach, and sits next to Theo.

Sally, Amara and Billy sit on my other side and cry. Amara holds my hand and leans her head on my shoulder to comfort me, 'I'm so sorry,' she sobs. I don't reply.

Alex paces back and forth, swearing and kicking a tree, whilst my Dad comforts my Mother. After a while, Nathan returns with Alpha Greg and a few of his pack members.

'Holy chaos! What in the world of wands!' he cries out. He can't believe Micah is dead. He lifts the shirt to assess him and just as quickly covers him up again.

'Micah, not Micah,' he says, falling to his knees. His hand runs down his face in disbelief and sadness. 'This is going to destroy Alpha Varan. Micah is his only son and his pride and joy.'

Alpha Greg looks at me, but I don't make eye contact. Instead, I continue to stroke my fingers through Micah's hair and rock. His pack members place a stretcher and a body bag on the ground and begin to put gloves on.

'Lylah,' Alpha Greg says, 'I'm so sorry. I cannot imagine what you must be feeling right now.'

I don't respond, but him mentioning that makes me realise I can no longer feel the sparks when I touch Micah's skin. My hand quickly touches my mark, only for me to feel its almost completely vanished.

'No. No, no, no!' I panic.

I claw at my neck as if digging into my skin will bring the mark back. Theo grabs my hands to stop any further bleeding.

'My mark! Please tell me it's still there?' I say to Theo.

He looks at the mark and wipes the fresh blood aside with his hand. He can only see two very faint scars. He looks at me, heartbroken and shakes his head.

'No!' I scream—Tears stream down my face. Theo pulls me into his chest and holds me. Alpha Greg helps his men to slide Micah's body into the unzipped bag.

'No!' I yell and push myself away from Theo. I lunge towards Micah's body, but Theo grabs me around the waist and pulls me back against his chest.

'He is mine! Micah is mine! You can't take him from me! I love him, please!' I beg as Theo tightens his grip. Everyone is a mess and cries. My mother tries to hug me along with Amara, but I push them away and continue to fight my way out of Theo's arms. Alpha Greg zips the bag and lifts it onto the stretcher. He and his men carry him away.

'You bastard! Bring him back! He is my mate. He is mine!' I yell.

I begin to hyperventilate, and the world begins to spin. I black out.

***

My father is carrying me home. I'm curled up against him. I can feel his heavy breaths of distress about what has happened to Micah. Even though I'm now awake, I feel so numb, so empty. I'm too weak to open my eyes. So I just remain as is. The sun is now rising.

'They were supposed to take over Storm Glenn. They were supposed to become parents and have a wonderful life together. How could this happen to them, to Micah, to our Lylah? They never deserved this fate,' he says.

'We will find the vampires and destroy them all,' Theo replies.

Alex approaches my Dad. 'We have sent the warriors to begin searching for the vampires again, as you asked, Alpha. We have doubled the number of warriors this time.'

'Good, I want every last vampire dead,' he says as he walks up the front steps of the pack house.

He stops in the doorway and turns to face everyone. 'Someone call for the pack doctor. Lylah is human. She can't heal quickly like the rest of us and one other thing. No one is to speak of this until I have informed Alpha Varan. I don't want him hearing second-hand that his son is dead. So I suggest you all get some rest. I will send for Alpha Varan to make his way here immediately.'

Alex shifts and runs towards town to fetch the doctor. Alpha Greg turns to his men. 'Take Micah to Kayla downstairs in the apothecary. She will probably go into shock, just like the rest of us. Tell her to prepare his body for burial as soon as she can. We don't want Micah's father seeing the extent of his wounds.'

My father nods, agreeing with Alpha Greg.

As my father enters the pack house, the others follow but separate, going to their rooms to mourn and rest. I'm carried upstairs and gently laid on my bed. My mother removes my boots and socks and sits beside me, and holds me while dad sits in the armchair and stares down at the floor in silence.

Later, Alex storms into my room with the pack doctor by his side.

'Alex has filled me in with what has happened. I'm so sorry to all of you for your loss. Micah was a true gentleman and was loved by everyone,' he says.

My Dad stands, 'Doctor Matlin, thank you for your condolences. Lylah has suffered quite a few injuries from the ordeal.'

'Yes, I see,' he replies and approaches my bed. Doctor Matlin looks me up and down, figuring out where to start. He gently lifts my foot. I flinch and pull my foot from his grip. Lylah has a sprained ankle. She should keep her foot elevated and avoid bearing as much weight as possible on her foot. She also has blood in her hair. Did she hit her head?' he asks.

I instantly have a flashback of my ankle being grabbed and yanked, making me fall to the ground, hitting my head on a rock. I subconsciously touch the back of my head and wince.

'Here,' my mother says, pointing to where I had just touched.

She helps me to sit up and turn to face her so Doctor Matlin can take a look. I begin to tremble, and tears slide down my cheek.

'She will need some stitches,' he says. He cleans the wound and gives me five stitches. 'I can see some wounds running down your shoulder. Is it okay if we remove your shirt?' he asks.

I nod.

'I'll wait outside your room,' my father says, leaving to give me privacy.

Chapter 16

My mother lifts the torn shirt from over my head and gasps when she sees three deep claw marks across my back. I didn't realise my back had been clawed through the fight. The doctor dabs the wounds with something cold and wet.

I bite my bottom lip, 'It stings,' I cry.

'I'm sorry, Lylah, but we must clean it to prevent infection,' Doctor Matlin says.

I never felt the wound until he began cleaning it. The stinging becomes a horrible burning pain. I roll onto my side and hug myself, 'Stop! It hurts too much,' I cry.

'Doctor, let me try and heal some of her wounds,' my mother says, stroking my hair.

'Of course, Luna,' he says.

She hovers her hands over me and says an incantation. The claw marks heal over but leave three long thick scars across my back. The inflammation in my ankle reduces by half, and some of the scrapes on my legs completely heal.

'I'll need to rest for a while before I can conjure more healing powers,' she says and kisses my forehead. 'Kayla might have some remedies as well that might help.'

'She has minor bruises on the rest of her body. But, with time and some rest, she will be okay again,' Doctor Matlin says.

I sit up and glare at Doctor Matlin, 'My mate is dead. Torn apart in front of me and drained of blood, and you say I'll be okay again? I will *never* be okay again. No matter what medicine or treatment you give me, no matter how much rest I have, no matter how much time passes. There is no cure for this,' I say.

'Forgive me, Lylah. I'm sorry for your loss. I will see myself out,' he says, bowing and taking his leave.

My father walks in looking very sad and broken. He would have heard what I had just said to Doctor Matlin.

'I'll mind link Bella and have her help me bath Lylah,' my mother says.

'Alright, I'll check on everyone else and send for Alpha Varan.'

'Make sure you rest too,' my mother says as he walks out.

He nods, but knowing him, he won't be resting.

Bella knocks and quietly enters. She nods at my mother and walks into my bathroom. They must be mind-linking. Bella runs the bath and adds a scented bath oil. She then helps my mother walk me over to the tub. I stand there numb, unmoving and stare blankly at the water. Nothing matters to me anymore. I don't want to do anything. All I want is Micah. I just want to curl up in the darkness and let it consume me forever.

Bella sees my lack of motivation, removes my daggers, leggings and underwear, and helps me step into the bath. I see the horrified look on Bella's face through the mirror when she sees the scars across my back. More tears quietly drip from her face, giving my mother a sad gaze. My mother's lips tremble, and she sobs as she begins washing my arms with a wet cloth. Bella takes my other arm and begins to wash me gently. The smell of fresh lavender has taken over the smell of death that had covered me. Bella keeps glancing and frowning at the scars on my back. I suddenly feel self-conscious. I hug myself, even though it does nothing to hide my scars.

The only sounds are sobs, crying, and the sound of tears splashing into the bath water or onto the stone-tiled floor.

Bella combs the shampoo through my hair and pulls out any twigs and leaves. My mind replays over and over the events of Micah's death. My body trembles, my chest tightens, and I struggle to breathe.

My mother cups my face and begins to take deep breaths, 'Breathe sweetheart, breathe with me,' she says.

I follow her breathing, and my chest releases the tightness. However, my body still trembles, and the tears continue to fall. Bella rinses my hair out, and mother grabs a towel for me. Once I'm dried, I sit on the end of my bed, wrapped in the towel. I notice my mother is unsteady, but she tries to hide it. She is drained from all her energy from healing some of the areas of Micah's body and then mine. My grandma, Anna, had said healing uses more energy than any other spell.

'Bella, can you take Mother to her room to rest, please? I want to be alone for a while anyway,' I say.

'Are you sure you want to be alone? I can have Amara keep you company?' she suggests.

'No, I need some space,' I reply.

Bella pauses and gazes at me as to whether she should give me some space, 'Okay, but I will be back to check on you, though,' she says.

'Sure,' I say, not caring.

'Alright, Luna,' Bella says. 'Let's get you to your room.'

My mother nods, and they leave. I walk morbidly over to my wardrobe and drop the towel on the floor. I put on a crop top, an oversized shirt, fresh underwear, and leggings. Then make my way back to my bed. I crawl under the sheet and cradle myself as I cry for Micah to come back to me.

***

'No! Get out of my way! Where is he? It can't be true? It can't be?'

I've been woken by Alpha Varans' thunderous yells that echo through the packhouse. I slowly remove myself from the bed sheet and hobble to my door. I peek my head out, trembling and gaze towards the downstairs staircase.

'You're lying, Alpha Maximus!' Alpha Varan shouts.

My hands shake as I hold the staircase railing and, step by step, slowly make my way down the stairs. I have to make an effort not to put too much weight on my sprained ankle.

'I'm sorry, Alpha Varan. We are all so sorry. I will take you to see him now in the apothecary,' he replies.

I sit and hug myself in the shadows of the staircase and watch them walk down the corridor to the apothecary.

'No! My son, my son!' I hear Alpha Varan's cries.

I close my eyes tightly as I try to keep myself from shedding new tears but fail miserably. I burst into tears. My heart hurts. It aches. I clutch my chest and feel my heart shatter like glass into a million pieces. It feels as if the flame in my heart has been snuffed out.

After listening to his cries for a while, he exits the apothecary and storms up the corridor.

'Where is she? Where is the little wench responsible for my son's death?'

'What did you call her?' my father shouts angrily behind him.

'You heard me! If that little useless, human wench of yours weren't my son's mate, he'd still be alive!'

I watch as my father shifts into his Lycan and holds Alpha Varan up by his throat. Alpha Varan grips my father's wrists and tries to release his hands. His feet struggle to desperately touch the ground. Alpha Varan shifts into his wolf instead, and they fight. They knock over every vase and table along the corridor. Theo, Leo, Nathan and Alex struggle to separate them.

Glass shatters everywhere. I stand and walk down the stairs to make myself known, and everyone freezes. Alpha Varan and my father shift back into their human forms. My mother and Amara approach and stand next to me. I look up at Alpha Varan with my red-puffy eyes, fall to my knees, and cry, 'I'm so sorry, Alpha Varan. I tried to save him. I tried to get back to him. There were too many. They were everywhere. I couldn't see them. It happened so fast,' I tremble.

Alpha Varan takes a step closer with fists clenched and looks disturbingly deep into my eyes with rage.

'You tried to save Micah?' he laughs. 'You're a useless human with no magic, no wolf and now no mate! I'll take my son home to Storm Glenn, where he will be laid to rest away from you!' he says.

I glare at Alpha Varan, 'No!' I say firmly and stand.

'No?' he replies, raising an eyebrow.

'Micah, maybe your son, but he is my mate, and as his mate, I get to choose where he will be laid to rest. I won't let you or anyone take him away from me. He will be buried here in the packhouse gardens where I can always be near him.'

'You little wench!- oomph!'

My father punches Alpha Varan in the jaw. I watch as he grabs his face and stumbles backwards.

'Lylah is right. As his mate, she gets to choose, and she has chosen. Insult my daughter again, and next time, you will have broken arms and legs to go with your broken jaw,' my father warns with a look that could kill.

'When do you intend on the burial?' Alpha Varan snaps.

'Midday tomorrow,' I reply and burst into tears running past everyone and into the apothecary.

Chapter 17

Kayla wipes the tears from her face as she sees me entering the apothecary. Her dark skin tone shimmers against the many coloured liquids bubbling throughout the apothecary in the beakers, flasks, pipettes, and test tubes. Her long, dense wavy hair sits in a large braid with thick gold chains. Kayla's obsidian eyes flicker with sadness as she holds her arms out and approaches to embrace me.

'Lylah,' she sobs. 'I'm so sorry.'

I allow her to embrace me, even though I don't want to be touched by anyone, 'I've come to see Micah,' I whisper.

'Of course,' Kayla nods and walks me down the spiral stone slope. There are tall wooden shelves along every wall that reach the ceiling. The shelves are mainly stacked with books with objects, such as the odd animal skull, candles, and jars. Tables are aligned with Bunsen burners, tripods, flasks, mortar, and pestle. There are bottles of potions and other substances. Bouquet garnies of parsley stalks, bay leaves, thyme, rosemary, tarragon, basil and more hang low within hands reach. There are cobwebs everywhere. You would never guess. Kayla lives down here. The air is hazy due to the bubbling of liquids and the mist floating from the cauldron. I halt as I see a heavy wooden table with an open casket. My hands tremble, and I try to ease my breathing as I slowly approach. I stop myself from approaching before turning to Kayla.

'I'd like some time alone with Micah, please.'

'Take your time, Lylah. I'll go upstairs to the kitchen,' she says.

I watch Kayla walk up the spiral ramp and exit the apothecary. I Turn my attention to the casket and gaze at the hundreds of flowers that surround the casket. Kayla has also added candles amongst them. I watch the flames dance and flicker in a trance.

'Micah can't be dead. He can't be gone. It's all just a dream. A really bad dream,' I say, approaching him as slowly as possible. The first thing I notice is Micah's sandy-coloured hair, neatly combed. His skin is the palest I have ever seen, but then I remember he was drained of so much blood. A lump forms in my throat, and I blink away the tears. His eyes are closed. I desperately want to see them. I reach out and stroke his cheek and feel broken at the thought I will never see his beautiful sable eyes again. His lips are pursed together. He looks content and peaceful. I place my hand over his that are clasped together. He is dressed in a black suit, tie, and white shirt. I lie my head near his shoulder and cry. I remain there for hours and think of all the time we spent together over the last three years until our last night when we made love for the first and last time together.

My chest begins to ache again. I'll never get to see Micah's eyes again. I'll never hear him tell me he loves me again, and I'll never be able to make love to him again.

I stand, lean over and leave my final kiss on his lips. 'I love you so, so much, Micah. I love you so much that it hurts. I will never forget you, and I will always love you.'

I take in all his facial features one last time and comb my fingers through his hair. I blow out the candles and slowly walk away up the circular ramp. I lean against the door as I close it and wipe the tears from my face. My sobs echo through the corridor. I'm glad no one is around to hear them. In a silent trance-like walk, I return up the stairs to my chamber. I sit in the bare corner of my room, hug my knees, and stare at the stone wall.

After a while, there's a knock on my door. Sally enters with a tray of food. She frowns when she sees me huddled in the corner.

'Lylah, I brought you some dinner. You should sit on the bed where it's warmer and have something to eat?' she suggests.

I don't respond.

'Okay, I'm going to shut the doors to your terrace. It will be nightfall soon,' Sally says and closes them. 'Your dinner is on your bedside table. I'll check on you soon,' she says, hesitantly leaving the room.

It's nightfall, and I haven't moved. Bella has come to check on me. She notices I haven't eaten, but she doesn't mention it. 'It's really cold in here, Lylah. I'm going to start the fire up for you,' she says, igniting the sticks and wood alight in my fireplace. The fire gives my room a beautiful glow. I silently watch the shadows on the wall form from the fire. Bella takes my tray of cold food and leaves my room.

It must be the middle of the night. Lacking energy, I crawl across my floor and climb into bed. I throw the sheet over myself and hide there for the rest of the night. I'm not sure if I slept. I'm unsure if I was remembering moments with Micah or if I had fallen asleep and dreamt them.

I sit up when I hear a knock on my door. I don't say anything. My mother enters. She looks at my puffy face and red eyes. My hair is unkempt, and I have dark rings under my eyes. I can tell she also has not had much rest. She walks over, sits next to me, and wraps her arms around me. We sit silent and hug each other. It's a silence where words aren't needed as the actions speak for themselves.

My Dad enters a few moments later, carrying a tray with a glass of juice and a bowl of cereal. He looks awful. The dark patches under his eyes match mine. He places the tray on my bedside table and opens the doors to my terrace. Expecting sunshine, but all we see is the sky full of dark heavy clouds. My Dad sighs and walks over to me, placing a kiss on my forehead and sits with Mum and me.

He leans over, picks up the glass of juice and passes it to me, 'Drink,' he says using his Alpha tone. Unable to disobey, I drink the juice and pass him back the empty glass. The juice was refreshing as much as I didn't want to eat or drink. I lick the remnants from my lips.

'Do you want help to get ready for Micah's burial?' Mother asks.

I shake my head, 'No, I can do it,' I reply softly.

'We will leave you to it then,' my father says, and they leave the room.

I put my thin white dressing gown on and sit out on my terrace. It's cold, and it looks like it will rain soon. I look down at the garden and see a plot has already been dug out, ready for Micah. My lips tremble, and I fight back the tears and the lump forming in my throat.

Flashbacks of darkness appear. I can't see Micah, but I can hear him. He whimpers in pain but continues to fight the vampires off. I reach my arms out, trying to feel him, to help him, but as I feel myself getting closer to him. I snap out of the flashback, and he is gone, 'Micah!' I yell, breathing heavily. Hugging myself, I return to my room and shut the terrace doors.

I give myself a moment before walking over to my set of draws. I gather black leggings, a black shirt and a black hoodie and put them on. My boots aren't in their usual spot. I search my wardrobe, check the bathroom, and then the terrace. Finally, I find them under my bed. My dagger glistens from the light, grabbing my attention. I walk over to my display of knives and pick up the dagger Micah gave me. It still has blood on it from where I managed to stab the bastard vampires. I glare, staring at the blood. If I ever see a vampire, I will kill them at first glance. They will regret killing my mate. I will make their lives hell. They will regret ever being born. Taking a cloth, I clean my dagger, grab the stone I use to sharpen my weapons and spend the next hour polishing and sharpening my dagger. Holding it, I run my fingers over the engraved eye. 'I miss you so much,' I whisper.

A knock on the door startles me. I stand and tuck the dagger into the waist of my leggings and open the door. It's Amara and Billy. Amara has her hair in a neat bun with small white stone flowers. She wears a black dress with a black cardigan and shoes. Billy is dressed in a black suit and has his hair combed to one side.

'We thought you might want some company going to the burial?' Amara says softly.

I nod and force a small smile. I might feel less uncomfortable entering the hall with others rather than by myself and having everyone stare at me. I approach my dresser and tie my hair up in a ponytail, and return to Billy and Amara waiting for me outside my door.

They walk down the stairs with me through the corridor and into the hall without saying a word. Everyone is there, dressed in black, including Alpha Varan. His hair is dishevelled, and he is distraught, pacing back and forth. Even though he hasn't treated me well, I still want to reach out and hug him and tell him how much Micah loved him. But then he comes to a halt and glares at me. I pull my hood over my head and walk up to my parents, who are talking to Theo and Leo.

Dad places his hand on my shoulder to comfort me. Moments later, Kayla enters the hall and calls for Billy, Alex, Theo and Leo to go with her down to the apothecary. They return as pallbearers carrying Micah's coffin. Kayla approaches and takes my hand. She nods at Alpha Varan for him to follow us.

Soft music begins to play. Alex, Billy, Theo and Leo carry the coffin to the pack house gardens while Alpha Varan and I stand behind the coffin and follow. Everyone else follows behind.

Rain plummets down upon us, and the ground becomes muddy. We reach the garden, and Micah's coffin is lowered into the plot.

Kayla tells Micah's life story up to the night he was tragically taken away from us and that he is up with the Moon Goddess now watching over us.

Everyone shifts except for me, Sally and Kayla, who have no wolves, and they all howl in unison, as is the tradition at a werewolf's burial.

Chapter 18

Everyone has returned to the hall to continue mourning. I remain behind, standing in the rain, watching Theo and Leo shovel the dirt onto the coffin until the plot is filled. Theo and Leo place a hand each on my shoulder, giving me a sympathetic gaze before leaving me be.

I fall to my knees and can't believe this is happening that my beloved mate, Micah is dead and now buried. I stare at the muddy grave in a trance until a lightning bolt strikes nearby, bringing me back to reality. I look to the flowers on my right, lean over and pick some before placing them neatly onto Micah's grave.

After a while, I notice guests beginning to leave. I must have been sitting out here for a while and lost track of time. I almost want to laugh at the thought of time now. Realising that I'm mateless and no longer have Micah in my life, that time no longer matters to me.

An oversized coat is placed over my shoulders. I look up to see my Dad. He looks down at me sadly. 'Lylah, you will become unwell if you stay in this weather any longer. Let me take you inside,' he says.

I look back at Micah's grave. 'It doesn't matter if I become unwell anymore. Nothing matters anymore,' I say.

'Lylah!' Dad replies angrily. He places his hands on my shoulder, and I stand. He looks deep into my eyes with a hurt look. 'Everything still matters, Lylah. You still matter!' he growls.

I shake my head, 'No, I have no wolf, no magic and no mate. I'm nothing, Dad. I'm useless. It should have been me who died, not Micah,' I cry.

'Lylah, stop this. You are my daughter. You mean everything to me, your mother and brothers. The entire pack adores and loves you. You don't need a wolf or magic to be accepted or loved because you already are. Micah loved you for you long before you even found out you were fated mates. You can come and see Micah whenever you want, just not in the middle of thunderstorms. Now come inside before you catch a cold,' he says, taking my hand.

As we enter the packhouse, I begin to shiver. Dad rubs his hands over my arms to warm me up. 'Most of the guests have left. Come into the hall by the fire,' he says. I nod and follow him into the hall, hugging his coat over my shoulders. He walks me to the fire, and I sit on the rug and quietly watch the fire and warm my hands.

Mum, Dad, Kayla and my brothers sit in morbid silence at the table watching me. No one is talking. I'm not sure where Billy and Amara have gone. Sally and Bella are in the kitchen with Beth making a tray of hot tea to serve everyone. Sally passes me a hot cup of tea when she returns to the hall. No longer wanting to be in the company of others, I drink the remainder of my tea and place it on a nearby tray before leaving the hall without saying a word. I return to my room, place my dagger under my pillow and lay on my bed.

Five days pass. I haven't slept or eaten. If I'm not lying in bed, I'm on the terrace staring at Micah's grave. The flowers I placed on the grave have become dull and lifeless, just like my soul.

There is a knock on my door. Kayla enters, holding a tiny olive green vial, 'Alpha Maximus told me you haven't been sleeping or eating?' she asks.

I shrug my shoulders in response. Kayla sighs, sits next to me and places the vial in my hands. 'It's a sleeping potion. I think it's important you have a good rest. Then afterwards, we can focus on filling your empty stomach,' she smiles.

I shrug my shoulders, and she sighs again. 'Please, Lylah. Drink it,' she pleads before leaving my room.

The vile is no bigger than my thumb. It's glass, with a cork on top. Every time I managed to fall asleep, I would wake up not long after from having nightmares about the night Micah was killed. I've been forcing myself to say awake ever since. Perhaps the potion might help me have a solid sleep without having any nightmares.

With nothing left to lose, I pop the cork off and scull the liquid down. It tastes like liquorice. I put the vial on my bedside table and lay on my bed. Within a minute, I'm fast asleep.

***

My mother sits by my side, stroking the hair from my face. I sit up, squinting until my eyes focus. It was the first time I had slept without any nightmares.

'You've been asleep for two solid days,' she smiles.

'Two days!?' I ask, surprised.

'I'll run you a bath, and perhaps you can join us for lunch?' she says in a hopeful tone.

I don't want to make her unhappy, so I force a small smile and nod.

'Great!' she says and enters the bathroom to run the water for me.

I gather a fresh pair of black track pants, shirt and hoodie and place them on my bed. Mother turns off the water and stops to place a kiss on my forehead before leaving my room. I enter the bathroom, throw my nighty in the wicker basket, and step into the bath. It's nice and warm. After washing myself, I remain in the water a little longer. I hold my breath and sink underneath, keeping my eyes open. I stare at the ceiling while allowing my mind and body to relax. My mind has other intentions, and I envision the red eyes, then suddenly, the image I'm envisioning transitions into Micah's face. It looks so real that I raise my hand from the water to touch him. I feel his skin as my hand cups his face.

'Lylah,' he whispers.

I sit up gasping, 'Micah?' I say, desperately looking around the bathroom to see there is no one here. I look at my hand. I swear I felt him. I touched him and heard his voice. What's wrong with me?

'Micah, please come back. I know I felt you,' I cry, but no one responds.

I drain the water and dry myself before entering my room. I roll onto my bed in my towel and hug myself for a few minutes.

'It was just a dream, a hallucination. It has to have been?' I tell myself.

I sit up, jump off my bed, and race out onto the terrace. The sun is shining today, and the air is warm. I look down at Micah's grave to see it's still in tack, and my shoulders slump. 'It was just my imagination, after all.'

I get dressed and tie my hair up before walking downstairs to join the pack house for lunch. Everyone is talking but quiets as I enter. I rub my arm, frown and take my seat beside my mother.

Beth places a plate of food down in front of me and gives me a sympathetic look.

'It's good to see you join us,' Theo smiles. I nod and pick up my fork. I have a few bites of the food but end up playing with most of it as I listen to everyone talk to each other. Nearly everyone seems to be smiling and talking as if Micah had never died. I throw my napkin down and abruptly stand and leave the dining room. Everyone pauses and frowns. I walk outside and go straight to the garden and walk around picking Micah a fresh bouquet. I place the lavender and daisies neatly on his grave. A headstone has been placed on the plot.

Micah Storm-Glenn
Beloved son to Alpha Varan and Luna Rosaleigh
(Deceased)
Loving mate to Lylah.

I trace my fingers over the words and look up when I hear giggles. Vicky and Tamara approach and lean over the grey stone wall that surrounds the garden.

'Looks like none of us gets to have Micah, not even you, Lylah,' Vicky snickers.

'It's such a shame she is a useless human. If she was normal like the rest of us and had her wolf, she could have saved him. It's her fault Micah's dead,' Tamara says.

I clench my fists, stand up and scream. Vicky and Tamara glance at each other before I run towards them and jump over the stone fence. I shove Vicky onto the ground and lunge at Tamara. My fist repeatedly makes contact with her face as I straddle her. A tooth comes flying out of her mouth. Vicky screams for help as I show no sign of stopping. Tamara's face swells and becomes purple from all the bruises on her face. But I don't stop. Her nose cracks as my fist make contact again. She tries to shift, but she struggles. Vicky has shifted and bites my arm. I punch her in the jaw and lunge at her. Tamara isn't moving and is most likely unconscious.

Everyone in the pack house runs outside, hearing the scream and whimpers.

'Lylah!' They shout, but I ignore them and continue to fight Vicky's wolf form. I hold her in a headlock and bite her leg, ripping out a chunk of her flesh. I'm grabbed from behind by many arms and held down by my Dad and brothers. I continue to kick, punch and scream at them. While Alex, Nathan and my mother help Vicky and Tamara.

'I'll kill them! Let me kill them!' I scream.

I may have punched my Dad and kicked him along with my brothers. I was so angry and upset that Micah was gone. All I could see were those red eyes in my mind. I wanted the vampires dead, all of them.

Kayla is kneeling beside me and pouring a small concoction into my mouth while I'm held down. It tastes terrible, like rotten fish. I try to spit it out, but darkness quickly consumes me.

Chapter 19

With a struggle, I manage to open my eyes. I'm feeling groggy and realise I'm in my room on my bed. My Dad is leaning against a wall with arms crossed and a not-impressed look on his face. My brothers stand in front of my door as if guarding it, and my mother wipes the blood from my arm where I have been bitten. I flinch from the pain and pull my arm away from her as she dabs too close to the bite mark.

'Lylah,' Dad says. 'I know you are grieving, but what on earth were you thinking? Attacking Tamara and Vicky like that? They are both seriously hurt!'

'Good! They got what they deserved. I hope they never come near me again!'

'Lylah!' Everyone says.

'They said it's my fault Micah's dead. Do you expect me to sit there and listen to them ridicule me and blame me for my mate's death?' I argue.

'No, but violence is not the answer, Lylah,' Dad replies.

'Oh? Are you sure about that, Dad? Because it seems to have worked. I can't see Tamara or Vicky bullying me anymore,' I say sarcastically.

He lets out a growl of warning.

My mother frowns, 'Lylah, let me heal this bite mark,' she says, reaching for my arm.

'No, don't touch me,' I say, moving away from my bed.

'Lylah…' she says.

I turn to face them all, 'I want you to leave me alone,' I say.

Theo, Leo and Dad stare sadly at each other.

'Lylah, you're hurt,' Dad says, taking a step forward.

'I don't care,' I say, walking onto my terrace. I stare at Micah's grave. 'Nothing matters anymore. Just leave me be.'

I hear them silently leave, not saying a word and keeping my back to them.

***

It's been four months since Micah's death. Every night I watch the sunset from my terrace, holding my dagger close to my heart. The only time I leave my room is during the night when everyone is asleep. That's when I climb down from my balcony and sit by Micah's grave in the moonlight. Some nights I fall asleep on his grave. It's the only way I can sleep without having nightmares of his death, rather than waking up hysterical, exhausted and drenched in sweat.

A tray of food is left outside my room each day, but I struggle to eat because of the deep depression I'm in. I'm angry that our pack warriors have found no trace of the vampires after all this time. I hate seeing them return each week, knowing they have found no leads. A few more humans have been killed since Micah's death. The humans are convinced it's wolves and have organised hunting parties that now hunt and kill wild wolves each night.

Everyone knocks on my door to see me most days, but I keep it locked and ignore them. I never want to go through the pain of losing a loved one again. So, I have disconnected myself from them all. My heart aches all day and all night. The flame I once felt in my heart had gone out the moment Micah died.

Every time I close my eyes, I see him, and it feels like a little more of me dies. Gazing up at the moon, I hear my name and flinch, 'Lylah.' I grip my knife closer to my chest. It hurts so much every time I hear Micah's voice. I hate that I'm always imagining his voice, it's like a cruel taunt, but I can't stop it no matter how hard I try.

'Lylah,' I hear the whisper again.

'Stop! Please, stop,' I say, falling to my knees and gripping my hair.

I hear a knock and look towards my door and know no one is ever awake at this time. I wipe the tears from my face, walk over, and wait a few moments. Then, taking a deep breath, I slowly open the door. There is no one there. As I'm about to close it, I hear it again.

'Lylah.'

'M-Micah?' I say, stepping out into the corridor.

A shadow going down the stairwell gets my attention. I chase after it and race down the stairs. My heart beats erratically as I look frantically in all directions to see where it has gone.

'Lylah,' I hear whispered to my left.

I follow the voice towards the grand hall. As I enter, soft instrumental music plays, but there are no musicians. I look around and pause in the centre of the hall. A chill runs down my back. I turn and gasp when I see the apparition of Micah smiling at me. He holds his hand out, and I take it. I'm pulled towards him and whirled around to the music. I smile and cry with happiness as we dance and gaze into each other's eyes. I feel the spark in my heart reigniting and hope and happiness for the first time since Micah died. We waltz throughout the hall, the music becomes louder, and our dancing becomes faster. My eyes don't leave Micah's, not even for a second. As the music slows down and ends, so does our dancing. Our lips come closer, and as they are about to touch, Micah begins to vanish.

'I love you,' is the last faint whisper I hear from him before I can no longer see him.

'No, no, no, no! Micah, don't go, please don't go! I need you! Please!' I beg.

I spin and turn, looking around the hall for him and run through the corridor. There is no sign of him. I sit in the stairwell, hug my knees and cry for a while before walking up the steps and returning to my room. I lay on my bed, turn on my side, and stare out the terrace into the night sky.

My heart feels like it's shattering all over again. I feel so broken, so lost without Micah. I remove myself from the bed, enter the terrace, and stare at Micah's grave.

'Tamara and Vicky are right. It's my fault Micah died. It's my fault. If I had my wolf or magic, I could have saved him. It should've been me who died. I don't want to be here anymore. I want to be with Micah,' I cry.

I steel myself, realising that there is a way I can be with Micah. The sun will be rising soon. I need to do this before everyone wakes. So, I climb down my balcony, sit on Micah's grave with my back against his tombstone, and hold the dagger against my wrist. My hand trembles as I push the dagger down harder and watch the line of blood appear. I then take the dagger from my other hand and cut my other wrist. Finally, I drop the dagger and slump down. I'm lying on Micah's grave and close my eyes. I smile, knowing I'll now be free of this nightmare and be with Micah again.

'I will be with you soon, my love,' I whisper and drift off to sleep.

***

I'm having the most beautiful dream. My head rests on Micah's lap, and we are in a field of flowers. I hum as Micah caresses my cheek. It's so peaceful. Little bluebirds fly over us, and the sunshine warms our skin.

'I love you so much, Lylah,' Micah says, smiling at me.

'I love you too,' I smile.

Suddenly, the world begins to disappear. The green grass and the flowers shrivel up and die. The trees in the distance begin to sink.

I sit up, 'Micah, what's happening?' I say, looking around and becoming distressed. He doesn't reply. I turn to look at him, but all I see is darkness and those red eyes. In a flash, everything vanishes. I sit up and scream. I look around, breathing heavily. I'm in the apothecary: Mother, Father, Kayla, and my brothers. Everyone is here surrounding me. They are all crying and gasp in relief as I sit up and scream. 'Micah! Where is he?' I say, frantically looking for him. Everyone looks away or at their feet. I look down at the healed cuts on my wrist, which are now scars.

'No! What did you do? Why did you bring me back? Why did you take me away from Micah?' I shout.

'Lylah,' My mother cries, 'Your father found you on Micah's grave and rushed you here. You're my daughter, Lylah. I had to heal you. We had to save you. You may not be able to live without Micah, but we could never live without you,' she cries.

I flinch at her words. I'm angry that they healed me and brought me back, but I'm also upset at myself for putting them through this. The pain I feel from losing Micah is a pain I just inflicted on my family.

I move forward and off the table. My Father and brothers move aside to let me through.

'I'm going to my room. I want to be alone,' I say.

A firm hand lands on my shoulder and tightens. I turn my head and see the weariness that has formed under my father's eyes. It's the first time I have seen my father with such a look.

'No! This is going to stop right now, Lylah. No more being alone, no more locking yourself in your room and never will you ever attempt something like this again. Do you hear me?'

I can hear the pain in his voice. He doesn't even try and hide it. His eyes are pleading with me. I burst into tears and hug him.

'I'm so sorry, Dad. I'm so sorry,' I say, crying into his chest. He wraps his arms around me and holds me tight.

Chapter 20

We are together in the dining room. It's quiet, but everyone is weary and exhausted after this morning's ordeal. Everyone has been watching me like a hawk throughout the day. Beth serves us dinner, and my Dad gives me a look after I have been pushing my food around for a while with my fork. I begin to eat my food, and he nods. I manage to eat over half my meal. It's the most I've been able to eat for a long time. I place my fork down and stare at my wrists as I caress my thumbs over the scars. Theo is sitting next to me and frowns at the scars but doesn't say anything.

With everyone now finished dinner, I stand. 'I'm very tired, and you probably are all tired too. I'm going to go to bed,' I say, leaving the hall. As I enter my room, Amara rushes in behind me.

'Amara?'

'Lylah,' she says, rubbing her arm nervously. 'It would give me peace of mind if you would allow me to sleep in your room with you tonight?'

'Amara,' I sigh, 'I'm not going to… you know,' I say, unable to finish the sentence.

'I-I know, but,' she bursts into tears and lunges at me and hugs me, ' I was so scared I was never going to see you again this morning, and it's been over four months since we've spoken. I've missed you. I miss having you around, and you gave me such a scare this morning.'

'Fine, you can sleep in my room, but only tonight.'

'Thank you!' she says, leaps onto my bed, and hops under the covers. I roll my eyes at her. Someone knocks at the door. I answer it to see Theo with his hands behind his back.

'Theo, don't tell me you want to crash the night in my room too?' I ask.

He looks over my shoulder to see Amara in my bed with a big grin on her face.

'Actually, I was thinking about the scars on your wrists and know it's something you wouldn't want others to see, just like the ones on your back you hide.'

I stiffen and become uncomfortable at him mentioning them. The horrible reminder I have to see each morning and evening and every time I change and bathe. I never walk around anymore in my tank top or shirts with thin straps unless I have one of my hoodies over the top so no one can see the scars.

'I thought about getting you some bracelets to help cover them up, but I know that jewellery isn't your style. So, I thought you might like to wear these each day instead?' he says, pulling leather bracers out from behind his back.

'Theo,' I say, taking them. 'These are your favourite set of bracers. You've had these for so many years, and you wear them every time you practise archery.'

'Yeah, well, I always thought they gave me luck. So, I want you to have them. Besides, Mother has been complaining she never sees me wear the ones she bought me last year for my birthday.'

'Thank you,' I say, forming a small smile.

Theo smiles, nods and walks away. I place the bracers on the table where my knives are and notice the dagger Micah gave me is there. I'm grateful my parents never kept it from me, although I can imagine it wasn't an easy decision for them. It would have been because they knew Micah made it for me and that I wouldn't be able to part with it. It's been thoroughly cleaned and sharpened. I could recognise my father's work any day.

I climb into bed, Amara cuddles right up to my back, and we fall asleep. I dream the same nightmare I have each night of Micah's death and wake up early in the morning to Amara shaking me. I sit up, drenched in sweat.

'You were having a nightmare, Lylah. You were thrashing your arms around, yelling. Then, you hit me in the face… twice,' she frowns.

'I'm so sorry, Amara.'

'You couldn't help it. Do you have these nightmares often?' she asks.

I nod, 'The same one, every night since Micah….'

'That's terrible, Lylah. You are suffering enough not having Micah here but reliving it again each night. I wish there were something I could do. Perhaps Kayla might have a potion that will stop the nightmares?' she suggests.

I shrug and get out of my bed and walk towards my bathroom. 'I'm going to have a bath. I'll see you afterwards at breakfast.'

'Okay,' she replies, and I close the bathroom door behind me, strip my clothes and look over my shoulder at the long thick scars down my back. I place a towel over the mirror to avoid looking at my scars and hop into the bath, only to stare down at the new ones on my wrists. I feel ugly and ashamed of myself. I realise I'll never be beautiful, and these horrible scars would make anyone cringe. No one would ever want a wolfless hybrid, especially one covered in scars with a broken soul.

I am now dressed in black pants with a matching crop top. I put my favourite hoodie on, but I keep it unzipped. I tuck my beloved dagger in my belt, push the sleeves of my hoodie up, and place the bracers on. I pull on the thin leather straps and tie the ends together, so the bracers remain firmly gripped to my forearms. Ready for the day, I walk downstairs to join everyone for breakfast.

Everyone is surprised but relieved to see me walk into the dining hall. They all smile at my presence. I knew if I tried to stay in my room or lock the door, Dad would only break it down and drag me down here for breakfast. I take the seat next to Theo.

'The bracers suit you. They also look better on you than on me,' Theo smiles.

Leo stands up and walks to the large window as we finish breakfast.

'Is that Alpha Greg and the warriors? He must have left half of them behind to continue searching for the vampires,' he says.

We all join Leo and stare out the window. Alpha Greg looks hagged and worn along with the few warriors he has with him.

'I don't have a very good feeling about this,' my father says and exits the dining hall to greet Alpha Greg.

We wait in the hall until Alpha Greg enters and sits with the warriors. They all look tired and worn out.

My father enters behind them. 'Beth will bring you all some food and refreshments,' he says.

'Thank you,' Alpha Greg replies. 'Unfortunately, I have returned with terrible news. We thought we had found a lead a few nights ago and followed it, but it turned out to be a trap. We were cornered, and a vampire with dark hair and a black cape appeared. It seemed he was the only vampire at the time. So we weren't too worried at first, but then he told us to bow down and pledge our allegiance to him. We laughed, of course; he became furious and emitted a black mist from his hands, and large dark shadows appeared. They were so fast, and their eyes were red. We think they were more vampires. We were attacked from all directions. As soon as we managed to kill a vampire, it instantly disappeared, only to reappear a moment later. Over half the warriors were killed. The rest of us only managed to get away. We returned to the area the next day, and all the warriors had been drained of blood with two holes pierced in their necks and were all dismembered. We buried them before the humans could find them.'

Everyone is silent from shock, processing the horrible news. My breathing intensifies and becomes heavy. Everyone stares at me. I slam my fist down onto the table in rage and scream.

'I'm going to find those bastards and kill every one of them until they no longer exist!'

'Lylah, these vampires are much quicker than us and seem to wield some kind of power we have never seen or dealt with before. Defeating them is going to take more than us. We will have to organise more packs to join us to fight them, and we will need more than wolves to help us,' he says.

'What else could help us?' my father asks.

Alpha Greg looks to my Mother and Kayla, 'Magic, and as much as we can get,' he says. 'I suggest you train as many pack members as possible each day to improve their strength and agility. Contact as many packs as you can. Have them do the same and be on standby. We will head out and hunt them down together as soon as we find the location or a lead to where the vampires reside. Then, hopefully, with Kayla and Hope's magic and more wolves, we can defeat them.'

Everyone agrees to the plan.

Beth enters and serves food and drink to Alpha Greg and the warriors. I walk to the serving trolley, pile some food onto my plate, sit back at the table, and eat.

'You just had breakfast,' Leo says.

I swallow my mouth full of food. 'I need to eat all the food I can, in order to start training each day and get my strength and fighting skills back on track for when it's time to kill the vampires,' I explain.

My father looks at me, 'Lylah, I'm sorry, but you're not going to go with us. You won't be able to keep up without a wolf, and unfortunately, you don't have magic either.'

I drop the food I hold onto my plate, stand and look him in the eyes.

'I'm a good fighter, one of the best around, and you know it! I will be going whether you like it or not, but it's your choice if I go with you or if I go alone,' I say firmly and storm out of the hall, not giving him a chance to reply.

Chapter 21

Pacing back and forth angrily in my room, I punch my wall, grazing my knuckles. I try to read a book for a while but can't concentrate. All I have on my mind is vengeance. Finally, I toss the book aside and walk out onto my terrace for fresh air.

I notice all the local male pack members heading towards the training grounds. My father must have mind-linked all the males over eighteen to begin daily training immediately. Why hasn't he told me he was starting the training today?

With determination on my side, I open the top drawer of my dresser and take out my boxing hand wraps. I put the loop over my thumb, wrapping my wrist and the palm of my hand. Next, I make the crosses across the back, wrapping the material between the fingers. I clench my fist to feel it's tight and secure, then wrap my other hand the same way.

I jump down from my balcony and jog to the training field.

As I arrive, men ask each other why I'm there. At the same time, other men check me out. I want to knock them all out, but instead, I flip them the bird. After that, everyone splits into different groups to train. Some go inside the gym and weight lift; others race laps, and others do push-ups and pull-ups.

My father glares at me across the field. I know he is angry I'm there, but I don't care. I go to the sparring group, which happens to be where my brothers are and line up for my turn. The men frown, and I smile daringly at them. Leo and Theo smile and nod in approval that I'm there. I have fought with them a few times, and the only way they can defeat me is in their Lycan forms. I've whooped their human forms a few times over the last year.

It's my turn against Mark, a well-known tool in the pack. He flexes his oversized arms before pulling his shirt off and making his pecks bounce up and down. As he continues showing off, trying to swoon me off my feet, I decide to swoon him off his by dropping to the ground and spinning my leg around, knocking him over.

Everyone laughs as Mark becomes red-faced while I nonchalantly look at my nails. Then, finally, mark stands up, cracks his knuckles, and narrows his eyes at me.

'I was going to go easy on you, but I think I'll enjoy spanking that sweet little ass of yours instead,' he says.

My brothers growl and begin to shift into their Lycans to rip his head off. I place my hands on their chests to calm them.

'You know I can handle this clown on my own,' I say, giving them a wink. They stop shifting and remain in their human form to let me handle Mark myself.

I bring both of my hands right above my chin. I make tight fists. I throw the first punch hitting his nose. Mark blinks a few times as blood begins to trickle from his nostrils. He wasn't expecting me to begin already.

He copies my position and holds his clenched fists up like mine, but not so well, as they are below his chin. I'm quick to learn he isn't used to this fighting style. I notice my father has joined the now-forming crowd and watches me closely. Mark throws a few punches. I duck for the first hit and move my head to the side for the next two. I send a solid kick to his stomach, sending him back. He runs towards me angrily like a bull. I jump to the side as he lunges at me, and I elbow strike the back of his neck. He falls flat on his face. Men begin to cheer and applaud, and others nod and smile.

Mark scowls at me. He is angry he lost the round and storms off, embarrassed a woman beat him. I smile with my hands on my hips until my Dad steps into the sparring area and readies himself in a fighting stance.

Oh, Wands! My father wants me to spar with him. He isn't just a werewolf or just a Lycan. He is the Alpha, making him even stronger.

'Fighting you puts me at an unfair advantage,' I say to him.

He swings a punch. I duck, and he only misses by a millimetre, making me stumble back. I stable my balance and raise my clenched fists above my chin.

'Yet you think you can take on Vampires? Until you can take me down, you don't stand a chance,' he replies.

I flinch. My father is most likely right, but I need to do this. I need justice. I need to seek vengeance for Micah's death, even if it means me dying.

Growling, I swing my fists towards his face. Out of the five strikes, he dodges four of them. I drop to the ground and swing my leg around to knock him over, but he sees it coming and jumps over my leg. I try to punch him again, but he grabs my wrist and throws me over onto the ground with ease.

He holds his hand out to help me up. I take a grip of his hand, and he pulls me up. 'You're a good fighter, a skilled fighter. But it's not enough to defeat our greatest enemy. Until you can take me down, you won't be ready. So I expect to see you here each day training and to spar against me,' he says and walks away.

Theo and Leo race over to me in disbelief, 'That's the first time I've ever seen you defeated,' Theo says.

'Well, there's a first time for everything, I guess,' I reply, wiping the grass remnants from my arms.

'Looks like you will be training with us every day, after all,' Leo says and gives me a high-five.

'I might be human, but I'm still the daughter of a Lycan,' I say, with a look of determination on my face.

I run across the field into the gym and lift weights for half the day. Afterwards, I practice throwing my daggers at the target next to the one where Theo is shooting his arrows. When everyone groups up to do push-ups and sit-ups, I join them and make sure to keep up with them.

I repeat the training every day for five months, followed by the sparring session with three different men and then finally against my father. Every day I become angrier and more hateful towards the vampires. Many more humans have been killed, along with more of our pack warriors. The humans no longer suspect wild wolves after having hunted and killed so many of them over the past months, yet there is an increase in humans being killed. There are reports of some small towns that have no signs of life at all. No bodies have even been found, and no electricity either. They are ghost towns now, and the humans are dumbfounded as to what has happened or how it's happened. But we know it's the result of the vampires wiping them out.

Alpha Greg returns once a fortnight with fewer and fewer warriors to inform us they still have not found the location of the vampire's lair. Furious, I take my anger out on the boxing bags. I think of Micah every single day. From the moment I wake to the moment I sleep and even when I sleep. The nightmares haven't stopped but have only gotten worse. Amara hears my screams and cries along with half the pack house each night during the nightmares. She is the first to reach me as our rooms are the closest and wakes me up. I spend hours each night sitting by Micah's grave before I sleep. Alpha Varan has come to visit the grave twice since his burial. He still hates me.

My father is waiting for me to spar with him. After having Alpha Greg return this morning with the same news as usual, I am beyond upset and angry.

I swing my fists, I kick and roll, and for the first time, I land each blow, but I don't stop. My father strikes and misses. He tries a high kick and a low. I dodge both and roll under his legs ending up behind him and kicking the back of his knee, making him fall over onto the ground. The crowd is silent from complete shock. My father remains lying on the ground for a few moments, stunned and bursts into a cheer.

'You did it. You actually did it,' my father says.

Theo and Leo stare, beaming at me proudly. I close my eyes and envision Micah's face as a gust of wind goes by, making my hair flow in the wind, 'Micah,' I whisper.

The red eyes flash through my mind, then Micah's last moments. I withdraw two old daggers from my boots and walk towards the trees.

'Lylah, where are you going? We need to celebrate,' my father says.

I come to a halt, turn and clench the daggers tightly at his words, 'My mate is dead, and I am yet to seek my vengeance. This is no time for celebrations,' I say, turning back and walking towards the trees.

Chapter 22

It's been over nine months since I have gone to the area in the woods where Micah and I would train. Nine months since the flame in my heart went out. Nine months since I lost my true love and fated mate. It hasn't gotten easier. It's only become harder living another day without him. My heart has never stopped aching; each day, the pain I feel only worsens. Kayla told me the mate bond could become physically painful for some when your mate dies. She has been giving me potions to help the pain, but in the last couple of months, they haven't worked as well as they usually would. I tend to keep away from everyone and find somewhere quiet until the pain passes, as I don't want them to worry more than they already do. It can sometimes last a couple of hours. I have to bite down on a stick I wrap with material to suppress any screams or cries. My heart is so broken that I realise that not even magic or potions could ever fix me.

Heading to the training field, I notice a she-wolf racing towards my father, frantically yelling and waving something in the air.

'Vampires!' I finally hear clearly. I run over to her as she reaches my father. Everyone has gathered around. She hands my father an envelope that has been sealed with red wax. No one had sealed envelopes with wax since long before my father was a pup.

'I was alone, doing my usual routine of berry picking and a vampire wearing black approached and gave me this to give you, Alpha Maximus. He said it's important we meet with them, and then within seconds, he was gone,' she said.

I try to take the envelope, but my father steps back and opens it.

'Alpha Maximus, we understand humans and werewolves have been killed frequently over the past year. I know you have had men trying to track us down so you can kill us as punishment for these deaths. For one, you will never be able to find our lair unless we bring you there ourselves. Two, it's important you know that we vampires are not responsible for these deaths. Demonic wolves called 'Blood Dwellers' that are part vampire, part demon and part wolf are controlled by a Demon Lord called Atticus. It is he who is behind these deaths. We have been tracking and trying to stop Lord Atticus from his killing sprees to no avail. He has no intention of stopping, and he is extremely powerful. We must meet to come together to end him and end all these senseless murders. Meet us at Blue Scale Rock tomorrow night during the full moon.

Sincere regards,

Lord Talon,' My father reads.

'Liars, they're lying! It has to be a trap? They must be planning an ambush? There are no such things as blood-sucking demon dogs! I saw their eyes, red like blood. I saw one dressed in black, sucking the blood from Micah. They killed him. I saw them!' I shout angrily.

My father looks at the note in his hand and reads it in his mind, assessing the situation.

'I don't think trusting a vampire is ideal. I think Lylah is right. They must be planning an attack since they know we are hunting them down.'

***

We wait patiently at Blue Scale Rock. The moon has only begun rising. My father halves us into two groups. He is upfront with my brothers and half the warriors but insists I stand back and stay with the backup, hiding fifteen metres behind him amongst the shrubbery and trees. My mother and Kayla are also with the second group of warriors. I protest at first, but he gives me a stern look to do as I'm told. Sighing, I trudge begrudgingly back to the others but hide in a nearby tree, so I can see and hear better for when the vampires arrive.

Sitting on the branch, I swing my leg impatiently. We've been waiting three hours now, and there is no sign of the vampires. I've been waiting for over nine months to get my revenge on them for killing Micah, and tonight is finally the night I can take my vengeance and kill them. I take my dagger Micah made and angrily carve into the thick branch. As I wait, a strange but warm invigorating sense overcomes me. I can't help but look around as I'm being drawn to something in my surroundings. But then I see two shadows step forward.

'They're here,' my father says.

Everyone steels themselves or stands in a fighting stance as two vampires approach. I shake my head of the familiar feelings I always felt around Micah and try to concentrate on the two vampires standing in front of my father with my dagger in hand, ready to strike. The male vampire has blonde hair combed back and wears a black suit with a red vest and shirt underneath. The woman has dark brown hair past her shoulders and wears a two-piece red silk dress. The top is a corset followed by a long silky skirt. They look ready to attend a ball rather than a meeting with werewolves at the edge of the woods. They only appear to be in their mid-twenties, maybe younger.

'Alpha Maximus. My name is Soren, and this is my blood flame, Nadia. We're pleased you and your warriors could make it to this meeting,' he smiles.

I keep trying to watch Soren and Nadia, but my mind keeps drifting away, looking around beyond them, desperately searching, but for what? I feel so confused. These feelings are the same as I felt when I was in the presence of Micah. A sense of calm, security, happiness… lust. An urge to run past the vampires and further into the woods overwhelms me. 'What is wrong with me? Stop it, Lylah, stop. You need to focus. Micah is dead. He isn't here, and this is your moment to seek revenge!' I say, slapping myself in hopes of removing these feelings that are suddenly consuming me.

'How do we know this isn't some kind of ambush?' my father asks Soren and Nadia.

'I guess we have no way to assure you we mean no harm and intend no harm towards you. We can only give you our word to trust us,' Soren answers.

Rotten Liars! I bet they have vampires everywhere in the trees and shrubbery, just like we have warriors hiding. They are probably waiting for the right moment to strike, but I won't let that happen. I'll make sure to kill them first!

My father laughs, 'You expect us to take your word? How do we even know you aren't responsible for the deaths of all those humans and werewolves? I suppose you want us to take your word for that, too?'

Soren and Nadia frown at one another before staring back at my father.

'Alpha Maximus, if I may? Nadia says, taking a small step forward. 'Blood Dwellers exist, they are real, and the one who can summon and control them is very real. Lord Atticus and his Blood Dwellers are a threat to all species, including ours. The only way we can put a stop to him is by working together. It hasn't been an easy decision for our coven to work with another species, but it's the best decision if we are to stand a chance to end Lord Atticus.'

The urge to go further into the woods consumes me. I subconsciously climb down the tree in a trance-like state. My father quickly grabs my shoulder as I nonchalantly walk past him.

Everyone, including Soren and Nadia, watch me with confusion.

'Lylah! What are you doing?' he growls, tightening his grip on my shoulder.

I blink a few times and realise I'm no longer in the tree but standing in front of my father. I look around with the same look of confusion as everyone else.

'I don't know...'

He sighs, 'Cleary,' he says, annoyed and pulls me beside him.

What in the wands was that? Why don't I recall climbing down the tree? I'm so confused. Why do I have this urge to run past Nadia and Soren? Why is my heart beating so fast? All the questions race through my mind as I stare at my feet. Suddenly the red eyes flash through my mind, and I flinch, jumping back in fright.

Soren, Nadia, my father and my brothers stare at me, and I look up at Soren and Nadia and notice they both have brown eyes.

'Why aren't your eyes red? That night when I saw you when you attacked us. Your eyes were red, like blood,' I yell.

My breathing intensifies as I fight these urges and feelings and have the memories of that night flash through my mind. I'm sweating, and I feel like I can't breathe.

'That's because it wasn't us. Vampires don't have red eyes. We have the same coloured eyes as any other human,' Soren says.

'You both said your names are Soren and Nadia, but this note is signed by a Lord Talon. Why isn't he here conducting this meeting?' my father asks.

'Lord Talon is the vampire lord of our coven, just as you are the Alpha of your pack. It's our job and pleasure to keep him safe. We know you have many other warriors waiting to attack us. This is a safety precaution. Not that you would be able to defeat Lord Talon, but we insisted that we conduct the meeting on his behalf,' Soren explains.

We hear the snap of branches and the sound of heavy breathing that matches mine. A man with long, dark thick hair heaves forward. I can't see his face. He is dressed all in black, including his cape, but his shirt has the top few buttons undone, exposing his hard muscular chest. I realise he is fighting himself to stay back. I can see the beads of sweat dripping from his forehead onto the ground. He shakes his head, 'No, it can't be,' he says in a deep husky voice. Butterflies erupt in my stomach and flutter, hearing his voice.

'Lord Talon?' Soren says, confused and worried.

'Lord Talon?' I mumble his name. He flinches his head up, and his red crimson eyes immediately make eye contact with mine.

Chapter 23

We all step back and gasp in shock.

'Wands! This cannot be happening right now of all the times, places and species!' Soren says, looking between Lord Talon and me.

'This is not good…' Nadia says with worry.

I point my finger at Lord Talon, 'Liars!' I yell, 'His eyes are red. You did kill them. You killed them all!' I shout, tears escaping my eyes. I withdraw my dagger.

I'm glaring at the vampire who killed my beloved Micah, my fated mate. His eyes flicker like fire, and he doesn't break eye contact with me. I want to kill him, but I feel drawn to him as if something is pulling me toward him. He is incredibly handsome and attractive, with a mysterious aura about him. My eyes change from light blue to dark blue every second with mixed emotions. I close my eyes tightly for a moment and tell myself he is responsible for Micah's death. He killed Micah. I have to kill him now while I have the chance. Lord Talon takes a step forward. I lunge angrily toward him and thrust my dagger towards his chest. He swiftly grabs my arm, and I feel a sudden but quick burn on my wrist, followed by the sensation of sparks where his hand is gripping me. I try to pull my arm from his grip, but he won't budge. I glare at him, making eye contact again. I gasp and lose my breath momentarily as I become lost in his now deep blue eyes. He stares at me in utter disbelief and shock as if he can't believe what he sees. It must be because he recognises me from the night he killed Micah.

The pack warriors rush forward to attack the vampires. Nadia screams, sending a wave of sonic energy at us. My father, brothers and warriors are thrown back and clutch their heads in pain. I fall to the ground in agony from the sonic wave. Lord Talon releases my arm. I immediately try to cover my ears to block out Nadia's scream. I didn't know something like this was even possible to do. I notice blood trickling out from some of the warrior's ears and noses. Lord Talon holds his hand up, gesturing for Nadia to stop. She immediately becomes silent.

'I am warning you all to cease fighting. We are not your enemy,' Lord Talon says. His husky voice creating butterflies in my stomach again.

He killed my fated mate but has the gall to claim he isn't our enemy? The slight burning feeling on my wrist begins to itch. I tug my leather brace down just enough to see a symbol I've never seen before on my wrist. It's a sword, but it has a circle around the handle like a halo.

'What in the wands is this? What does it mean? What did you do to me?' I shout angrily at him.

Lord Talon steels himself, and a sad look flashes across his face as he fights to avoid eye contact with me before returning to his straight face, now showing no emotion at all.

My father and the warriors take this chance to strike the vampires. They shift into their wolves and Lycans and attack. Soren punches a wolf in the stomach with so much strength that the wolf flies five metres into the air.

'Tumultuous Volley!' I hear my mother shout. A large cloud appears above the vampires, and lightning begins to strike at them. They manage to dodge the strikes. A glass vial is thrown by Kayla towards them and smashes at the ground near their feet. Green smoke emits, and the vampires cover their mouths, stepping back and coughing.

Kayla grabs my arm, and a look of terror appears on her face as she stares at the symbol on my arm. Not wanting to lose this opportunity, I yank my arm away and run toward Lord Talon. I swing my dagger and slice his arm. He holds the deep cut and gives me a hurt look, but it's not the look of physical pain but emotional pain. A feeling of guilt takes over me. He killed Micah. He deserves this! He deserves to die! Why do I feel guilty and sad that I hurt him?

Soren tosses the warriors into the air like ragdolls and punches a few more, sending them flying back. Nadia screams again, sending us onto our knees, clutching our ears. The vampires then back away. They are retreating. Like hell, they are getting away.

I force myself up onto my feet as they flee and chase after them. The pain from the sonic wave is excruciating. My nose begins to bleed, but I ignore it and think of Micah. I think of his death and how close I am to his murderer and avenging his death. The vampires are darn fast, faster than werewolves, for sure. They suddenly decrease their pace, just enough for me to catch up to them. They must be planning something. Nadia has stopped screaming. My eyes focus on Lord Talon. They are talking to each other, but I can't hear them.

'I'll kill you! You monster!' I shout, lunging through the air toward Lord Talon, but flinch when that look of hurt appears on his face again. It makes me lose focus, and I falter to the ground and roll.

I hear my mother screaming my name, looking for me back through the woods. The vampires have come to a stop and stare at me silently.

'Monsters!' I say in a harsh tone. This time they all flinch. I race towards Lord Talon. He stands still as if he has no intention of moving as my dagger is about to strike his heart. I'm suddenly grabbed from behind—my dagger drops from my hand. I try to grab it, but it lands in front of Lord Talon's feet. Soren tightens his grip on me as I try to reach for Micah's dagger. Lord Talon notices the urgent look in my eyes as I try to grab it. He picks it up and runs his hand over it, admiring the craftsmanship.

'Don't you touch that! Give it back!' I snap.

'Why? So you can kill me?' he says, still looking over the dagger.

I elbow Soren in the stomach, surprising him. He lets me go from the impact he wasn't expecting. I roll and swing my leg around, knocking him over. Nadia is about to scream, but I knock her down quickly with a high kick. My fist is an inch away from making contact with Nadia's face. But my arms are grabbed, and I'm pushed onto my stomach with great strength. I try to roll, but I can't. So instead, I kick Soren's shin. 'Agh! This one's feisty and a decent fighter. You'll need all the luck you can get with this one,' Soren says to Lord Talon.

'What the hell is that supposed to mean?' I yell, kicking him in the other shin.

'Alright, that's it!' he says, tying my wrists behind my back.

'Let me go!' I scream and try to fight him off of me, but his strength is too powerful.

'Soren. What are you doing?' Lord Talon asks him.

'I'm clearly wrapping your present up for you. Complete with a bow,' he replies, smiling, tying the last knot.

'You bastard!' I yell at Soren. 'I'm not an object you can tie up and give away!'

'Oh, really?' he smirks, stands me up and shoves me forward into Lord Talon's chest. Sparks tingle all over as our bodies touch. Furious, I step back but fall over.

I watch as Lord Talon tucks my dagger under his shirt and gently grabs my arm to stand me up.

'Give me my dagger back!' I yell. The arrogant bastard completely ignores me. Still holding my arm, I try to pull away but fail. I don't like that I can feel sparks from his touch. It's something I only ever felt with Micah because he was my fated mate.

Lord Talon looks at Soren. 'We can't take her with us,' he says.

'It's too late. You don't have a choice now. You know what will happen if you don't stay near each other.'

'I know, but her pack won't allow it. They will want her back.'

'If her pack want her to live. They will have no choice but to let us take her with us,' Soren says.

'Of course, you monsters would rather murder me than give me back to my pack alive!' I yell.

Nadia walks right up to my face, 'You don't get what has happened, wolf! So I suggest you keep your yappy little mouth shut for now as you'll be thanking us for it later!' Nadia says.

'Me? Thanking murderous monsters!' I laugh, 'I think not!' I reply, glaring at Nadia.

'I knew this was going to be a bad idea. We need to keep moving. Let's go,' Lord Talon says, pulling my arm.

'No! I'm not going with you.'

'You don't have a choice,' Lord Talon says.

'Then kill me!' I say. He stops and turns to look at me. My eyes begin changing shades of blue again as a strange sensation runs through my body from his deep gaze. I force the feelings aside and glare, 'I'd rather die than go with you, and I will be sure to make your life hell if you take me with you. I won't stop trying to kill you until you are dead!'

Lord Talon reaches his hand out to cup my cheek, 'Your eyes. They change?' he says, gazing deeply into them. 'They're beautiful.'

My heart races.

As his palm brushes against my cheek, sparks explode between us, and I find myself staring at his perfect lips. I blink a few times and breathe heavily. This can't be happening. This isn't right, yet it feels so right. I step back and glare into Lord Talon's eyes.

'I'm going to very much enjoy killing you,' I tell him.

Lord Talon gazes deeper into my eyes as if trying to read me. His lips form a small smirk, and he swiftly lifts me to carry me and cradles me against his chest. I want to kiss him, I mean, punch him in the face, but my hands are tied behind my back. 'We'll see,' he says, and with great speed, runs into the distance with Soren and Nadia by his side.

Chapter 24

Trees, mountains, and rivers fly by us from the intense speed the vampires run. They are so fast that I cannot even fight, argue or speak for Lord Talon to put me down. Finally, after an hour, they stop in an open field with low grass. There are some trees and mountains in the distance. I can hear water flowing nearby. I give the darkest glare to Lord Talon as he gently puts me down. He doesn't respond. I'm relieved our bodies are no longer in contact, stopping the sparks between us.

'We can't risk the girl seeing the entrance to our lair. So you're going to have to blindfold her. We also need to feed,' Soren tells Lord Talon.

They all stare at me silently.

'Don't you dare even think about it! I refuse to be your meal!' I yell at them.

Soren and Nadia give Lord Talon a sympathetic look.

'It's fine,' Lord Talon says to them. 'I'll find a deer. In the meantime, you two feed and watch the girl while I'm gone.'

'It's Lylah! Not girl!' I huff. Lord Talon smiles, but I scowl, making him frown.

'Lord Talon, now that you have your blood flame, drinking from wildlife won't be enough to..., '

'I know!' Lord Talon growls, cutting Soren off. 'But what other choice do I have? I'm not going to force her,' he says with sadness and storms off towards the trees.

'Make sure you don't come back!' I shout behind him.

He flinches but keeps moving toward the woods.

Nadia races towards me in a blink. She lifts me by my throat and slams me against a tree. I'm struggling to breathe. 'You're a real piece of work, wolf! If you ever speak to our master like that again, I will rip your head off and feed you to the Blood Dwellers myself!' she growls.

My vision begins to darken from the lack of oxygen. I laugh. Soren and Nadia give each other a strange look.

'Do you think I care if you kill me? I don't think you realise how much I welcome death or how happy I would be to die and finally be at peace. Death is my best friend. So, hurry up and get it over with,' I say.

Nadia releases her grip, and I fall to the ground gasping for breath.

'She's bloody crazy,' Nadia says, approaching Soren.

Soren's fangs extend longer. He strokes Nadia's cheek and yanks her into his chest before biting into her neck and drinking her blood. In return, Nadia bites into Soren's neck, and they drink from each other and let out the occasional moan. I feel sick to my stomach. They're so disgusting. Repulsed, I look away and realise it's the perfect chance to escape. I shuffle my tied wrists toward my feet. Bending my knees towards my stomach, I lift my wrists over my feet, bringing my tied hands in front of me. I grab my old warped dagger from my boot and quietly sneak away. I have no idea where I am. Once I'm out of view of Soren and Nadia, I run as fast as possible. The sound of water becomes clearer. I skid as I force myself to a stop before I fall into the wide river. It must be at least thirty metres wide. The water is flowing rapidly, and there are a few large boulders. It looks dangerous and deadly, but I need to get over to the other side to get away. I have no choice but to risk crossing it. The water is freezing, I use all my strength to wade through, but the rapids are incredibly strong. I imagine Micah on the other side of the river holding his hand out to take mine.

'Lylah!' I hear my name called out in a desperate tone.

'Micah,' I say, pushing myself through the water towards him. His smile fades to concern as he looks to my right. I turn to see what it is. A log slams into the right side of my forehead. I'm pushed under the water by force. The rapids push and swirl me around. I gasp for breath every time my head bops above the water. I grab onto a boulder, but it's slippery and even harder to grip when your wrists are bound together.

'Lylah! Please! You don't understand your situation. You have to come back. You will die if you don't stay by my side,' I hear Lord Talon yell in desperation.

Blood from where the log hit me trickles down and drips onto the boulder. I feel dizzy, and my fingers are slipping. Suddenly I see Lord Talon, Nadia, and Soren run to the river's edge. Their eyes have turned black. They close their eyes and breathe as if taking in the most alluring mouth-watering scent. Their fangs elongate, staring at me like they are about to devour me alive. I panic and lose my grip on the boulder. I notice Lord Talon blink a few times and shake his head out of his blood lust trance. His eyes are dark blue again. His panic matches mine as he sees I'm being washed away by the rapids. He leaps with ease from one boulder to the next toward me. I'm pushed underwater but can't fight the rapids to swim back up for air. A hand swiftly plunges into the water and grabs my bound wrists. Tingles dance down my arms as I'm pulled out of the water and cradled close against Lord Talon's chest. I cling onto his shirt breathing heavily into his chest from almost drowning. He smells amazing, like mint and lavender. I hate that I like how he smells. He's a vampire, for wand's sake. He should smell like rotting flesh and sewerage.

Lord Talon continues to leap high into the air until he lands, crashing onto the ground by the river. He is sitting and holding me tight against his chest. I feel his hot breath against my neck. It makes my heart race and stomach flutter. I look up, and our eyes connect. Just like mine are flashing from light blue to dark blue, fighting these mixed feelings of hate and desire. His are flashing from dark blue to black, fighting his desire and blood lust for me. I realise Lord Talon has been feeling the sparks every time we touch. I don't understand. Micah is my mate, so why am I feeling the same sparks I felt with Micah? His handsomely structured face comes closer as we stare into each other's eyes. His eyes dart from the bleeding wound on my forehead to my lips.

Warm liquid runs down my cheek. I use my hands to wipe the blood away. I flinch as Lord Talon swiftly grabs my bound wrists and slides his tongue along the trail of blood as his other hand grips my thigh. His tongue and his touch send my insides soaring. I moan and quickly steel myself in the realisation of what is happening. No, no, no! Only Micah is allowed to make me feel this way. Only Micah is allowed to touch me this way. I yank my hand away from his grip and smack Lord Talon as hard as I can across his face.

His eyes change from black to dark blue. He stares at me in shock. 'Y-Your blood…' he says, licking the remnants from his lips. 'In the two hundred and sixty-four years I've been alive, never have I tasted blood so powerful. Who... what are you?' he asks.

I'm furious at Lord Talon for tasting my blood. I'm furious I feel things that I have only ever felt with Micah. I'm furious he kidnapped me, and I'm furious he killed my mate. I place my hand on his abdomen his eyes go black with lust.

'I'm Lylah, and I'm your worst bloody nightmare!' I yell as I grab my dagger tucked into his waist. I slash it across his chest and jump out of his lap. He looks down at his shirt, which is beginning to soak with his blood and touches it. Then he looks at me with intense sadness. I refuse to let it affect me this time. I imagine Micah's last moments drowning out Lord Talon's pleading eyes.

'This is for everyone you killed! This is for Micah!' I yell, leaping into the air. I hold my dagger with both hands, ready to plunge it through Lord Talon's heart. I suddenly become frozen in the air before the dagger could pierce Lord Talon's chest. What in the wands! I look down at the ground. I can't move my arms or legs. Lord Talon stands and steps toward me. His hand makes a gesture, and I rise even higher from the ground until I am at eye level with him. Our faces are only inches apart.

'You cut me again! I just saved you from drowning, and you still see me as a threat?' he says in an angry but hurt tone.

'No, I see you as a murdering monster! Now, put me down so I can finish killing you,' I say, glaring at him.

'Who's Micah?' he asks angrily.

'You should know. You are the one who killed Micah after all.'

I hear hissing sounds behind me. Soren and Nadia have finally crossed the river. Their eyes remain black, and they run towards me with their fangs protruding, ready to devour me.

'Great, just great!' Lord Talon says, throwing his hands up in the air, 'You cut my arm. I save your life. You cut me again, and now I have to save your life again, but this time from Nadia and Soren draining you of your blood because, for some strange reason, your blood tastes and wreaks of immense power. So which part of me are you going to try and cut off after I save you this time?' he asks, crossing his arms.

I smile and look down at his crotch. The look on his face when he sees me eyeing off his balls is priceless.

Chapter 25

Lord Talon raises his hand in the air and lowers me to the ground. As he takes my dagger from my hands, I try to grip it tighter, but his telekinesis stops me. I look at him, surprised, as he takes my dagger and cuts the rope from my wrists. I give him a confused look. The wind picks up and blows his long dark wavy hair across his face.

'Whether your wrists are bound or unbound. Either way, it will not stop you from trying to kill me or running away, but your wound, Lylah,' he says and softly caresses his fingers beside it. His eyes suddenly turn black from blood lust, and his breathing intensifies, but he quickly regains control, stopping himself from tasting my blood again. I want to slap his fingers away, but I can't. Instead, the warm feeling from his touch makes my eyes close. 'You need your wolf to heal it, so Soren and Nadia stop blood lusting for you. They are blood flames and should only be craving each other's blood for feeds. They shouldn't be blood lusting after you like this, and if they are, then so will other vampires. I need you to know you aren't a prisoner, Lylah, but you have to stay by my side at all times if you want to live.'

I'm suddenly released from his power and now able to move. He turns his back to me as if protecting me and uses his power to hold Soren and Nadia away from me. They hiss like feral animals.

How am I supposed to heal when I don't have a wolf? Should I just run and escape while I can? But what if Lord Talon is telling the truth that vampires will hunt me for my blood? Why would I have to stay by his side in order to live? Is it to protect me from his kind, or is there something else I'm unaware of? My biggest question is why he would even want to protect me. Why does he want me to live? Why does he seem to care if I die?

Soren is fighting against Lord Talon's telekinesis and can move slowly against his power. I wonder how he is able to move even if it is slowly against the telekinesis when I couldn't even budge an inch.

Then I remember how Soren was able to make warriors from my pack fly high into the air with a single punch, which makes me realise Soren has super strength! They all have their own unique power.

Lord Talon turns his head to look at me, 'What are you waiting for? Shift! Isn't that how your kind heals quickly?' he yells.

I bite my lip and look at my feet. I don't know what to do. I turn around and look at the mountains contemplating whether to run. Then I turn back to face Lord Talon. He looks at the mountains and realises I'm considering to flee.

But then suddenly, Nadia screams, sending me onto my knees as I clutch my hands over my ears in pain. Lord Talon is still trying to hold them both away from me, but he is beginning to struggle.

'You can't run away, Lylah! You will die! You need to shift to heal so Soren and Nadia can control themselves,' he yells.

Tears begin to form, 'I-I can't shift,' I reply.

Lord Talon stares at me with confusion. 'What are you talking about?' he asks.

'I haven't got a wolf. I can't shift, and I'll never be able to shift. I-I'm human,' I say and wipe the tear from my cheek.

'That can't be right. I could taste the power flowing through your blood. You aren't human,' he says.

Nadia stops screaming and resumes trying to wriggle free from Lord Talon's power.

'I'm telling you I have no wolf. Therefore, I cannot shift. Therefore, I cannot immediately heal! So, you will have to find another way to stop these monste-' Lord Talon gives me a look to not dare finish the words. 'To stop Soren and Nadia,' I rephrase.

'Well, wands! You know how to make things worse, don't you?' he says.

'What in the wands is that supposed to mean?' I say angrily and storm right up to him. My hands are on my hips, and I stand in front of him, glaring into his eyes.

'You need to wash the blood from your hands and face in the river. It might help stop the blood lust. Just don't bloody fall in the water this time,' he growls.

Furious, I yell at him, 'No! You didn't answer my question. How on this earth did I make this situation worse? Huh! You're the one going around murdering everyone! You're the ones who kidnapped me! But no, it's me who has made things worse for you! You're the one who destroyed my entire life!'

I grab my dagger from his waist, but this time I turn to stab Soren and Nadia.

'Wands!' he curses as he grabs my wrist and retrieves my dagger, releasing Soren and Nadia from his power. They lunge toward me, but Lord Talon pulls me into his chest, wraps his large cloak around me, and leaps high into the air over them. He lands safely on the ground holding me protectively but immediately runs.

'Why are you so stubborn? For moon's sake, Lylah, can you not go five minutes without trying to stab someone?' he growls, clutching me as tight as possible against his chest.

'Well, why are you doing this? Why do you keep saving me? Why don't you just let them kill me? I don't understand what you need me for,' I argue back, clinging onto his shirt and leaning against his warm, muscular chest.

Lord Talon's breathing calms, and his voice softens, 'There is a good reason why I won't let anyone harm or kill you. In time you will know.'

'Know what? What don't I know?' I ask, confused.

'Now is not the time for you to know. I'll already be sleeping with one eye open around you as it is. The last thing I need is to sleep with both eyes open,' he frowns.

'You say that as if I will be staying with you long term. I need to go home! My family will be looking for me, you know! They are strong and not like normal werewolves.

My father is a Lycan and the Alpha, and my mother is a witch and werewolf! They will come for me, and they will kill you all! So, I suggest you put me down, let me finish killing you because you will be killed anyway at the hands of my parents. Then I can return home to be miserable and lonely like before all of this, but at least I'll have some kind of peace knowing you are dead.'

Lord Talon slows down his pace and stares intently at me, 'You're a hybrid and the daughter of Alpha Maximus?' he says, surprised. 'Could it be witch's magic I could taste in your blood?'

'Sorry to burst your bubble *Lord Talon* but I already told you I'm human. Which means I can't shift nor can I cast magic!'

'Have you tried?' he asks.

'Are you kidding me? Have I tried?' I let out a manic laugh that disturbs Lord Talon enough to come to a stop and put me down.

He watches me as I take a few steps back. 'Aqua bedew! Inferno Flamo! Lifto Levitatous!' I say out loud and flick my hands towards him. But, of course, as expected, nothing happens. 'So, you can see, *Lord Talon,* if I were able to wield magic like my mother and her mother before her, I would have already cast you on fire and turned you into a pile of ash!' I shout.

He holds his elbow with one hand and holds his chin with the other hand, and stares at me in thought. 'A beautiful girl, born from a Lycan and hybrid wolf-witch that can't shift or wield magic. Yet, has blood full of immense power like nothing I've ever tasted before?'

He can't truly think I'm beautiful? I'm sure he would change his mind the moment he sees my scars. Not that he would ever be given a chance to see them. As he stares at me in thought, his demeanour changes. He now stares at me with sadness, but I don't want his pity.

I look away, upset, 'Yes, I get it. I'm a freak, okay!? No need to remind me,' I say, turning to walk away before he can see the tears forming in my eyes.

In a flash, Lord Talon suddenly appears in front of me, bringing me to a halt.

'I don't think you're a freak,' he says, surprising me, 'You mentioned you were miserable and lonely back home. Why?'

'You already know why. It's because of you I'm miserable and lonely! You will never be able to stop me from killing you. I'm unstoppable,' I say, bravely taking a step closer to him, ignoring the rogue tear escaping my eye.

Lord Talon stares at me, confused as to how he has caused me so much pain and loneliness. He then takes a step closer, closing the gap between us and uses his thumb to wipe the escaped tear running down my cheek—his dark blue eyes boar sadly into mine. 'You might be unstoppable, Lylah, but you're not unbreakable,' he says.

'How would you know?'

His eyes look even deeper into mine. My breath catches, and my heart deceives me and flutters in my chest.

'Because you're already broken,' he says.

I burst into tears and fall to the ground onto my knees and cry. Lord Talon kneels in front of me and pulls me onto his lap. I know I should stop him, but I don't. He holds me tenderly in his arms until I can no longer cry.

Chapter 26

Lord Talon

The moment Soren, Nadia and I arrived at Blue Scale Rock. We could see the werewolves and Lycans were already there. My feet begin to move on their own, and the sweetest scent comes over me. Sweat begins to form across my forehead as I try to stop myself from walking any closer to the pack.

'Lord Talon, is everything okay? You don't look so good,' Soren says.

'I'm not sure. I feel strange,' I tell Soren.

'Stay here, Lord Talon. We will conduct the meeting, and you can join us when you can,' Nadia says. I nod and gesture for them to go as I fight myself to keep still. What is wrong with me?

I listen to the meeting, but the scent comes closer and becomes more alluring. Against my will, I walk toward everyone. Beads of sweat drip from my forehead, and I suddenly realise what has happened. I've found my long-awaited blood flame. My fated mate that I've desperately waited over two hundred years for. I shake my head, 'No, it can't be,' I say.

'Lord Talon?' Soren says, confused and worried.

Then, I hear the sweetest voice that sounds like a bird singing as the sun rises, 'Lord Talon?' the she-wolf mumbles.

My head flinches up, and my eyes have turned crimson red from the Blood Flame bond and immediately connect with the most beautiful eyes that stare back into mine. Everyone else gasps in shock at my red eyes. At first, the beautiful she-wolf is briefly mesmerised as our eyes connect from the mate bond, but then she fights the bond, confused, and looks at me furiously.

'Wands! This cannot be happening right now of all the times, places and species!' Soren says, looking between me and the she-wolf.

'This is not good…' Nadia says worriedly.

My blood flame points her finger at me and glares, 'Liars!' she yells, 'His eyes are red. You did kill them. You killed them all!' she shouts, crying and withdrawing a glamorous dagger attached to her belt from a sheath.

Her eyes change from light blue to dark blue every second with mixed emotions. She closes her eyes for a few moments, and I step toward her to touch her and hold her. I can't believe my precious Blood Flame is an arm's length from my reach. Her eyes suddenly open, and she unexpectedly lunges angrily toward me and thrusts her dagger towards my chest. I'm devastated she is trying to stab me. This isn't how this is supposed to go.

I swiftly grab her arm to stop her from stabbing me but also to mark her, claiming and accepting the beauty of a wolf as mine. It makes the mate bond between us even stronger. Once you find your blood flame, the male's eyes will turn crimson red and remain that way until you have marked your Blood Flame. She flinches at the sudden but quick burn she feels on her wrist, followed by the sensation of sparks where my hand grips her. She gasps, and her breath catches momentarily as she becomes lost in my deep blue eyes. I stare at her in utter disbelief and shock as I still cannot believe I have found my beloved Blood Flame.

The pack warriors rush forward to attack us. Nadia screams, sending a wave of sonic energy toward them. The pack falls to the ground clutching their hands over their ears.

My blood flame falls to her knees. I release her arm, so she can cover her ears to block out Nadia's scream.

'I'm warning you all to cease fighting. We are not your enemy,' I tell them.

I notice my Blood Flame tug at the leather brace she wears to see my mark. She looks very confused and worried. I could see a glimpse of a scar near my mark, but she quickly pulls the leather brace back up and glares at me again.

'What in the wands is this? What does it mean? What did you do to me?' She shouts at me.

I stiffen and feel heartbroken that she doesn't know what has just happened between us. That she doesn't realise how special this moment of finding your Blood Flame is. I make a straight face, now showing no emotion at all.

The wolves and Lycans shift and attack the moment Nadia's scream stops. Soren punches a wolf in the stomach with so much strength that the wolf flies five metres into the air.

I hear a woman shout, 'Tumultuous Volley!'

A large cloud appears above us, and lightning begins to strike around us. We dodge the strikes, but then a glass vial is thrown towards us and smashes at the ground near their feet. Green smoke emits, making it hard to breathe. We cough and cover our mouths, stepping back.

A woman with gold chains through her hair grabs my blood flame's arm, and a look of terror appears on her face as she pulls at the bracer and stares at the symbol on my arm. She knows what it is and what it means and then looks at me with sadness. My blood flame yanks her arm away from the woman and runs toward me with a look to kill. She swings her dagger, and due to me being briefly in shock, she is about to stab me again. She slashes me across my arm near my shoulder. I hold the deep cut and give her an emotional hurt look. Her eyes begin to flicker repeatedly, from light blue to dark blue. As if she is confused and fighting her thoughts.

Soren tosses the warriors into the air like ragdolls and punches a few more, sending them flying back. Nadia screams again, sending the wolves and Lycans onto their knees again, clutching their heads and ears. We take the opportunity to retreat. I hesitate as I don't want to leave my blood flame, but she keeps trying to kill me. I don't know why, as Blood Flames are soul mates and meant to love each other for eternity.

Leaving her behind would also be deadly to both of us as we would begin to burn up and eventually die if apart too long. It's not normal for Blood Flames to be apart.

As I turn to look back, we are a long distance ahead of the wolves due to our immense speed, but I can see my Blood Flame chasing after us in the distance. I smile that she is following, hoping she has realised we are Blood Flames and that she wants to be with me.

'We need to slow down,' I say to Soren and Nadia. They look behind me and smile as well when they see the she-wolf following us.

'I can't believe you've found your Blood Flame, and she is a she-wolf!' Soren says as we come to a halt to wait for her.

'I'll kill you! You monster!' she shouts, lunging through the air toward me. She flinches as she sees my smile fade to one of sadness. Her eyes flicker in shades of blue, and she loses focus. She falls to the ground as she fights the mate bond.

We stare at her silently.

'Monsters!' she says in a harsh tone. We flinch at her hurtful words. She lunges toward me, but I keep still with no intention of moving to see if she truly wants me dead or to kill me. I have been waiting a very long time for my Blood Flame, and if she doesn't want to be with me, if she truly hates me, then she may as well kill me because the moment our eyes met, I knew I could never live a day without her by my side. I knew at that moment she had stolen my heart, and I knew from that moment onward I would protect her and love and cherish her no matter the cost.

As her dagger is about to plunge through my heart. Soren suddenly grabs her from behind. Her dagger drops from her hand and lands in front of my feet. She desperately tries to grab it back and won't take her eyes off it. Desperation flashes through her eyes as I pick the dagger up and run my hand over it, admiring the craftsmanship.

'Don't you touch that! Give it back!' she snaps.

'Why? So, you can kill me?' I say, still looking over the dagger.

She elbows Soren in the stomach, surprising him. He lets her go from the impact he wasn't expecting. She drops and rolls, swinging her leg around, knocking Soren over. Nadia is about to scream, but she knocks her down with a high kick. I watch her fist clench and fly towards Nadia's face. But Soren grabs her arm and pushes her onto her stomach. She kicks Soren's shin. 'Agh! This one's feisty and a decent fighter. You'll need all the luck you can get with this one,' Soren says to me.

'What in the wands is that supposed to mean?' Lylah yells, kicking him in the other shin.

'Alright, that's it!' he says, tying Lylah's wrists behind her back.

'Let me go!' she yells and tries to fight him off.

'Soren. What are you doing?' I ask him.

'I'm clearly wrapping your present up for you. Complete with a bow,' he replies, smiling, as he ties the last knot.

'You bastard!' she yells at Soren. 'I'm not an object you can tie up and give away!'

'Oh, really?' Soren smirks, stands her up and shoves her into my chest. Sparks tingle all over us as our bodies touch. I enjoy every second of it until she steps back, furious and falls over.

I tuck her dagger under my shirt into my belt and gently grab her arms to stand her up.

Chapter 27

'Give me my dagger back!' she yells and tries to pull away. I want her to feel the sparks. I want her to know I'm not a threat. She has a sudden look of sadness, and I begin to feel guilty. All I want is to see her smile, to see her happy.

I look at Soren. 'We can't take her with us,' I tell him.

'It's too late. You don't have a choice now. You know what will happen if you don't stay near each other,' he replies.

'I know, but her pack won't allow it. They will want her back.'

'If her pack want her to live. They will have no choice but to let us take her,' Soren says.

He is right. The only way for her to live is to stay with me. If Lylah returns to her family without me, she will begin to burn up as if she has a fever, which will worsen until she burns to death. She is mine now, my love, and I won't let my Blood Flame have that fate even if it means her hating me.

'Of course, you monsters would rather murder me than give me back to my pack alive!' she yells.

Nadia walks right up to her face, 'You don't get what has happened, wolf! So, I suggest you keep your yappy little mouth shut for now as you'll be thanking us for it later!' Nadia tells her.

As angry as I am at Nadia for speaking to my Blood Flame like that, she is right. My Blood Flame still hasn't registered that we are fated mates or that she will die if she leaves me.

'Me? Thanking murderous monsters!' she laughs, 'I think not!' she says, glaring at Nadia.

'I knew this was going to be a bad idea. We need to keep moving. Let's go,' I say and gently pull Lylah's arm.

'No! I'm not going with you,' she yells.

'You don't have a choice,' I tell her.

'Then kill me!' she says.

I stop and turn to look at her. Her eyes are changing shades again. Then she suddenly glares, 'I'd rather die than go with you, and I will be sure to make your life hell if you take me with you. I won't stop trying to kill you until you are dead!' she warns.

Enchanted by her eyes, I ignore her threat and caress her cheek, 'Your eyes. They change?' I say, gazing deeply into them. 'They're beautiful,' I add.

Sparks explode between us as my palm brushes against her cheek. She breathes heavily and then steps back, glaring into my eyes.

'I'm going to very much enjoy killing you,' she tells me.

I gaze deeper into her mesmerising eyes. *Mine!* I form a small smirk and swiftly lift her and cradle her in my arms against my chest. Thankful her wrists are bound behind her back so she can't claw my heart out from my chest. It feels amazing holding her in my arms. I've never felt such warmth, such love like this before, and she is all mine!

'We'll see,' I smile and with great speed, run into the distance with Soren and Nadia by my side.

We stop in an open field with low grass. I ignore the glare from my Blood Flame as I place her down.

'We can't risk the girl seeing the entrance to our lair. So, you're going to have to blindfold her. We also need to feed,' Soren says.

We all stare at my Blood Flame, silently sharing the same thought, knowing she isn't going to let me feed freely from her.

'Don't you dare even think about it! I refuse to be your meal!' she yells at us.

Soren and Nadia give me a sympathetic look. They know that vampires can no longer sustain enough nourishment from drinking the blood of animals or others once they have found their Blood Flame. It will only give me little strength drinking any other blood now. I need to feed from her blood to keep up my full strength.

'It's fine,' I tell them. 'I'll find a deer. In the meantime, you two feed and watch the girl while I'm gone.'

'It's Lylah! Not girl!' she huffs.

I smile, hearing her pretty name, but then she scowls at me, making me frown.

'Lord Talon, now that you have your blood flame, drinking from wildlife won't be enough to.... '

'I know!' I growl, cutting Soren off. 'But what other choice do I have? I'm not going to force her,' I say in a sad tone and storm off towards the trees.

'Make sure you don't come back!' Lylah shouts behind me. I flinch, hurt by her words, but I keep walking.

Lylah watches Nadia and Soren feed on each other while I quickly catch a deer and feed from its blood, but when I return, Lylah is nowhere to be found.

Frantic, I race around, looking for her. 'I told you to keep an eye on her!' I yell at Soren and Nadia.

They both cower.

'Lylah!' I call out, desperate to find her.

I pick up her sweetly scent toward the river. As we approach, we all become consumed with blood lust. Our eyes turn black, and our fangs elongate with a hunger for her blood. I see Lylah struggling to hold onto a boulder in the river. But my eyes won't budge from the blood dripping down her face. Her blood wreaks magnificently of immense power. I close my eyes and breath to focus and snap out of my blood lust. I then leap from boulder to boulder with ease and grab, Lylah's bound wrists as she sinks further under the water. I pull her into my arms and hold her tight as I leap across to the other side of the river. Sitting with her on my lap, my eyes turn black with blood lust again, and our eyes connect and flicker. I'm trying to control the urge to not bite her neck and feed from her, but also to not kiss her. Lylah looks at me with great confusion, and I notice she slowly takes in my facial features. My eyes dart from the bleeding wound on her forehead to her small plump lips.

Lylah then wipes the blood from her face with her hand. I lose all control, grab her wrists and devour the smeared blood with my tongue while my other hand grips her thigh seductively. It's the sweetest, most delectable blood I have ever tasted. I feel my strength and power intensify just from licking the small amount of blood from her hands. Her back arches and she moans as I lick and suck her hands. The bulge between my legs begins to pulsate. I need her so badly. If she didn't hate me so much, I'd devour her body right now in many ways.

Suddenly, Lylah stiffens in realisation she has just allowed me to continue touching and tasting her and that she has been enjoying every moment of it, just as much as I have. She yanks her hand away from my grip and smacks me swiftly across my face.

I'm slapped out of my blood lust trance. I lick Lylah's blood from my lips and taste the power resonating through it. This isn't normal werewolf blood. I stare at Lylah in shock 'Y-Your blood….' I tell her. 'In the two hundred and sixty-four years I've been alive, never have I tasted blood so powerful. Who…. what are you?' I ask her.

Lylah maintains eye contact while placing her hand on my abdomen, and my eyes go black with lust.

'I'm Lylah, and I'm your worst bloody nightmare!' she yells, grabs the dagger tucked into my waist, and slashes it across my chest, jumping out of my lap.

I look down at my shirt, soaking my blood and touch it. Then, feeling heartbroken, Lylah cut me again. I look at her with intense sadness. My eyes plead with her as to why she would do this to me, to her Blood Flame.

'This is for everyone you killed! This is for Micah!' she yells, leaping into the air. As the dagger is about to plunge through my chest, I hold my hand up, using my telekinesis to freeze her. Lylah looks down at the ground. She can't move the rest of her body. I step toward her and make her rise even higher from the ground until she is at my eye level. Our faces are only inches apart.

'You cut me again! I just saved you from drowning, and you still see me as a threat?' I say, hurt and angry.

'No, I see you as a murdering monster! Now, put me down so I can finish killing you,' she glares.

'Who is Micah?' I ask, angry at her mentioning another man's name.

'You should know. You are the one who killed Micah after all!'

I don't understand why she thinks I go around killing everyone and why she thinks I killed this, Micah. I don't even kill the animals I feed on. I drink what I need and let them go.

Chapter 28

Soren and Nadia have finally crossed the river. Their eyes remain black, and they run towards Lylah with their fangs protruding, ready to devour her. They should only be blood-lusting for each other as they are Blood Flames, but Lylah's blood isn't like everyone else's. Her blood is special, and she is unlike anyone I have ever met.

I'm annoyed and hurt. Lylah keeps trying to kill me and fighting the bond, and now her blood is making other vampires blood lust after her, 'Great, just great!' I say, throwing my hands up in the air, 'You cut my arm. I save your life. You cut me again, and now I have to save your life again, but this time from Nadia and Soren draining you of your blood because, for some strange reason, your blood tastes and wreaks of immense power. So which part of me will you try and cut off after I save you this time?' I ask sarcastically and cross my arms.

She smiles at me for the first time but looks down at my balls. My body stiffens, and I pail. She wouldn't dare, would she?

I lower Lylah to the ground and retrieve the dagger from her hands, cutting the rope from her wrists. She looks at me, confused. The wind picks up and blows my long hair around.

'Whether your wrists are bound or unbound. Either way, it will not stop you from trying to kill me or running away, but your wound, Lylah,' I say and softly caress my fingers beside it.

My eyes flick to black from blood lust, and my breathing intensifies. I want to taste her again, but I regain control, stopping myself. I watch as she closes her eyes as I caress her face. 'You need your wolf to heal it, so Soren and Nadia stop blood lusting for you. They are Blood Flames and should only be craving each other's blood for feeds. They shouldn't be blood lusting after you like this, and if they are, then so will other vampires. I need you to know you aren't a prisoner, Lylah, but you have to stay by my side at all times if you want to live,' I tell her and release her from my power.

I turn to face Soren and Nadia and freeze them before they can reach her. They hiss like feral animals, desperate to drink her blood.

Soren is able to use his strength against my telekinesis to move slowly closer to Lylah. I look at Lylah as I wonder what is taking her so long to shift. 'What are you waiting for? Shift! Isn't that how your kind heals quickly?' I yell.

She bites her plump little lips and looks down, then looks over at the mountains with a look that tells me she is contemplating running away again.

But then suddenly, Nadia screams, sending her falling to her knees and clutching her hands over her ears in pain. Nadia uses her sonic scream against me as well. I'm beginning to struggle to hold them.

'You can't run away, Lylah! You will die! You need to shift to heal so Soren and Nadia can control themselves,' I yell.

'I-I can't shift,' she sobs.

I stare at her with confusion. 'What are you talking about?' I ask.

'I haven't got a wolf. I can't shift, and I'll never be able to shift. I-I'm human,' she says, wiping a tear from her face.

'That can't be right. I could taste the power flowing through your blood. You aren't human,' I tell her.

Nadia stops screaming and resumes trying to wriggle free from my control.

'I'm telling you I have no wolf. Therefore, I cannot shift. Therefore, I cannot immediately heal! So, you will have to find another way to stop these monste- ' I glare at her, and she stops herself from referring to us vampires as monsters. 'To stop Soren and Nadia,' she rephrases.

Of course, she has no wolf. Of course, the Blood Flame blessed to me hates me and wants me dead, and her blood is unique, sending other vampires into a blood craze.

'Well, wands! You know how to make things worse, don't you?' I tell her.

'What in the wands is that supposed to mean?' she says angrily and storms right up to me, glaring into my eyes.

'You need to wash the blood from your hands and face in the river. It might help stop the blood lust. Just don't bloody fall in the water this time,' I growl.

'No! You didn't answer my question. How on this earth did I make this situation worse? Huh! You're the one going around murdering everyone! You're the ones who kidnapped me! But no, it's me who has made things worse for you! You're the one who destroyed my entire life!'

She grabs her dagger from my waist, but this time turns to stab Soren and Nadia.

'Wands!' I curse and grab her wrist and retrieve the dagger, releasing Soren and Nadia from my power. I pull Lylah swiftly into my chest, wrapping my cloak around her, and leap high into the air over them. I land safely on the ground holding Lylah protectively but immediately run.

'Why are you so stubborn? For moon's sake, Lylah, can you not go five minutes without trying to stab someone?' I growl, clutching her tighter.

'Well, why are you doing this? Why do you keep saving me? Why don't you just let them kill me? I don't understand what you need me for,' she argues back, then clings tighter onto my shirt and leans against my chest. It hurts but also feels good as she is against my wound.

I calm my breathing. I feel terrible for telling Lylah she made everything worse. When in fact, she has only made my world better by being my Blood Flame.

'There's a good reason why I won't let anyone harm or kill you. In time you will know,' I tell her.

'Know what? What don't I know?' she asks, confused.

'Now is not the time for you to know. I'll already be sleeping with one eye open around you as it is. The last thing I need is to sleep with both eyes open,' I frown, thinking of how she will probably freak out and keep me on her kill list when she finds out we are mates.

'You say that as if I will be staying with you long term. I need to go home! My family will be looking for me, you know! They are strong and not like normal werewolves. My father is a Lycan and the Alpha, and my mother is a witch and werewolf! They will come for me, and they will kill you all! So, I suggest you put me down, let me finish killing you because you will be killed anyway at the hands of my parents. Then I can return home to be miserable and lonely like before all of this, but at least I'll have some kind of peace knowing you are dead.'

I slow down and stare intently at Lylah, 'You're a hybrid and the daughter of Alpha Maximus?' I say, surprised. 'Could it be witch's magic I could taste in your blood?' I wonder.

'Sorry to burst your bubble *Lord Talon* but I already told you I'm human. Which means I can't shift nor can I cast magic!'

'Have you tried?' I ask.

'Are you kidding me? Have I tried?' she lets out a disturbing manic laugh. I put Lylah down and watch as she takes a few steps back. 'Aqua bedew! Inferno Flamo! Lifto Levitatous!' she says out loud, flicking her hands at me.

Did she seriously just try and cast spells on me?

'So, you can see, *Lord Talon,* if I were able to wield magic like my mother and her mother before her, I would have already cast you on fire and turned you into a pile of ash!' she shouts.

Thinking, I stare at her in thought. 'A beautiful girl, born from a Lycan and hybrid wolf-witch that can't shift or wield magic. Yet, has blood full of immense power like nothing I've ever tasted before?'

As I stare at her in thought, I begin to sympathise with her, that she seems unable to use any abilities.

She looks away, upset, 'Yes, I get it. I'm a freak, okay!? No need to remind me,' she says, turning to walk away to hide her tears.

I appear in front of her in a flash, bringing her to a halt.

'I don't think you're a freak,' I tell her. Lylah flinches as if surprised by my words, 'You mentioned you were miserable and lonely back home. Why?' I ask her.

'You already know why. It's because of you I'm miserable and lonely! You will never be able to stop me from killing you. I'm unstoppable.' She says, bravely taking a step closer to me. The tear she tries to hold back escapes.

I stare at her, confused. I don't understand how I have caused her so much pain and how she could be lonely in her pack surrounded by family. I take a step closer, closing the gap between us. I wipe her rogue tear from her cheek with my thumb. Her eyes close from my warm, gentle touch. When she opens her eyes, she finds me staring sadly into them. 'You might be unstoppable, Lylah, but you're not unbreakable,' I tell her.

'How would you know?' she asks.

I stare deeper into Lylah's eyes; her breath catches, and I can hear her heart race. There is such sadness in her eyes. My heart begins to ache, knowing my precious Blood Flame is suffering immensely. To think that my precious Blood Flame is enduring such terrible pain causes me great anguish.

'Because you're already broken,' I say to her.

Lylah bursts into tears and falls to her knees, and cries. I'm not sure what to do. We are Blood Flames, destined mates, yet, she hates me and even wants to kill me. I know she can feel the sparks when we touch. I know she is fighting the pull between us, but why? She is meant to want me. Why does she seem confused as to why she can feel a mate bond between us? Does she not know how Blood Flames work? Does she not realise we are fated mates? I want to kiss her small, plump lips and tell her everything will be okay. But instead, I kneel in front of her and pull my beautiful Blood Flame onto my lap. Surprisingly, she doesn't even try to push me away or fight me. Instead, she lets me hold her and continues to cry.

Chapter 29

Exhausted from crying and recent events, Lylah sleeps soundly in my arms. I carry her toward my lair but stop by one of the lakes along the way. Sitting by the water's edge, I hold her tight, savouring the moment as I know she will continue being stubborn and keep fighting against the bond. I stroke her hair from her face and caress her cheek, taking in all of her features. Her platinum white hair, high cheekbones, small but plump lips, her soft skin. The Gods have blessed me with the most beautiful woman I have ever seen. Even though she is stubborn and argumentative, I've never felt so happy. She is perfect, and my feelings toward her are already strong. I pray to the Gods she will fall in love with me regardless of the bond.

Scooping water from the lake in my hand, I gently wash all the blood from her face. Thankfully the wound on her head has stopped bleeding. Hopefully, now having no blood on her, Nadia and Soren will return to their senses, and she won't cause my coven of vampires into a blood lust craze when we arrive.

Now that I have freshened Lylah up, I resume my journey to my lair. I approach the well-hidden entrance to the labyrinth of tunnels with a smile, knowing I'm about to bring my Blood Flame home. My coven of vampires will be thrilled to have their lady of the coven to now serve. The entrance is at a very old and long-forgotten medieval cemetery. Using my telekinesis, I make a large flat rectangle of stone that looks like the top of a grave slide across the ground. It reveals stairs of stone leading underground. I enter, walk down, and then, using my mind, slide the stone slate again to close it. There are fire torches and candles lit throughout the tunnels. It takes an hour of walking through a multitude of passages that twist and turn. If you didn't know your way around, you would never find your way out. Lylah begins to stir awake and stares at me angrily as she realises I have been carrying her while she slept.

'Put. Me. Down.' Lylah says in anger.

I halt my steps and let her go. I watch her as she takes a few steps back and turns around a few times, looking at all the different tunnels.

'W-where are we?' she asks worriedly.

'We are going home to the underground,' I tell her.

'I already told you I need to go back home! My family will be looking for me. They will come for me,' she says.

I take a deep breath and try to speak in the gentlest tone possible.

'I'm sorry, Lylah. They're not coming, and even if they did, they would never be able to find the underground.'

'What do you mean they aren't coming?

I step towards her, but she steps back. I sigh and walk around and then past her, 'I will explain it later when we get back home to our lair, and once you have settled in, I will explain what I can to you,' I tell her.

She runs up behind me, and I hear her heartbeat pound erratically, 'Our Lair? The lair you are going to is your home, not mine. I will not be staying, and I definitely won't be settling here anytime soon. I'm going home, and you can't stop me!' she says and turns around to walk in the way we came.

I slowly follow behind Lylah and watch her become confused and lost from taking a few wrong turns. It seems to have made her even angrier. She turns to face me and tries to shove me, but I don't budge. She growls and stomps her feet as I continue to gaze at her calmly. Her glare deepens, and the little hellion pulls a dagger out from either boot and begins trying to slash me open again.

I continue to dodge her moves as she swings her arms rapidly towards me. I can hear her daggers whipping through the air with each strike. She is incredibly quick with her moves. I lean backwards as she attempts to strike across my throat but misses. 'How many daggers do you have?' I ask.

'Wouldn't you like to know!'

'Yes, I would, hence why I asked.'

Lylah smirks, 'I have enough to kill you.'

'I bet you do,' I say, grabbing her ankle as she attempts a high kick into my chest. She spins around, making me let go of her foot and throws a dagger at me. I tilt my head as it flies past. She only just missed me! I'm in shock Lylah almost got me. I'm feeling proud this feisty little spitfire is all mine. Beautiful, feisty, and well-skilled. Her fighting me is starting to turn me on. Whoever taught her to fight taught her well, most of my coven wouldn't stand a chance against her as they don't have unique abilities. All vampires are blessed with great speed, but for some, they are blessed with another power. It's usually the higher ranked that are blessed with it. Nadia has her sonic scream, Soren has super strength, I can move objects with my mind, and my dear friend Cedric can open portals.

'You missed,' I tell her.

'Clearly, but not this time!'

As Lylah runs toward me with determination. I grab her wrist, then the dagger and flip her around, so her back is against my chest. I take the dagger and push myself against her until she is pressed against the wall. Lylah gasps and her heartbeat fastens as I hold her hands above her head and slide my other hand slowly down her body. 'Let me go!' she says, half moaning from my touch.

'Are you sure you want me to let you go? You seem to be enjoying this,' I say, my breath hot against her neck, triggering more sparks and sensations between us.

'You bastard!' she says, her breath hitching as my nose glides across her neck. My fangs protrude on their own. I realise the bond is drawing me to sink my teeth into her nape and taste her properly.

I find five old daggers and withdraw them from her whilst running my hands over her body, checking every pocket, belt, and any other area one would conceal a knife.

I can't help myself. I playfully nip but don't bite Lylah's neck. Her back arches and she leans back against me as if she is no longer trying to fight the desire between us.

'All done,' I say, casually stepping back and walking away while inspecting all the daggers.

'All done?' she says, annoyed and follows abruptly behind.

'Yes, I seem to have collected all your weapons. Now we can proceed to our lair,' I smile. 'These daggers are old and rusty. If they weren't slightly bent, affecting your aim. You probably could have killed me,' I tell her.

'Killing you was the whole point!' she says through gritted teeth.

'Oh, well. Better luck next time.'

She lets out a scream in frustration that echoes through the labyrinth.

'Feel better?' I ask.

'No! I will feel better when you are dead and when I'm out of this place!'

I show no emotion and keep a blank face. 'Fair enough,' I tell her and turn around, continuing forward. 'This way,' I say.

But she ignores me and continues to go the wrong way. I touch my chest and arm as it's still hurting since she cut me. It's strange because they should have healed well and truly by now, but they haven't healed at all. I'll have to have a good look back at the lair.

With a blink of speed, I appear in front of Lylah and lift her over my shoulder.

'Put me down!'

'Our home is this way, not that way. That way leads to a pit of venomous snakes, but if you prefer to find out for sure, go ahead,' I say, putting her back down.

'This isn't my home,' she says, then she looks at the tunnel she was pursuing and now seems nervous and unsure to go down there.

'This, here with me, is your home now, whether you like it or not, Lylah. When we are in a better situation, I will then take you home to visit your family. But in the meantime, you will adjust and instantly fall in love with the beauty of the underground just as you will one day, hopefully, if the Gods answer my prayers, fall in love with….' If I tell her 'me', she will fight and push me away even more.

Lylah gives me a puzzling stare.

'With the coven. Everyone in our coven,'

Lylah's shoulders drop, 'There are even more than you three in your coven?'

I smile assuringly and nod.

'Wands!' she curses, crossing her arms.

Chapter 30

Leaving the labyrinth of tunnels, we now enter a section with great stone pillars. They are all carved with all kinds of symbols and glyphs. The steps become softer as we now walk over sand. Lylah is intrigued by the carvings. She stops, stares at some of them, and runs her fingers over others as if trying to figure out what they mean.

We are about to enter my favourite part of the underground. I'm excited to show her our home, but she looks sad and miserable. I can see she is forcing herself not to cry. She keeps looking over her shoulder and becomes even more depressed every time she looks back. My heart begins to ache as I realise she misses her family and home. Her shoulders slump, and she won't look at me, keeping her eyes on her feet.

As we are about to step into the final part. I give Lylah a small smile, but she looks away, making me frown.

'Welcome to the Underground, our home,' I tell her as we step into the vast underground cave.

I watch as her mouth drops open, and she looks around in utter shock and surprise. The sound of water flowing and splashing echoes throughout the cave.

A massive lake glistens before us. Waterfalls on opposite sides of the lake are gushing out water from holes in the cave wall. The water in the lake is so clear you can see fish, the odd stingrays and even turtles swimming around. There is a big island on the left full of trees and flowers and some rabbits chewing on the grass. Green vines grow throughout the walls of the cave. Small tunnels of light seeping through the walls shine against beautiful large precious crystals reflecting the light. There are old bridges made from wood and rope to crosse the water to go to the island or waterfalls. The one across the centre leads to the largest island where my lair, my castle, is. I continue to watch Lylah's reaction.

'What do you think?' I ask her.

'I've never seen anything like this before. It's like I have fallen into an enchanted world.'

She steps to the water's edge and points, 'Is that a turtle?' she asks, surprised.

I smile and nod.

'Those bridges don't look very safe,' she says.

'There safe enough,' I assure her.

She holds onto the rope rail with each hand and steps onto the first plank. She begins to wobble as the bridge sways, and she panics. Standing behind her, I grab her waist to steady her.

'Don't touch me,' she says and angrily turning, she slaps my hand away, steps back, loses her balance and falls into the water. Lucky for her the bridge is only a foot above the water. 'That was your fault!' she yells when her head pops up out of the water. She clings onto a wood plank on the bridge and pulls herself up.

'I was just trying to help, so this wouldn't happen,' I say to her.

She glares at me as she wipes the water from her face. 'You're the reason I'm here! I don't ever want your help,'

I try not to flinch and glare back at her angrily. 'Fine, you don't want my help. Then you can get across the bridge yourself!' I say to her.

She looks over her shoulder and frowns at the long bridge. She then looks back my way but at the exit behind me. I step forward, blocking the start of the bridge so she can't get past me.

'Don't even think about it,' I warn her. My eyes flash with darkness, and my heart hardens to stone at the thought of her ever trying to leave me.

Lylah stares at me as if she wants to stab me. Unsurprisingly, she reaches into her boot, then pats around her belt to reach for a dagger but then remembers I removed them all.

What would normally take ten minutes to cross, takes Lylah two hours to cross as she slowly crawls and grips each plank one at a time and very carefully at a snail's pace.

Each time she moves onto the next plank, I roll my eyes or sigh and casually take a step forward. I could easily scoop her up and sprint across the bridge within seconds. But we are angry at each other, which will only escalate her anger toward me.

As we reach the bridge's end, Soren and Nadia enter the underground.

'I see she hasn't managed to kill you yet?' Soren jokes.

'Not yet anyway,' I reply as they approach behind me.

'Oh, I will. Don't you worry about that,' Lylah says, jumping from the last plank onto the large island. She rolls and lays flat on her back, relieved to have made it across.

We stand and stare down at her.

'What happened back there anyway?' Nadia asks. 'We have never craved to drink anyone else's blood before except for each other's as we are blood flames. I don't understand why we became so feral with blood lust for your Blood Flam-,'

I narrow my eyes at Nadia. I don't think telling Lylah she is my Blood Flame is wise and that it's the same thing as werewolves finding their mates. She is dealing with a lot as it is. She isn't ready to know yet.

'I mean for Lylah's blood,' she rephrases, taking the hint.

'Lylah's blood is very powerful, which I assume is why all vampires will be unable to resist it. Drinking her blood will strengthen any vampire from the power flowing through her and greatly enhance our powers. The small taste I had from her hands made me feel stronger than ever, and the taste was incredibly delectable, the purest, most powerful blood I've ever tasted.'

Soren laughs, 'Lylah, actually allowed you to taste her blood?'

Lylah sits up, 'I never allowed the jerk to taste my blood. He decided to rudely help himself to the remnants on my hands after wiping the blood from my wound.'

Soren laughs even louder and elbows me, 'You sly fox. Even you became feral with blood lust and couldn't help yourself.'

'Well, of course, I couldn't help myself! I am her Blood Fl-' I close my mouth abruptly before spilling the beans to Lylah. 'It doesn't matter now anyway. What matters is making sure, Lylah, under no circumstances, ends up with any injuries, not even a scratch. The smallest drop of blood could send the coven into a blood lust frenzy, and it would kill her if they managed to get to her.'

Lylah stares at me fearfully and gulps. 'I shouldn't be here,' she says, standing up. 'I'm going home!' she storms past us, but I scoop my arm around her waist and pull her into my chest.

'Let me go,' she says, trying to loosen my grip.

I turn her around to face me and place my hands firmly on her shoulders. 'Look at me, Lylah,' I say.

She stops fighting me and locks eyes with mine. Although she is quite fierce and strong, I can still see she has a soft and vulnerable side, which gives me hope that Lylah and I could work. That she could one day accept the bond and the feelings between us.

'I will not let anything happen to you. I will not let anyone harm you. You are safe here with me, and I will have Nadia as your personal maiden who will stay with you when I am not around or when you don't want me around,' I assure her.

'What!' Nadia and Lylah shout.

'Lord Talon. You can't be serious that I'm to be her personal maiden? Surely there is another in our coven far more suitable than I?'

'Lord Talon, I'm going to have to agree with Nadia,' Lylah says, 'I don't want her as my maiden, nor do I need a babysitter or anyone to look out for me. Just lead me out of the labyrinth, and we can be done with each other for good!'

I gently but firmly grab her chin and watch her eyes change to a light blue from my gaze and touch, 'For your own sake and safety, Lylah, you will stay here with me whether you like it or not.'

Her eyes narrow at mine, and her eyes change to the darkest shade of blue possible. She tries to shove me away and then turns and storms towards the bridge to leave.

I face Nadia, 'As the Lord of the coven; my word is final. You are to be Lylah's maiden and shadow her every move when I am not with her, and if I find out you have left her side for the briefest second or she has sustained the tiniest scratch. Then you will reap the consequences.'

Nadia forces a smile and nods, 'Yes, Master.'

I blink, appearing in front of Lylah and try to take her hand. The sound of the slap across my cheek echoes throughout the cave.

'You're a Liar! I'm your prisoner. I don't want to be here. Please, just please let me go,' she begs, falling to the ground.

'If it were that easy to let you go, then I would have already,' I tell her truthfully.

Lylah looks up at me with a defeated look, 'I hate you,' she says.

My whole body flinches in pain and hurts at her words, and I don't even try to hide it from her. It would have been much less painful to let her stab me in the heart with her blunt, rusted dagger. I take a deep breath, gently take her arm, and grip tighter each time she tries to pull her arm away, 'So be it,' I reply and enter up the steps of our castle.

Chapter 31

As we enter the castle, I use my mind to lower the portcullis gate behind us. The heavy chains clink as it lowers, getting Lylah's attention. She looks over her shoulder. Then, as she sees the portcullis close, she panics and races back towards it, but she is too late. It slams down shut. Her hands grip the metal, and she lowers her head. 'This isn't happening. It's just another bad dream—a nightmare. I'll awaken from it soon and find myself in my chambers in my packhouse, and then I can look back at all this and laugh… either that or cry,' she tells herself, nodding her head assuredly.

'Lylah,' I say gently. She turns to look at me, and we somberly stare into each other's eyes. Her eyes have not even the tiniest bit of joy or happiness. Her soul is completely lost and broken, but now I have added to the damage already done, making her completely miserable. 'I'm sorry,' I tell her, feeling terrible for her.

If only I could tell her that leaving me would kill her. That we have to stay together in order to live, but she doesn't even know we are Blood Flames yet. It's all too much for her to handle right now. Once the time is right, I will tell her everything. Lylah looks away, no longer wanting to look at me. No matter what it takes. I vowel to myself that I will one day heal her broken soul.

As we enter the castle, we walk up a corridor and towards a set of stairs. Vampires from my coven stop what they are doing and bow as we walk passed. Although they all sneak a curious peek at Lylah, who pays no attention to anyone, keeping her eyes on her feet. She would be exhausted, and I need to speak to the entire coven before I introduce them to her. I avoid the main rooms, proceeding up the stairs to another level.

A long horrendous moan, which turns into a wailing cry, then a manic laugh, echoes throughout the castle. Nadia, Soren and I give each other a solemn stare. Lylah is disturbed by the sounds but doesn't say anything.

My best friend Cedric has lived alone in the underground crypts for one hundred and twenty-eight years. Ever since the day we sealed Lord Atticus into the dark portal. Although it was a great victory banishing him. It was also a very tragic time for the coven. My brother, Lord Atticus, had killed our father and tried to take over the coven. Father wanted me to take over if he were ever to die. He knew he had one good-hearted son and one evil. My father knew the death and destruction my brother would cause the world one day. He wanted to prevent that from happening. So he declared me as the heir to the coven. My brother became enraged, but our father had warned him many times to stop summoning his Blood Dwellers to hunt down humans. It was critical that humans never find out about our existence. We can live for thousands of years, but we can still be killed in the meantime. My brother summoned his Blood Dwellers and killed our father in front of the entire coven. We fought against him and were defeating him, so he fled the moment he could. Months passed, and we found out he had been killing more humans to make himself more powerful each day. When we found him again, Alanis, Cedric's Blood Flame, was brutally killed at my brother's hands. Afterwards, he ripped her heart out and threw it at Cedric's feet.

Cedric, heartbroken and wanting revenge, began to open a dark portal. My brother set his Blood Dwellers onto him, slowing down the opening of the portal, and I used my powers to slow my brother's movements which in turn slowed the Blood Dwellers down. Soren kept grabbing Blood Dwellers attacking Cedric and throwing them far into the distance, but they would vanish in thin air and reappear. The same would happen when he punched them. Again, they would disappear and reappear.

As my brother got closer to Cedric and the portal became bigger. Just as I used my power to push him into the portal, he grabbed Cedric's face with clawed fingers and ripped it off before being forced into it. As soon as it sealed up, the Blood Dwellers vanished. I remember racing over to Cedric. He was on the ground, crouched over, and rocking himself. When he looked up, we all gasped and stood back. All his facial bones were exposed. The only skin he had on his face was on across his forehead. Even his nose and eyelids were gone. It was as if we were staring at a zombie or a skeleton but with his eyeballs intact.

'Alanis! Alanis!' he wailed, picking up her heart. He holds it against his chest and continues to rock himself.

He knows he is missing skin from his face, but he doesn't comprehend the extent of his injuries as the only thing going through his mind is the grief and anguish of losing his Blood Flame, Alanis.

We returned him to our castle. Cedric stayed in his room all week, refusing to let a healer see him. He was even refusing to drink blood. After a week, we heard the most horrendous wail from his room, only to discover him looking at his reflection in a bowl of water. He threw the bowl away and ran through the castle until he reached the crypts. He has never left the crypts since. We tried to get him out many times. He would hiss and bite at us like a wild animal. Over time we would visit him each week. We would always find him in nothing but a ragged loin cloth, drinking a rat's blood and eating it. 'Monster,' he would hiss at himself and hit himself repetitively as if punishing himself and would pull at his hair. He continued to try and attack us each day. Clearly, he wanted to be left alone to live out his days in the crypts. It's been over one hundred and twenty-seven years since we last went to the crypts to see him. I banned everyone from going down there so he would be left undisturbed. From the day he saw his reflection in the water, he has let out a loud and long wail and cry, which then becomes a manic laugh even up to this day. He had become completely mad.

Lylah continues to follow me quietly. We walk through the next corridor, and again any vampires about stop and bow in my presence. We go up one more set of stairs before arriving at my chambers. I push the door open and gesture for Lylah to enter. She enters the room, avoiding eye contact with us, and sits in a gentlemen's chair, depressingly staring at her feet.

'I think some rest might do you some good, and through the door on the right, over there,' I point, 'You will find a bath if you wish to use it. Nadia will remain outside your chambers. Let her know if you need anything,' I say to her.

Lylah doesn't respond. I frown and close the door. Nadia leans against the wall and nods, indicating they will be fine.

Soren follows me downstairs and into the healer's room, where Becky is organizing herbs.

'Master,' she bows, 'You're back. Did the pack attack you as I warned you they most likely would?' she says, looking me over.

'Well, yeah, but it wasn't them who caused any injuries. I was cut twice, but they haven't healed at all,' I tell her.

'You're telling me someone cut you? No one has ever been able to even lay a finger on you. You must tell me all about this fierce warrior. He has me intrigued already,' she smiles.

'Shouldn't you be more intrigued as to why I haven't healed?'

'Yes, I suppose that has me intrigued too. Now show me your wounds.'

I remove my cape and pass it along with my black shirt to Soren.

'The wound on your chest is deep. The one near your shoulder isn't too bad. I don't understand how you wouldn't heal from a knife wound, though?' Becky says.

I think about the knife and how it's been handcrafted using many materials. I stand and begin to empty my pockets of five old rusty daggers and then the fancy handmade one and place it on the table in front of Becky.

'What in the wands, Lord Talon? Since when did you carry so many knives?' Soren asks.

'Since Lylah attempted to kill me for the one-hundredth time, I had to put her against a wall and pat her down to find and remove them all. It was either that or continue to dodge rusty daggers thrown at my head for the rest of the trek home.'

'She must love her daggers,' he laughs.

'So it seems,' I say, staring at Becky inspecting the fine dagger.

She turns towards me. 'Who's Lylah?' she asks curiously.

'She is the one who cut me with that dagger you hold.'

'A girl!' she says, smiling and shocked.

'Not just a girl, Becky. Lylah is my blood flame who also happens to be the daughter of Alpha Maximus, the Lycan,' I tell her.

Becky bursts into laughter.

'Your blood flame keeps trying to kill you and is also a werewolf?' she asks.

'Sort of,' I reply, unimpressed she is laughing at the situation.

'Why would she want to kill you?' she asks, now becoming serious again.

'She thinks it was me who killed some of her pack members and all the humans that were murdered. She thinks I've made Atticus and the Blood Dwellers up. She saw them one night months ago and remembered their red eyes. Then, of course, she turned out to be my Blood Flame, so-'

'Your eyes turned red,' Becky says, finishing my sentence. 'Well, this is a bit of a conundrum for you, then?'

'It gets worse,' I tell her, 'She doesn't know we are Blood Flames or what Blood Flames are. She also keeps fighting the bond between us and seems confused by it.'

'Wow...' she says, not sure what to say. Finally, she opens a cabinet, pulls out two shot glasses and a potion bottle of lion's breath, pours the potion into the shot glass, and hands me one.

'What is this for?' I ask.

She smiles, 'For all the stitches you're about to get. Bottoms up, Bucko!' she says, clinking her shot glass against mine and shotting down hers.

Chapter 32

Becky rolls her eyes at me after she manages to give me the final stitch. 'You're the Lord of our coven, who's supposed to be strong and powerful, yet here you are being the biggest sook over a few stitches.'

'You just gave me six stitches on my arm and another fourteen on my chest! So that's more than a few stitches.'

'The lion's breath was supposed to make you brave and not sook the entire time. Must have been a dud bottle,' Becky laughs.

I glare into her brown eyes, but she smiles, tucks her short brown hair behind her ear, and shrugs.

'Okay, Becky, you've had your fun. I'm out of here,' I tell her, taking my shirt from Soren and putting it on.

She purses her lips which are thickly coated with red lipstick, 'Don't you want to know why your wounds haven't healed yet?'

I turn to face her, 'You know why?'

Becky walks to the table and brings the well-made dagger to me.

'This isn't an ordinary dagger, Lord Talon. This dagger has been crafted to kill any supernatural. The spine and quillon are silver, and the dagger's blade is made from Moonstone. The grip of the dagger is even made from dragon bone. Moonstone will cause our wounds to heal slowly at the same pace as humans, just like silver does to werewolves. If we were to be stabbed by this in an artery or main organ. We wouldn't heal quick enough to survive. Instead, we would die. How she knows that Moonstone is a weakness to vampires baffles me. It's secret knowledge only a few know of.'

'That might explain why Lylah was so desperate to get it back. She kept pleading I return it to her as if it were her most precious thing in the world.'

'Do you think she made this dagger?' Becky asks.

I take the dagger from Becky and tuck it in my belt. 'I honestly don't know, but I know not to underestimate her.'

'I look forward to meeting this she-wolf,' Becky smiles.

Soren glances at me, and I look back at Becky.

'Lylah doesn't have a wolf. She can't shift. Her mother is also a witch, but Lylah can't cast magic either.'

'Are you serious? That would make her a human? How does she know she has no powers? Has she even tried?'

I burst into laughter, 'Has she tried? Are you kidding me? Yes, she even tried using me as her guinea pig to cast the spells on. But thankfully, she was right, and nothing happened.'

Becky squints and looks me up and down. 'If her spells didn't work, then why are your ears pointy?'

I quickly grab my ears through my thick wavy long hair to feel them. The soft round edges feel the same as normal. Becky laughs, and I realise she is joking.

'Really, Becky? You still have the maturity of a one hundred and twenty-year-old vampire,' I scowl.

She laughs, 'Says the two hundred and sixty-four-year-old vampire who whimpers over a few stitches.'

I roll my eyes and face Soren, 'I don't have time for these shenanigans. Soren, inform everyone in the coven to meet in the hall immediately and then go to the kitchen and organise a tray of food and a drink for Lylah.'

'Yes, Lord Talon,' he bows and dashes away quickly.

I make my way to the hall and sit in my regal chair. Its gold framed and lined with red velvet. There's a slightly smaller version of the same chair beside mine, which now belongs to Lylah as her being my Blood Flame makes her the lady of the coven.

Over a hundred vampires enter. They whisper and ask each other if they saw the girl who returned with me and if they know who she is. I hold my hand up, and they all become silent. I adjust one of my large ruby rings on my finger.

'As you are all aware, due to gossiping amongst each other. I have returned home with a new member of our coven.'

They all turn and talk amongst each other, curious as to why and who she is, as they noticed she isn't a vampire.

'But first, the meeting with the Alpha Lycan and his pack we organised did not go to plan, and we were attacked.'

The vampires look at each other annoyed to talk, and whisper that I, their Lord and Master, was attacked. I gesture my hand again for them to stop talking.

'They still believe we are responsible for the deaths of the humans and some of their pack members. But, during all this, Alpha Maximus's daughter, Lylah, was there, and it turns out we are Blood Flames.'

'Master has found his Blood Flame,' they gasp.

'We finally have our lady to serve,' others say.

'Yes, our coven is now complete with our Lady, but she has no idea what a Blood Flame is or that I am her Blood Flame. Lylah has been through a lot and is not in the right frame of mind to know just yet. So, it's very important no one is to tell her or explain what it means. Once she has settled in and become more comfortable, preferably with her no longer trying to kill me,' They all gasp. 'Then I will tell her and explain it to her, then.'

'She tried to kill you, Master?' Tobin asks in shock and steps forward.

'Only a few times,' I smile, twirling Lylah's dagger with my fingers.

Everyone is confused as to why I seem calm about the situation. 'Lylah has very impressive fighting skills. So, be sure not to make her angry when she decides to explore the castle grounds. Lylah can go anywhere she likes within the castle but must never leave the castle grounds without Nadia or me under any circumstance. Is that clear?'

Everyone nods and bows.

'Now, go back to your duties,' I say, standing and walking away up the stairs.

I find Nadia sitting in a wooden chair outside my chambers.

'Did Lylah receive her tray of food?' I ask.

'I took it from Soren and brought it into her. She hadn't moved from the seat. So, I placed it on the table beside her. I tried to talk to her, but she remained silent, so I left and waited here since.'

I nod, 'Okay, you can go and return in the morning to keep an eye on her.'

'You're going to spend the night in there?' Nadia asks in surprise.

'It is my chambers, Nadia. My clothes are covered in blood. I need to bath and change anyway, and besides, maybe being near her might help?'

Nadia snorts a laugh at the idea.

I glare, making her silent, knock on the door and enter. I close the door and then face Lylah to find she hasn't moved or eaten any of the food.

'You must surely be hungry?' I ask, trying to muster up a conversation with her.

Lylah ignores me, staring at her feet.

'Okay, then. If you don't want to talk, I have other things I need to do anyway. Like, take a bath,' I say, walking to the other side of the room and unbuttoning my shirt.

Lylah flinches and stares at me when she realises I'm undressing. I throw my blood-drenched shirt into a basket and turn to see her eyes looking over my body.

'You're welcome to take a closer look if you like?' I smile.

Surprisingly she stands, blushing and marches towards me, not with a smile but a scowl.

'What do you think you're doing getting naked in my room?' she growls.

Our faces are only an inch apart. If only Lylah knew how sexy she looks when she is angry. I look down at her lips. I want to kiss them, suck them, taste them even.

'This is my room, Lylah and thanks to your wonderful artwork across my chest and arm. I need a bath.'

She looks guilty as she stares at the wound on my chest. Her hand reaches out to touch it but then stops and withdraws her hand back. I swiftly grab it and place it on my chest over the wound—sparks from the contact fly between us.

Lylah breathes heavily. 'Why do I feel this?' she asks.

'I'm not a threat to you, Lylah,' I say, tucking a strand of her white hair behind her ear. She gazes at me as her chest rises from the touch. 'That's why you feel this,' I whisper.

Lylah steps back. 'Wait, this is your room? I don't want to be in here. You could at least be a gentleman and give me my own chambers!'

I smile, 'You don't have a choice to be in here,' I step towards her, keeping eye contact.

She steps back nervously with each step I take forward until her back hits a wall. I place a hand above her head and lean in to whisper in her ear. 'But, if you let me, I can show you how much of a gentleman I can be.'

Lylah's chest rapidly rises. Her eyes flash to a light blue and flicker. The bond is trying to force us both to slam into each other, but I can see she is fighting against it. Lylah concentrates on slowing her breathing, and she mutters random words through her breath as if to distract her mind.

Then, Lylah looks into my eyes with full control of herself, 'You are anything but a gentleman, *Lord Talon*.'

'Hmm,' I smile. 'Yet I'm sure you've been having many sensuous thoughts of me ever since we've met?'

Lylah flinches, 'The only thoughts I have of you are ill ones!'

I move my face closer to hers, and her eyes flicker a light blue again. I smile. 'I very much doubt that. Your eyes tell me otherwise,' I tell her, tilting my head to the side.

'I-I', she stutters with a blush.

I turn and walk towards my bathroom, unbuckling my trousers. I let everything drop to the ground, giving Lylah a full glimpse of my backside as I enter the bathroom. I hear her breath hitch, which makes me smile wider. I close the door behind me.

'Damn it, Lylah!' I hear her growl at herself.

Chapter 33

As I soak in the bathtub, I hear Lylah pacing back and forth in the room. Once clean, I step out and open the bathroom door in my full glory. Lylah comes to a halt. I casually put the towel over my head and dry my long wet hair.

'Damn you, Lord Talon! Do you have no shame!?' Lylah yells.

I remove the towel, look down at myself, and then back at Lylah, whose cheeks are now the rosiest red from blushing.

'Clearly, Lylah, I have nothing to be ashamed of,' I smile mischievously at her.

'You!' she says and abruptly turns, opens my antique wardrobe and rummages through my belongings. I lean against the door frame and cross my arms as I stare at her sweet little ass as she is bent over going through my clothes. I could stand and watch this view all night. I smirk.

As Lylah grabs my clothing and turns her head, she realises what I've been quietly viewing.

Lylah storms toward me and shoves my clothes into my chest, 'Don't you ever stare at my ass again! Now in the world of wands! Will you please? Get dressed!'

'Only because you said please,' I smile.

Lylah rolls her eyes at me, and I put my arms through the shirt.

'Not in here! Go in the bathroom and dress, for wand's sake. I don't need to see your… appendage dangling in my face!' she says as I notice beads of sweat forming across her forehead.

Lylah steps back quickly, trying to put space between us. She is fighting the pull between us, and me being completely naked right in front of her is proving difficult for her to fight.

'Fine, if you insist,' I say, bundling my clothes up and returning to the bathroom.

I hear Lylah sigh in relief as I close the door.

Now dressed, I enter the bedroom to find Lylah sitting back in the gentlemans chair with her arms crossed. I casually walk to a set of antique black drawers, pull out a long-sleeved casual shirt and walk over to Lylah. 'You can sleep in this until I organise some clothes for you,' I tell her, placing the shirt on her lap.

'Or you could lead me out of here, and I can go home and sleep in my chambers in my packhouse,' she retorts.

Lylah stiffens as I kneel in front of her.

I stare meaningfully into her dark blue eyes. 'Lylah, I promise I will take you back home to see your family as soon as possible. But for now, I need you to trust me. I swear to you I will never harm you. I just need you to give me a chance. Just one chance is all I'm asking of you,' I plead.

'How am I supposed to trust you when you killed all those people? How am I supposed to trust you when you have kidnapped me?'

I gently take her hands.

'I have never killed anyone in my entire life, Lylah. I don't even kill the wildlife I feed from, and I told you I will take you back to see your family.'

'I saw you there! You were even wearing black clothing and the same cape. I saw your red eyes, just like I did the night you destroyed my life… ' she quickly pulls her hands from mine and looks away. 'I want you to go.'

'Lylah. I swear to you. It wasn't-'

'GO!' Lylah yells, pointing to the door.

Sighing heavily in defeat, I storm out of the room and slam the door behind me. I pace the hallway outside my chambers.

How can I prove to Lylah that I'm not a murderer? How can I prove to her she can trust me?

I sit on the ledge of the large, arch-stone window near my chambers and peer out at the lake. It's the middle of the night, and all is still and quiet. There isn't even a ripple in the water. Then, after an hour, I hear shouting and sobs from my room. I quickly open the door. As it creaks open, I see Lylah asleep under the bed covers. She is wearing my shirt and her clothes are on the nearby chair. The leather braces she wears, for some odd reason, are also with her clothes.

'No, please,' she mumbles while she turns and tosses, gaining my full attention again.

She is having a nightmare.

Her arms swing as if she is holding her dagger.

'Get away from him! Micah! Please, please don't die. Please don't leave me,' she cries.

She is drenched in sweat and extremely distressed. I caress her face.

'Micah?' she asks, regarding my touch.

I'm not sure who Micah is to her. Perhaps a cousin or a brother? I remember Lylah said he was killed that night which she has mentioned a couple of times. Is this possibly what broke Lylah? I know my brother kills with great violence, so I can imagine the trauma it would have caused her to have witnessed a loved one killed by him and his Blood Dwellers.

Lylah screams and sits up, waking in terror, and bursts into tears.

I kick off my shoes, coat and shirt, leaving my trousers on, get into bed next to her and scoop her onto my lap. Her forehead rests above the deep cut she gave me across my chest, and salty tears drip onto the wound. I wrap my arms around her back, and she places her hands on my chest, sending a soar of sparks igniting throughout my body.

'Shh, shh.' I say, hushing and stroking her back.

After quite some time of comforting Lylah, her crying and sobs cease. Her hot breath against my chest has been sending my insides crazy. My fangs had protruded a few times against my will as the bond was pushing me to bite and feed from her. Even though I could barely keep my eyes off the nape of her neck, and I could have fed off her, I didn't. I had to force myself to focus on what was important, and even though I need to feed soon, I'd rather starve and become feral and weak than feed from her without her consent. Her blood is hers to give, not for me to take, even if we're Blood Flames. I want to earn her blood and earn her trust.

I lay comfortably back in the bed, keeping Lylah pressed against my chest. She sleeps soundly for the rest of the night with no more nightmares.

By the morning, she has snuggled her face further into my neck and has her hand firmly pressed against the stitches over my wound. My hand caresses her back until she starts to stir awake. She sits up swiftly when she realises we are in bed together.

'What are you doing in here? I told you to go!' she says in confusion.

'You were having a really bad nightmare. You were shouting and crying. So I rushed in here and held you, and then you fell asleep on me,' I tell her.

She looks even more confused now, 'I did?'

'You don't remember?' I ask.

'I-I remember the nightmare, but nothing afterwards,' she confesses.

'The nightmare you had. It was from that night you lost Micah?' I ask.

Her eyes bolt up into mine, and she nods.

'Every night, I have the same dream, the same nightmare. Ever since you killed Micah over nine months ago.'

I wish she would stop referring to me as the one who killed him, but until she sees the Blood Dwellers for herself, she will continue to blame me and keep trying to kill me. Although right now, she is more placid than usual, she does look miserable and overtired, probably from the nightmare.

'Lylah, was Micah a relative of yours? A brother perhaps?' I ask.

She shakes her head no, and now I'm the one staring at her, greatly confused.

'Then who was he?'

'Micah is my mate, my fated mate,' Lylah whispers.

And just like that, the colour from my face drains, and the utmost horrible feeling consumes me. I struggle to breathe and quickly withdraw myself from the bed, and without saying a word, I grab my clothes and flee the room. Nadia is sitting in the chair, waiting to take over her post. She is startled as I almost tumble over, looking out of place.

'Master? Are you okay? Did Lylah stab you again? You look paler than usual, and your breathing is quite heavy?'

I don't answer. Instead, I rush downstairs and attempt to clothe myself. I pace around, scrunching my hair in my hands. Lylah has a mate! She had a mate! This doesn't make sense. I am her Blood Flame.

'Lord Talon?'

'Soren!' I say, placing my hands on his shoulders.

'Has something happened?' he asks with concern looking at my dishevelled and half-dressed state.

'It makes so much sense now,' I say, shaking him. 'This is why Lylah is fighting the bond. This is why she is confused when we touch or when we are near. She had a mate, and what Lylah feels with me, she once felt with

Micah, and she doesn't understand why she feels it with me. But what does that mean if she already had a mate, and then he died, and now she is my mate? I guess what matters is I am her mate now, and she has been given to me by the God's. It's my duty to love and protect her; hopefully, one day, she will put her guard down and love me too.' My back stiffens. 'Oh, wands! I'm such a cauldron! She is hurting and grieving. She has been broken and suffering from the loss of her mate, and what do I do? Strip off, bare naked in front of her!' I fall back into a chair and drag my hands down my face in deep despair.

Soren's mouth is gaped open in shock at what I'm saying.

'Lylah has a mate?'

'Had, a mate.'

'You stripped off naked in front of her?'

'Don't even go there, Soren.'

Soren tries to stop a smirk from forming.

The stitches on my chest itch. I look down to see the wound has completely healed. I brush my hand over it, and the stitches fall to the ground.

Soren and I stare at each other, completely dumbfounded. I need to show Becky.

Chapter 34

Lylah

'Micah is my mate, my fated mate,' I say to Lord Talon, barely in a whisper.

He becomes pale, swiftly retreats from the bed, picks up his clothes, and exits the room.

I'm relieved he fled. I feel like I'm betraying Micah when he is around me, but I can't stop these thoughts I have of Lord Talon, no matter how hard I try. It has completely drained me. I'm exhausted from fighting myself from wanting to touch his skin, kiss his lips and more. I shouldn't be feeling warm and fuzzy around him. It's like something is wrong with me. I approach an arch-stone-shaped stain-glassed window and push it open. I look down and instantly regret it. I'm so high up. This is a situation I don't want to be in.

Mateless, grieving, kidnapped with feelings towards my captor… Wait a minute! Isn't that an illness? Finding your captor attractive and developing feelings towards them? Wands! This explains everything. I have Stockholm syndrome! A huge sense of relief overcomes me, knowing why I have forbidden feelings towards my captor and mate's murderer. I need to focus again. Now I have an explanation. I don't feel so confused. I just need to keep ignoring and fighting off these feelings and focus on Micah's revenge. Being here, kidnapped, might not be such a bad thing after all. I can use this to my advantage and kill Lord Talon. His attraction toward me is obvious. I think even Nadia and Soren have also noticed. I've got the perfect plan. I need to get my dagger back from him and pretend I've lowered my guard down, and then I will strike him with my dagger. Once he is dead, the Stockholm syndrome might stop. Then I can return to my pack and live out my days as a pack warrior with at least having the peace that Micah's murderer is dead. Yes, this will be my plan. I nod to myself. First things first. My dagger.

There's a knock at the door as I swing my legs out from the bed.

'It's me, Nadia,' she says and enters the room holding some clothing items. 'Is Lord Talon okay? He looked like he had seen a ghost when he raced out of the room.'

'I don't know why he reacted like that. He asked me who Micah was, and I told him, and then he fled. It was like he didn't know he had killed my mate.'

'Wait! You have a mate?' Nadia asks in clear shock.

'Did have until he killed him.'

Nadia stares silently at me for a whole minute.

'Is this why you kept trying to kill, Lord Talon? Because you think he killed your mate?'

I nod.

'I see, but Lady Lylah,' Nadia says, daringly taking a step closer to me. 'Lord Talon never killed, Micah. He has never killed a soul. He is gentle and kind and has a good heart.'

'Why are you even here, Nadia? I don't need you to babysit me.'

'I brought you some clean clothes to wear since your clothes from yesterday are covered in mud. I thought you would appreciate some clean clothes to wear,' Nadia says and lays out three dresses on the bed.

I laugh at the fancy vintage silk gowns. 'Sorry, I don't do dresses. So I'll stick with my muddy clothes, thanks,' I say, crossing my arms, turning my back to her and approaching the window again.

Nadia sighs, 'At least wear one just for today while I have your other clothes washed.'

'Fine,' I reply, lacking the energy to argue with her.

I storm into the bathroom. The lighting is dim. There are a few bundles of candles on each stone ledge. The tiles are black with gold patterns, just like all the furniture in Lord Talon's room. Even his four-post bed is black with gold embellishments, swirling up the posts and along the bed frame.

Once the elegant clawed tub is filled with warm water, I remove the oversized long-sleeve shirt over my head, toss it aside and step into the bath. On the ledge beside some candles, I see a bunch of bottles. I reach for each bottle and smell them until I find the lavender.

I lather my body and sink under the water, holding my breath for as long as possible. Then reach over for a towel and step out. Nadia is still standing by the bed.

'Oh look, you're still here?' I say with sarcasm.

'Someone needs to lace up the back of your dress for you,' she explains.

I step back, clinging tighter to my towel with a worried expression. My scars are my own to see and not for anyone else to look at. There is no way I'm letting these vampires see my constant reminders of Micah.

'I don't need your help. I will manage it myself,'

'but, Lady Lylah,'

'Stop calling me Lady Lylah. You make it sound as if I'm in charge around here. I told you to go, now go,' I point to the door. Nadia nods and leaves.

I sigh in relief and loosen my grip on the towel as I walk over to the bed. I put the undergarments on, and then the sound of a moaning cry and wail echoes throughout the castle. I shiver. Who in the wands is that? I heard it yesterday as well. It had completely creeped me out, but I forced myself not to seem bothered by it around Lord Talon. I saw the sad stares they gave each other at the time. Whoever, it sounds so sad, so lonely, so… broken. I wonder what his story is. Why is he so sad? Maybe he lost a loved one like me? His wailing cry resonates through me. A tear forms and rolls down my cheek as I feel the same pain, loneliness, empty feeling, and brokenness. The cries stop.

The dresses are way too fancy. I take the floor length, A-line, maroon velvet dress and step into it. The neckline is low and accentuates my small breasts. There is gold lace that runs underneath my bust. The same lace graces the ends of the sleeves. I frown at the scars on my wrists. The sleeves only reach three-quarters down my arms leaving my scars exposed. I peer at the other dresses, but the sleeves are much shorter, only sitting over the shoulder. It's probably going to look a little silly, but I decide I don't care what the vampires think. I take my leather braces and put them on. Then I reach around my back to pull on the lace and tie it up. Looking over my shoulder into the mirror, I see the back is poorly pulled and tied. I shrug, deciding it's good enough. I comb my fingers through my hair to neaten it as much as possible. Now for my mission! My stomach suddenly grumbles with hunger. Fine, breakfast and then I can focus on getting my dagger back from Lord Talon. I open the chamber door and gingerly skip past Nadia guarding my door. She watches me confusingly, then chases after me but keeps her distance. Damn, Lord Talon. Making Nadia follow me. It's like Mum and Dad always having Theo and Leo follow me or wait for me after school. It's utterly ridiculous.

I walk through one hallway after another and one hall after another and realise I've been walking around in circles when I notice the same gallery wall full of goth-like portraits.

I turn around to face Nadia. 'Why didn't you tell me I've been walking around in circles?' I growl.

'Oh, I thought you were doing it on purpose, admiring all the decor and portraits.

I burst into laughter. 'Do you think I really care about any of that? I've got far more interesting things to do than admiring the décor of the castle I'm held prisoner in.'

'May I ask what you would find more interesting then?' Nadia asks.

'The kitchen,' I say as if the answer should be obvious.

'Oh, down those stairs and then take a right,' she says, flinging her dark silky hair over her shoulder.

I silently march down the stairs. I notice Nadia constantly gazing at me. So, I stop at the bottom of the stairs.

'Why do you keep glancing at me? It's beginning to frustrate me,' I ask her.

'Oh, I'm just surprised. That's all.'

'Surprised by what?'

'Now that you aren't covered in dirt and wearing a dress. You are actually quite fascinatingly beautiful to look at. I wasn't expecting you to look this beautiful,' she smirks.

'Really?' I say, stepping closer to her. 'What were you expecting? Huh?'

'I-um...'

My glare deepens, and she takes a step back.

'Nadia,' Soren says, saving her ass.

He wraps his arms around her and kisses her passionately. Occupied eating each other's faces, I take this opportunity to sneak away from them again.

Chapter 35

Lord Talon

'Becky, it's healed,' I say as I enter the room.

She is brewing something in a small cauldron, and it smells horrendous.

'What's healed?' she asks, walking around the table and toward me.

I unbutton my shirt and watch her jaw drop. 'What did you do?' she asks.

'I didn't do anything,' I tell her.

'Something must have happened? Tell me everything you did from last night up till now.'

'I was sitting on the window ledge watching the lake until I heard Lylah yelling and crying in her sleep. I raced in there and held her in my arms, and I spent over an hour comforting her until she fell asleep on me. I did notice the pain from the wounds had gone by then but didn't think much of it as I was too worried about Lylah. I woke up with Lylah sleeping against me. We spoke, and she told me Micah is her mate who she thinks I killed, and I bolted out of there freaking out she had a mate, then ran into Soren and told him. My chest itched from the stitches, so I ran my hand over it, and they all fell out, and I saw it was completely healed. Not even a scar, so I came straight here.'

Becky walks away, walks around the room in thought, and then approaches me again.

'Do you have that dagger of hers on you?' she asks.

I nod, withdraw it from the back of my belt, and hand it to her.

She takes her own small knife she uses for chopping up herbs.

'Hold your hands out,' she says.

'Why?'

'I want to see if you have somehow become immune to the moonstone, which is unheard of, or if some magic has been used on you.'

'How can you find out?'

'Well, I will show you if you hold your hands out,' she replies.

I hold the palms of my hands out. Becky makes a cut across one palm with Lylah's dagger and then another cut with the other knife on the other palm.

'Now we watch and wait,' she says.

We watch the wound Becky cut with her knife slowly heal over a minute, but the cut from Lylah's dagger remains unhealed.

'You are not immune to moonstone. You have been healed by magic,' she says.

'But how?'

And then it dawns on me, and we both say in unison, 'Lylah!'

'Lylah said she couldn't cast magic, though? She even tried to use spells on me, and nothing happened.'

'Lylah is either lying and knows she can use magic and is trying to fool us, or it could be starting to awaken? Nadia is the one shadowing her, isn't she?'

'Yes, she is.'

'Maybe ask if Nadia has seen any signs of Lylah using magic and keep observing her. If her magic is only beginning to awaken now, she might not be able to control it. Her emotions will play a big part in controlling it, and I think she may struggle with that. As you just mentioned, she already had a mate who has died, and now she is here in this castle away from her loved ones and with the one she thinks killed her mate.'

'Wands! This is not good. Maybe we should tell her then that she healed me? Maybe if she isn't lying and it's awakening, she can be more aware of it and perhaps more in control of it?' I suggest.

'I have to meet this new Lady of the coven who has stolen your heart, well not stole it per se but trying to stab it,' Becky laughs.

I roll my eyes at her.

'So let's have her join us for our morning feed. I'm sure she will be hungry. Besides, I'm hungry for my bloody breakfast anyway,' she laughs. 'Get it bloody, breakfast?' she elbows me.

I ignore Becky's lame joke. 'Let's get Lylah from my chambers then.'

Before I walk up the second set of stairs, I find Soren and Nadia frantically dashing from one room to another. Something is wrong. Within a flash, I appear before them and hold Soren and Nadie by their throats.

'Nadia, why aren't you outside my chambers guarding Lylah?' I ask through gritted teeth.

'She didn't want to stay in there. So I-I followed her for a while, and she asked where the kitchen was. I was taking her there, and then she just… disappeared. She has escaped, Lord Talon. I'm sorry. I didn't mean to let her out of my sight.'

'Escaped!? It's impossible for her to escape if she thinks the labyrinth is confusing, this castle has just as many rooms, hallways and passageways. What were you doing when she disappeared?'

'I'm sorry, Lord Talon. I couldn't help myself and had to kiss my Blood Flame, if only for a moment. Then we realised she had fled. Most likely to find her way out of here,' Soren confesses.

'Damn it!' I say, letting them go. 'Find her now!' I shout at them.

They nod and continue to dash throughout the castle, looking for Lylah.

Half the coven is now looking for her. I help search for Lylah as well. I triple-check each room I enter. I'm incredibly worried and trying to keep my emotions at bay. I don't want my coven to see how much she has affected me in so little time. I hold my forehead feeling woozy from not being able to feed from Lylah and not having a feed in general.

'Lord Talon. Let's go to the kitchens and get you some blood to drink,' Becky says.

I nod and let her hold my arm to keep me upright.

As we enter the kitchen, my jaw drops at the most beautiful site I have ever seen. Lylah sits at the large wooden island with loaves of bread, cheeses, butter, grapes and other foods. Her hair is the neatest I've seen, and she is wearing a dress! God's help me. She is more stunningly beautiful than I could have ever imagined. I take in the sight and lower my eyes to her chest. The dress shows off her very fine, delectable goods. My fangs elongate in need of a taste of her. Lylah plucks a grape from a stem and pops it into her mouth. She closes her eyes, and I watch the look of pleasure on her face. The vein on her neck moves as she chews the grape, and my eyes zone in as my fangs are now fully elongated.

Lylah swallows the grape and realises she is being watched. She looks toward us, but her eyes focus on Becky's hands wrapped around my arm. She then looks up, making eye contact with Becky and gives her a deathly glare. Only to then jump up off the seat when she looks at me. My eyes are black, my breathing is heavy, and my fangs are fully extended. She knows I'm becoming blood-crazed.

'Oh!' Becky says, now looking at me. She runs towards a small room and returns with a jug of blood and a cup. She pours the blood and hands it to me. I scull it down within a second. So, she pours me another. I drink it but more slowly as the blood craze dissipates and my energy increases just enough to stop the wooziness. Finally, my fangs retract, and my eyes are blue again.

I hand Becky the cup, march over to Lylah and stand in front of her. Lylah steps back in fear. She gasps as I grab her, pull her into my chest, and wrap my arms around her tightly.

'I was so worried when I couldn't find you. I thought you had escaped?'

Lylah angrily pushes me away and steps back.

'As if I would try and escape on an empty stomach. It could take me days or weeks to get out of this horrible place. I'm smart enough to at least fill myself up with food before attempting to flee so I at least I won't die from starvation along the way,' she says.

'Why did you run away from Nadia then?' I ask her.

'Are you kidding? Do you expect me to wait around watching Nadia and her lover boy make out in a corridor all darn day while I waste away with hunger? Besides, they were practically eating each other's faces. I thought you vampires had decorum, but clearly, it's the other way around. You might have to put them in etiquette classes as those two have no shame at all,' she says and sits back at the table and continues to eat. 'At least your food here isn't too bad,' she munches and then makes eye contact as I sit opposite her at the table. 'Why were you going all blood-crazed before? I haven't got any new cuts or scratches, so it couldn't be me that triggered it?'

Becky approaches and takes a seat next to me. I watch Lylah's eyes become a darker blue as she glares at Becky.

'Lord Talon, here, hasn't been feeding on his Blood Flame like he should be. So, it weakens him. The blood I served him before will only be able to sustain him for so long. But once he regularly drinks from his Blood Flame, he will be as good as new. Won't you, Master?' Becky says, now holding my arm again and smiling at me.

A growl, much resembling an angry wolf, is heard. Becky and I stare at Lylah.

'And who in the wands are you!?' Lylah growls.

Chapter 36

Lylah

'I'm Becky. I've heard so much about you,' she beams and squeezes herself closer to Lord Talon.

A burst of jealousy from Becky touching Lord Talon's arm ignites within me.

'I'm sure….' I say while telling myself not to care that Becky is practically rubbing herself all over, Lord Talon. He keeps glaring at her and giving her back-off looks. But she persists in fluttering her eyes at him anyway.

Not wanting to stare at her face or acknowledge her. I ignore her and look at Lord Talon.

'You should find that Blood Flame of yours and feed off it. It's quite silly, starving yourself of blood when a human is living here against her will. The last thing I need is you trying to bite me,' I say sarcastically.

Becky bursts into laughter and begins elbowing Lord Talon in the ribs, 'Master, you should take this human's advice and feed off your Blood Flame. In fact, you should do it right now?'

'Becky, that's enough!' Lord Talon growls. 'I can live off the blood of animals for as long as I need to!'

'Suit yourself. The offer was practically right there. I'm sure you will change your mind eventually, though. When we find Lord Atticus, you will be too weak and may have no choice but to take what you need in order to have the strength to defeat him,' she says, walking away and leaving the kitchen.

Lord Atticus is the one the vampires blame Micah's death on. How could that be when I saw Lord Talon kill him? Maybe they are trying to fool me into thinking they aren't responsible. That must be it. I stand, walk over to a rustic tap, and pump some water to wash my hands from the butter and cheese.

Lord Talon stands and watches me quietly. I discreetly look him over but can't see my dagger in the front of his belt. He has to have it on him somewhere, but how will I find it?

I casually walk past him and through a hall. Like a shadow, he follows me closely without saying a word. I peer at the stairs and smile as an idea pops into my head. I walk up ten steps and stop to face Lord Talon.

'Can you stop following me?' I ask.

'No,' he replies casually.

'Why not?'

'I want to follow you.'

'Why?'

'I want to learn more about you,' he says.

Nadia and Soren appear at the bottom of the staircase.

'You found her!' Nadia says, relieved.

We both ignore her.

'You already killed my mate and kidnapped me. I don't want you to know anything more about me!' I say, walking back down towards him but purposely pretending to fall.

Just as I thought he would, he catches me. I ignore the tingles and sparks from his touch, and I use this chance to pretend to wrap my arms around him, not to fall but feel the back of his belt. We tumble down the stairs as I grab my dagger and pull it out. Lord Talon lands on his back as I land straddled over his lap. I hold my dagger with both hands above him and plummet the dagger towards his chest.

'Lord Talon!' Soren and Nadia shout.

Lord Talon uses his telekinesis to freeze my action and gestures his hand making me slowly rise in the air off of him. Even though Lord Talon glares at me, I can also see the hurt in his eyes. I become frustrated at myself again as guilt consumes me. I almost want to cower, but being still like a statue, I can't even do that. Finally, he stands up, angrily removes my dagger, and then grabs my chin.

'How did you know Moonstone is deadly to vampires? How did you make this? It's made from all the materials to weaken and kill every supernatural.'

'I didn't know Moonstone was deadly to vampires. It wouldn't matter what dagger I had. I would use anything within my reach to kill you,' I tell him.

Nadia and Soren hiss at me.

Lord Talon gestures for them to stop and back away. They obey his orders.

His glare deepens, 'Only a few vampires have this knowledge of Moonstone. Who gave it to you? Who made it?' he asks.

'It was a gift. It was specifically made for me to have,' I reply.

Lord Talon crosses his arms and steps closer, waiting for me to say more. I look away. 'Micah made it for me. He knew my collection of daggers wasn't in the best shape. He crafted it himself after collecting all the specific materials. It took him months to make. He was adamant I was to keep it on me at all times. As if he knew something....' I say in shock at my sudden realisation.

'He knew... Micah knew something was going to happen, but how? He made this dagger for me for a reason. He knew it would protect me but from what?' I say to myself, completely forgetting Lord Talon is standing before me.

I gaze up into Lord Talon's eyes as mine flicker in confusion. Did Micah know I was going to be kidnapped? My mind flashes back to when I first met Alpha Varan. He was pleasant until I told him I had no wolf. Later that day, after I cried. Micah promised me that his father would one day have the utmost honour and respect for me. He reminded me a few times over time that his father's views of me would one day change. Then I remembered later that night before Alpha Varan left. He was talking to my father about when Micah was a child. That Micah would always talk about his dreams and how he was adamant they always came true. Then his father said how the pack members of Storm Glenn began to say Micah was strange and worried he might not be mentally fit to be an Alpha.

So, Alpha Varan made Micah swear he would never talk about his dreams again, otherwise be punished. So, he never mentioned his dreams again after that. Suddenly a particular line Alpha Varan said comes back to my mind, and it hits me like a ton of bricks. 'I know his dreams are just dreams. But I always hated how he used to tell me he would die young.'

Even though I'm still a few feet hovering in the air, my body trembles against Lord Talon's ability and my breathing intensifies as a panic attack consumes me. 'Micah predicted his death. He was able to see into the future, into mine and his. He knew he was going to die. He knew he was going to leave me!' I sob.

Lord Talon steps back nervously and stares at Soren and Nadia briefly with worry before turning back to face me. I realise I'm back on the ground, assuming Lord Talon has let me go. But unbeknownst to me, I broke free from his hold and didn't even realise, as I'm too angry to hurt, that Micah knew he was going to die and never told me. I pace back and forth repeatedly and grab my hair.

'Why didn't he tell me? I could have saved him. We could have never gone camping, and he'd still be alive,' I burst into tears and fall to my knees.

Lord Talon approaches me. I stand and step back. 'Don't come near me,' I shout and run upstairs and slam the chamber door behind me.

I spend the entire week in Lord Talon's chamber, refusing to come out. I had the same nightmares each night and every time I woke from the dream. I swore I could feel Lord Talon caressing my back or stroking my hair, but every time I sat up and turned, no one was there.

I picked at the food placed on the trays Nadia brought to me each day. I was too depressed to eat. I felt betrayed that Micah never told me about his dreams and predictions. I'm unsure what to do with this knowledge, and part of me wishes I had never figured it out.

The daily wailing cry echoes throughout the castle. I've figured out it's coming from below the castle, maybe from the underground crypt. I'm tempted to find my way down there to see who it is and why they are so sad and miserable.

My thoughts are disturbed by a knock at the door. Lord Talon enters and slowly approaches.

'Lylah,' he says.

'I don't want you in here. I want you to leave me alone, preferably forever,' I say to him.

He ignores me and steps even closer. 'Lylah, what you said last week about... your mate having the ability to predict the future and predicting his own death. I just wanted to tell you that I'm sorry. I can't imagine how horrible that would be for you to find out. I'm sorry,' he says meaningfully.

'You're sorry? You're the one who killed him!' I shout and storm past him out of the room.

'I've told you many times I never killed him. I swear to you, Lylah!'

I march down the stairs, 'Where are you going?' he asks.

'I'm going home!' I shout.

Sparks flow through me as I'm swiftly lifted over Lord Talon's shoulder and carried into the dining room.

'Let me go,' I yell angrily.

'You're going to join me for dinner, Lylah. You've barely eaten all week,' he says. I go to protest but notice he is slightly swaying as he carries me.

He puts me down and pulls my seat out at the end of the table. I plop down in the chair with my arms crossed. Lord Talon takes his seat opposite me. I keep my scowl on him, but he pays no attention to it, making me angrier. His vampire servants place cutlery, a napkin in front of me, and a goblet in front of him.

'Lady, Lylah,' they say and bow.

'I'm not a lady,' I growl at them.

Lord Talon tries to hold in his laugh. 'You've got that right,' he smirks.

I swiftly grab the butter knife. It whips through the air with great speed towards his head but using his ability. The knife comes to a sudden halt and hovers in the air right in front of his face.

'I see we're going to be in for quite the dinner,' he smiles as he takes the hovering knife and places it on the table beside his goblet.

Chapter 37

A plate of vegetables with a steak is placed in front of me, whilst a serving of blood is poured into Lord Talon's goblet. I refuse to make any eye contact with him. Instead, I watch the flames of the candles on the table flicker.

Halfway through silently eating my meal, five vampires I've never met before enter the dining room, marching. One leads the others as they approach Lord Talon and bow. Nadia and Soren enter behind them and sit at the dining table.

'My Lord,' The lead vampire says.

'Mervin, tell me you have returned with good news? Where are the others?' he asks.

'My Lord, they are all dead. Along with many more human casualties.'

'What!? You were supposed to observe the whereabouts of Lord Atticus and return to me as soon as he was found.'

'Forgive us, Lord Talon. When we found him, he was in a rural town. We were well hidden and observed him. He killed every single human as if it were a sport and drank the blood from some of them before he had them ripped apart. We tried to leave without him noticing us. When we turned around, we were surrounded by his Blood Dwellers. He had known all along we were there and watching him. He left only us alive and told me to send you a message. Pledge your loyalty to him, or the entire coven dies.' Mervin says, placing a map in front of Lord Talon. 'He will be expecting your answer during the full moon tomorrow night at this location here,' he points.

If Lord Talon and the coven have been telling the truth, then I need to know for sure, and the only way is for me to find and meet this Lord Atticus myself. I stand from my seat, quickly approach the map, and desperately snatch it up to look at the location. It has the underground marked on the map. So I can see where I am. I look at the mountain Mervin pointed to and assess the distance it would take to get there. If I leave tonight, I might stand a good chance of getting there during the full moon tomorrow night.

'Lylah,' Lord Talon says.

I look up from the map to see that Lord Talon has appeared in front of me. He holds his hand out for the map. I step back and hug the map to my chest.

'You are going to go, right?' I ask him.

'There's no reason to go. I will never serve Lord Atticus, nor will I ever pledge my loyalty to him. He is a monster, a demon, and he needs to be returned to the depths of darkness. But, even with the abilities some of us have. It's not enough to defeat him. The last time we defeated him, there were more of us and more of us with abilities. Most of the coven are normal vampires. We tried to reach out to your father, to join forces in hopes that it will be enough to take down Lord Atticus.'

'Wait! You've defeated him before? When?' I ask.

'One hundred and twenty-eight years ago,' he answers.

I gasp, 'That's over a century ago! Why have the werewolf community never heard of him before? Surely it would be written in our history if it's happened before?'

'We were able to handle it somewhat quietly ourselves at the time. It all happened suddenly,' he says and looks away with a grim look, remembering the morbid events.

'You have to go!' I tell him.

'No, I don't, and I won't,' he says adamantly.

'You want to prove to me you never killed Micah. Then this is your chance. Take me to see Lord Atticus. I need to see him. I need to see his Blood Dwellers. I need to know for sure,' I tell him.

Lord Talon gazes into my eyes, quietly in thought. My eyes plead with his. Now that I'm directly staring at him and taking in all his features, I notice he is more pale than usual. He looks tired, weaker even. His long dark hair drapes down past his shoulders. I then wonder if his hair is as soft as mine. Then my eyes reach his lips before meeting his gaze again.

He is incredibly mysterious to look at as well as handsome. My hand slowly rises, and I suddenly realise I'm about to touch him. I shake my head and realise Lord Talon has stepped closer and raises his hand, tucking my hair behind my ear. I close my eyes from his touch, from the warm and familiar feeling I miss and crave so much from Micah.

'No,' he says, taking the map from my hand and walking back to the table.

I open my eyes, and my breathing becomes erratic, 'What in the wands do you mean no!'

He turns to face me, 'It's too dangerous. I'm not strong enough to protect you from him.'

'Give me my dagger, and I can protect myself.'

Lord Talon laughs. 'You wouldn't stand a chance against him, Lylah. Have you not been listening? He has been killing humans and drinking their blood. This means he is only becoming more powerful and much stronger.'

'Becky said if you drink from your Blood Flame, you would regain your strength, that it would increase your power.'

'It's not that simple, Lylah,' he sighs.

'Why not?'

'Why is it not simple? What is a Blood flame then?'

Everyone in the dining hall stares at me. If a pin were to drop, we would all hear it.

'She needs to know,' Nadia says, reassuring him.

Lord Talon closes his eye for a moment before releasing a deep breath. 'Lylah, a Blood Flame is the equivalent of a werewolf finding their mate. Vampires call them Blood Flames instead.'

A sudden sense of jealousy and hurt overtakes me. Lord Talon has a fated mate. He never told me. Why have I never seen her? Why hasn't he been feeding off her?

'Vampires have mates?' I say, confused.

'Yes,' he replies.

I look over at Nadia and Soren and remember they mentioned they are Blood Flames.

'How did you know you were Blood Flames? What does it feel like?' I ask them.

Nadia blushes, 'Well, at first, it feels like you are being pulled toward each other. It feels as if your mind is racing with your heart. An overwhelming sense of desire and love consumes you. It's as if you are dancing on the clouds in the heavens. Once you make eye contact, the male's eyes turn red from blood lusting over you. Their eyes remain red until they touch you, leaving a mark on your wrist. Their eyes will then return to normal. Feeding off animals no longer becomes necessary once you find your Blood Flame as the only blood that strengthens us is from our Blood Flames.'

I flashback to Nadia and Soren feeding off each other, and then I suddenly turn pale and grab my wrist.

Nadia and Soren realise from the look on my face that I know now. I turn to face Lord Talon with a horrified look.

'No…' I say, gripping my leather brace that covers the mark and the scar. My eyes well up with tears. 'It's not true,' I fall to my knees and stare at Lord Talon as tears run rapidly down my face. 'Please tell me your eyes didn't turn red the moment we saw each other? Please tell me you didn't mark me. Tell me we are not mates?'

His eyes bore into mine, welling up with tears, but he remains silent.

'Please!' I scream, 'Tell me!'

He closes his eyes tightly, and a tear rolls down his cheek. He looks away.

I stand up, wipe the tears aggressively from my face, and walk right up to him.

'This is why I've never met your Blood Flame. This is why you haven't fed from her and why you're becoming weaker. Because I am her?' I say to him. 'I'm your mate?' I sob.

Lord Talon nods as he stares sadly into my eyes.

So many memories of Micah flash through my mind. The first time we met, the first time we touched, kissed, danced, made love, replays over. I'm struggling to breathe, and then I remember what Micah told me the night he died. 'Your life doesn't end here with me. More is waiting for you, and I want you to find it. You will go on adventures. I know you will find someone and fall in love all over again. I want you to find happiness. I want you to live again and know it's okay to be happy without me.'

'Micah knew. He saw this. He knew I would have another mate,' I say, stepping back.

'Lylah,' Lord Talon pleads, reaching his hand toward me.

I shake my head no and run from the dining hall.

Nadia tries to chase after me, 'No,' Lord Talon says, 'Leave her. She needs some space to process all of this.'

Chapter 38

I run from one hall to another and then one corridor to another through many rooms and down staircases I haven't seen before. I have no idea where I'm running to, but I don't care. I just want to get away. I've passed many vampires along the way, but I completely ignore them as they stare curiously at me.

Once out of sight, I lean against the grey stone wall in the shadows before sliding down to the ground and hugging my knees. Lord Talon is my mate. That's why he hasn't killed me. That's why he wants to keep me alive and protect me. This is why I've been developing feelings toward him. Lord Talon knew this whole time since we met that we were Blood Flames.

No wonder he looked devastated and heartbroken every time I tried to kill him. I feel terrible, among many other feelings. I'm angry that Micah and Lord Talon kept things from me. I feel I'm betraying Micah by being attracted to Lord Talon. I'm upset and heartbroken that Micah isn't alive. I'm frustrated at myself for not figuring all this out when the signs were in front of me this whole time—such as Micah being able to predict the future and Lord Talon being my mate.

Sobs and low-wailing moans gain my attention. I stand and cautiously walk down a narrow passageway, following the sounds. It's quite dark. There is only dim light from the odd-lit candle.

I take a candle and continue down the narrow passageway that leads down steep stairs. Although I can't see the rats, I can hear them. Finally, I reach the bottom of the stairs and enter a rectangular room. There are life-size statues behind each stone coffin. I realise they replicate the vampire inside each coffin. I walk from one to the other, curiously taking in their features. Then suddenly, I turn and jump in fright as the wailing cry starts again, but it's coming from this very room. There, in the shadowy corner, comes the heartbreaking wails and cries. I slowly walk toward the moving shadow holding the candle out in front of me. My heart is racing in fear and tells me to turn and run, but curiosity has already won this game, forcing me to step closer.

As I approach, the candlelight reveals someone crouched over with their back to me. It's a man. He has brown hair and is wearing nothing but an old rag around his waist. He is very underweight, and his bones stick out all over. He appears to be eating something, but it's hard to see with his back to me and hovering in the dark.

I place a hand on his shoulder, and he flinches, 'I hear your cries echo throughout the castle each day. What is causing you so much pain?'

He slowly turns, and I scream as if my life depends on it. His face has no skin, no lips, and no nose. It's that of a skull with his eyeballs still intact. His teeth and skinless chin drip with blood. He holds out to me the dead rat he has just been feeding on. I drop the candle in front of him, turn and run, only to slam into a warm, masculine chest that sends tingles throughout my body.

'Lylah!' Lord Talon says, pulling me tightly into his chest.

He sadly stares at the creature in the corner before he wraps his cloak over me and dashes through the castle with great speed until we enter his chambers.

'W-who was that?' I tremble as Lord Talon puts me down.

'That's Cedric, a dear old friend of mine,' he tells me.

'I don't understand. Is Cedric a vampire?' I ask, confused.

'Yes, he hasn't left the crypt in one hundred and twenty-eight years. He went mad after Lord Atticus killed his Blood Flame, Alanis and then ripped his face off just before we trapped Lord Atticus into the dark portal. He mourns for his life back every day for Alanis and for his appearance. He knows he resembles a monster and has stayed isolated and alone in the crypts. No matter how often I would try to see or talk to him. It would only cause him more distress. So I forbid anyone from going to the crypts so he could be left undisturbed.'

I gaze at Lord Talon with sadness, 'He lost his mate, just as I did mine, and also by Lord Atticus,' I say. Feeling Cedric's pain.

I close my eyes and whimper. Tingles and sparks run through my body. I open my eyes and see Lord Talon with his face close to mine as he caresses my cheek. 'The pain

Cedric is going through must be unbearable,' I say, grasping my leather-bound wrist as I think back to the unbearable pain of not wanting to live another day without Micah and attempting suicide. I hug my wrist to my chest.

'Lylah,' Lord Talon says as he presses his body against mine. Immense desire and sparks flow between us, and he takes the wrist I hold from against my chest. 'This. You and me, being Blood Flames. It's not a punishment. This mark,' he says as he unties the laces of the leather brace. 'It's a blessing from the Gods. I have been waiting for you for a very long time, Lylah. All I ever wanted, more than anything, was to find my soulmate, and I've finally found you.'

My leather brace falls to the ground as Lord Talon keeps eye contact with mine. He brings my bare wrist to his lips and closes his eyes as he kisses the mark, causing my heart to ignite with flames. I have the sudden urge to not only rip my clothes off but also his. My body begins to ache for his touch. He gasps as he opens his eyes and sees the thick scar under the mark across my wrist. His breathing intensifies, and he quickly grabs my other wrist. I begin to panic and pull my other wrist away, but it's too late. He rips the brace off and throws it aside before holding my wrists out in front of him. My breathing becomes erratic like his.

'Let me go,' I whisper, feeling ashamed and broken.

'No. Lylah. Please tell me you didn't try and kill yourself.'

'I couldn't do it anymore. I couldn't live another day without him. The pain of losing him became too much. It only became harder as time went by. I was desperate to end my pain and be united with him again.'

Lord Talon releases my wrists and gently tilts my chin to look at him.

'Lylah, is this why you wear these leather braces?' he asks, his eyes well up with heartbreak, anguish and despair.

I nod. Lord Talon's hand drops, and he pulls me into his chest. I burst into tears, and he spends hours stroking his fingers through my hair and down my back, comforting me as I mourn for Micah. I know in my heart I can't live my life until I get justice for Micah. I will never have peace until Lord Atticus is dead.

I gaze up with pleading eyes. 'Please, you have to meet Lord Atticus tomorrow night. You have to take me with you.'

'I'm not risking your life, Lylah, and if he finds out you're my Blood Flame, he will want you dead.'

I remove myself from Lord Talon's arms and approach the window. 'Don't you see this is my chance to avenge Micah's death? This is my chance to help my heart heal.'

Lord Talon approaches and spins me around.

'Lylah. If I take you to him, unless I pledge myself and our coven to serve him. He will kill us both. I'm not strong enough to defeat him, and neither are you!' he growls.

I shove Lord Talon's hands from my shoulders and angrily walk to the other side of the room to sit in the chair.

'Lylah?' he says. I look down at my feet to avoid eye contact.

He sighs with sadness and defeat as he walks to leave the room. He pauses and places something on the chest of draws by the door. 'I know you miss Micah. I know you love him, and I know it hurts. You will get your justice, I promise you. Your time will come, but it won't be tomorrow,' he says and closes the door behind him.

I approach the drawers to see my dagger. I hold it to my heart and walk to the window. Everything is quiet. The lake's water is still. There's no wind, nor do the trees sway. I look down at the small balconies below, then at the long curtains beside me. I tuck my dagger in my belt and smile. If Lord Talon won't take me, I'll just take myself. I yank at the curtain, pulling it off the rail, then the other. I tie them together and toss one end out the window. I look around as to where I can tie the end I hold.

The bed's post gains my attention. I tie it as tight as possible, race back to the window, and climb out. Once I climb down to the end of the curtain, I begin to swing myself until I can jump onto the balcony. I land with ease and look up. I must be at least twelve meters down from the chambers. I climb through the window into the room. It has lots of shelves with books and a small empty bed. I open the door. There's no one around. I speed walk through the corridor and down a stairwell. The double front door is only down the next hallway. As I'm approaching, I hear someone talking. I quickly hide behind the display of knight's armour until the two vampires are out of sight. I open and step through the front doors and quietly close them behind me. I race to the end of the island in victory, only to be met with the dreaded bridge.

I close my eyes, take a deep breath and run as fast as possible without looking. The bridge rocks and sways beneath my feet, but I keep my eyes closed. I feel the hard ground under my feet and open my eyes. I kneel, kiss the ground, and quickly thank the Moon Goddess for not letting me fall off the bridge before bursting into a run. I race past the pillars, through the sand and enter the labyrinth. I sprint up and down every path, desperate to find my way out, but to no avail. I'm lost. I'm worried Lord Talon will find me and return me to his castle. I lean my back against the wall. I don't want to give up. I have to keep trying. Then suddenly, I hear his voice in a low whisper calling me.

'Lylah,' I hear Micah's whispers coming from the path to my left.

'Micah,' I breathe out heavily and race towards his voice.

Chapter 39

I arrive at a set of stone steps that lead to nothing but a dark dead end. I feel the ceiling and realise it's a large paver. Using all my strength, I push it open and climb out. I look around and see I'm in a very old graveyard. I know where I am. I saw it on the map. I run east toward the mountain where Lord Atticus awaits Lord Talon.

After hours of running and jogging, I have to rest. The sun will be rising soon. I lay next to a large tree and sleep for a while before I continue east. By the time it's nightfall, I'm exhausted. Lord Talon would have come to check on me through the night to find I'm gone and see I've escaped through the window. I continue to look over my shoulder every so often, knowing Lord Talon could catch up to me any time now. That's if he knows I'm heading toward Lord Atticus. He might think I've possibly escaped to return home to my pack.

I'm feeling very hot and flustered. At first, I thought it was from all the running, but no matter how much I rest, it only worsens. Constantly sweating, I'm relieved to come across a lake. I dive straight in, but the cold water does nothing to cool me down. I focus my mind, thinking of Micah to keep me moving.

The moon rises. I can see the mountain up ahead. I don't realise how tall the mountain is until I reach the base and glance up. I huff as my shoulders drop in dismay. I take one step after another. My skin almost feels like it's burning. I'm only halfway up when I hear twigs breaking and the rustling of nearby bushes. I can't see well, not having wolf vision. So I steady myself and listen to figure out in which direction the movements are coming from, only to realise it's everywhere all around me. I'm being surrounded, but by what?

Red eyes appear in front of me, blinking—my heart races. I swiftly pull my dagger from my belt. 'You!' I say and lunge toward it, striking it across the throat, only for it to vanish and reappear moments later.

'What!' I say, stepping back.

Someone claps behind me. I turn to face a man stepping out from the shadows towards me with a smile.

'It's not very often someone attempts to strike and kill my pet Blood Dwellers,' he says and holds his hands, palms down beside him.

Black demonic dogs flicker, appearing under his hands. He pats them gently. They have fangs three times as long as vampires. I watch as the Blood Dwellers twitch and flicker as if they are apparitions. Their eyes are red, blood red. The same eyes that had surrounded Micah and me. The Blood Dwellers are real.

'Lord Atticus,' I say under my breath, now staring at him in shock.

His hair is dark, and he is dressed all in black. I can't quite put my finger on it, but some of his features seem familiar, or am I remembering his features from the night he killed Micah? I do remember seeing dark hair and the side of his face. He is wearing the same black cape as Lord Talon. I can't help but feel they somewhat resemble each other. Is that another reason why I was so sure it was Lord Talon who killed Micah?

His eyes meet mine, 'So, you've heard of me? I'm glad word is getting round,' he smirks sadistically.

I clench my dagger tighter and glare at him.

He smiles, 'If looks could kill,' he laughs. 'I can't help but sense some animosity in the air. In fact,' he says, taking a step closer and shaking a finger at me. 'We've met before. I remember your blue eyes changing shades, your white hair, and, most of all, your scent,' he says, flashing past me with great speed.

I swing my dagger around to stab him, but in a flash, he has disappeared and reappears behind me. I quickly face him.

He tilts his head and stares at me curiously as I step closer to him. Then, he begins to walk around, circling me like a vulture waiting to pick at its prey.

'I'm glad you're here,' he says.

He then vanishes from in front of me, and I hear and feel him inhale my scent against my neck behind me. He presses himself against my back. I thrust my dagger back, but he vanishes again.

'That night, your scent, your smell led me to you. I couldn't stay away. I had never smelt blood so sweet in my two hundred and sixty-two years of being alive.'

My mind flashes back to that night, riding through the woods on Micah's back. The trees whipped past us. I had been struck lightly by some of the low branches, but it had only left a few tiny scratches on my arm. They were small enough that you wouldn't even bother putting a bandaid on them. It must have been enough for vampires to pick up the scent from the tiny drop of blood on my arm, triggering any nearby vampires into a blood-lusting craze. Lord Atticus was within the radius of us. It was me who brought on Micah's death!

My breathing intensifies at the realisation that my blood had triggered the events leading to Micah's death.

'Why didn't you kill me? Why didn't you drink my blood instead of Micah's!? Why did you have to kill him?' I scream.

'I was going for you, but that damn boy got in the way trying to stop me. He knew you were my target. I'd never had such a challenge trying to kill someone before. I knew if I were to taste you, I would have to get through him first, so I did just that. I was going to finish feeding off him, and then it would have been your turn, but then I heard your pack howling nearby after they could hear your screams. That darn wolf boy was hard enough to kill as it was, let alone a pack of them, so I had no choice but to stop feeding from him and retreat.'

In a rage, I run toward Lord Atticus, jump in the air and kick him in the chest, making him step back in surprise. Catching him off guard, I raise my clenched fists at my eye level and manage to swiftly hit him with three blows in the stomach before he grabs my wrists tightly and slams me up against a large tree.

I'm sweating profusely at this point, and my arms are burning. It hurts.

'How did you know I was here?' he asks. 'It's not you who I was expecting, and unless you know Lord Talon, there is no way you would have known I'd be here.'

'Why do you and Lord Talon wear the same cloak?' I ask.

He tilts his head, 'So you do know him,' he smiles, 'But how? We don't normally associate with your kind. Well, with me as the exception, I enjoy drinking the blood of werewolves. It's much tastier than humans,' he smirks.

I manage to free my hand from his grip as he chuckles and slap him hard across the face. He steels himself and looks at me angrily. 'Well, aren't you feisty?' he says through gritted teeth.

He grabs my arm and squeezes it. I cry out from the pain. We look down at my arm to see my skin burning. Lord Atticus makes eye contact with me in surprise as he begins to realise something. He then looks at my wrist and runs his thumb over the symbol.

'You've been marked. You're Blood Flamed with one of my kind. Who is your Blood Flame?' he growls.

'Let her go!' Lord Talon shouts.

Lord Talon appears from the shadows of the trees. He is sweating just as much as I am and sways slightly. He needs to feed. I realise I have never allowed him to feed from me, which has weakened him greatly. I don't understand why we are both sweating and burning, though.

Lord Atticus bursts into laughter, looking between us, 'Brother, you did come after all,' he smiles.

'Brother?' I mutter under my breath, now looking between the two of them.

Lord Talon looks guilty and worried as we make eye contact.

'I must congratulate you, brother,' he says and swings me around so my back is pressed against his front. He holds me so tight I can barely move. 'You have found you're Blood Flame after all. You never did stop talking about how all you wanted in life was to meet your Blood Flame. It made me sick to my stomach every time you mentioned it. Yet here she is in my arms and not yours. I can't wait to taste her,' he says, sliding his tongue slowly up my neck, and his fangs extend. I cringe.

'Stop! I'll pledge my loyalty to you. I'll give you lordship of the coven. Just let her go! That is what you wanted all along. That's why you are waiting here for me.'

Lord Atticus pauses in thought, 'That's true, but I must admit, ever since that night I smelt her blood, I've never stopped thinking about it, craving it, yearning to taste it,' he confesses.

Nadia and Soren appear from behind Lord Talon as Lord Atticus scrapes his fangs playfully across my neck to stir his brother up further. I discreetly grab my dagger and hold it firmly.

'Nadia, Soren, it's been a long time. You'll have to give Cedric my regards,' he chuckles before sinking his teeth into my neck.

At the same time, I plunge my dagger deep into his thigh, making Lord Atticus withdraw his bite and yell.

'That was for Cedric. He sends you his warm wishes, too,' I smile as I step back.

Lord Atticus hisses and glowers at me. A few drops of my blood glide down his fangs. He tilts his head back, and his tongue wipes the blood, tasting it. His eyes become black with blood lust. He lunges toward me for more, but I kick him in the lower stomach, turn and run towards Lord Talon. Nadia screams, sending Lord Atticus back, and Lord Talon uses his ability to slow his brother and his Blood Dwellers down as they race back toward us. I notice everyone's eyes are black now, including Lord Talon's, as I run toward him. Not sure what to do, I turn right and run down the mountain as fast as possible. Before I make it to the base of the mountain, my skin begins to cool and warm tingles and sparks flow through my body as Lord Talon scoops me up and dashes into the distance. I gaze up at him as the burning in my arms dissipates. I'm so happy to see him. He's fighting the blood lust and trying to get me as far away as possible from Lord Atticus. But then he suddenly collapses, drained of strength and energy.

'Talon!' I shout as I crawl over to him.

I help sit him up.

'Lylah,' he whispers and gently cups my cheek. We gaze tenderly into each other's eyes. I turn my face into his warm hand and close my eyes. My hand cups over his as I allow his touch to ignite my heart into flames.

Chapter 40

My breath catches, and I realise at this moment how much I truly care for Lord Talon, that I've fallen for him so hard, like ocean waves crashing into rocks. Like lightning that has struck the ground. Like the sound of thunder that ripples through your body. I'm in love with Lord Talon. I place my forehead against his and use my free hand to cup his cheek. We breathe heavily in unison as a sense of overwhelming love and desire takes over us.

My walls come crashing down, and my lips slam into his with a fiery passion. My lips coax his open, and our tongues entwine and dance as if they were meant to be.

We gasp for air as we part, and I pull Lord Talon's shirt from over his head and toss it. Our hands explore every inch of each other as we kiss again. I straddle his lap and begin to undo his belt as he pulls the laces undone on the back of my dress and yanks it down, exposing my breasts.

Now, completely naked, we both pause with our foreheads touching, taking in as much of each other as possible.

'Talon,' I say. The way I say his name without his rank makes the desire in his eyes burn even more. 'I want you to feed from me.'

He steels himself and gazes into my eyes to see I'm serious. He enters his member between my legs, and we make slow but passionate love, maintaining eye contact the entire time. We touch and caress every inch of each other, and then as we are about to climax, his fangs grow. He bites down and drinks as he releases his warmth inside of me. I cry out in euphoria and bliss as I release and feel him feed from me. His hold tightens around me as he continues to drink. He moans with contentment and fulfilment as he withdraws his fangs.

His lips crash into mine, and I taste my blood's sweetness and can taste the power. It has no metallic taste as I would expect blood to have.

Lord Talon is at his full strength again. He holds me against his chest and caresses my back.

'What's this?' he asks as he gently touches the three thick long scars. I stare at him with worry and quickly reach for my dress. I hold it against my chest and withdraw myself from his lap.

'Lylah, what's wrong?' he asks, standing up and walking toward me.

'Nothing, I just don't want you to see them, okay.'

'See what, exactly?'

'To see how hideous and ugly I am. You've already seen these ones,' I say, holding my wrists out. 'That was hard enough to show,' I hug myself.

'Lylah, you are the most beautiful woman I have ever met. No scar or amount of scars could make you any less beautiful,' he says, gazing into my eyes.

I'm caught off guard by his sweet words. He steps around me, and my back arches as he places a tender kiss on the scars. 'You are perfect, Lylah. Scars and all,' he whispers and continues to kiss my back.

I turn to face him. 'The scars don't bother you?' I ask.

'The only thing that bothers me is the sombre look on your face, and I'm going to make it my mission to make you feel nothing but happiness from this moment onwards,' he says and pulls me in to kiss me.

I smile endearingly at him as we part. 'Now, let's take you home to your family,' he smiles.

'Wait! You mean back to my packhouse?'

He smiles and nods. I jump happily into his arms and cover his face in kisses.

'I want you to have the justice that you and Micah deserve. Without Cedric, we can't open the portal to send Lord Atticus back into the abyss of darkness. The only way to stop him is to kill him, and the only way we can accomplish that is by bringing the vampire and the werewolves together. But first, we should bathe,' he smiles and gestures his head over to a small lake.

Before he walks towards the lake, I notice the deep cut on his arm and shoulder has vanished. I trace my finger over the area of his chest where I had cut him.

'It's gone?' I say to him.

He takes my hand, kisses it and smiles. 'That night after the nightmare. I was comforting you and then without you realising it. You had healed me.'

I step back, 'No, that can't be, right? I have no magic.'

Lord Talon's gorgeous smile widens, 'When you tried to stab me after we fell down the stairs. I had used my power to stop you from killing me. When you became upset after realising Micah was able to see the future. You broke free of my power yourself. Again, you didn't notice you had done it yourself.'

'I thought you put me down? That you had let me go?'

'No, it was all you, Lylah.'

In absolute shock, I quietly walk to the lake and step into the water. Did I heal Talon? Was I able to break free from his power? I stare at the water and hover my hands above it as Talon watches me curiously.

'Aqua Bedew.' I say, but nothing happens.

I splash water in Talon's face. 'Liar,' I say to him.

'I'm not lying, Lylah.'

I decide to ignore him for a while. As I bath in the water, I think of how coincidental it was that I was sweating and burning, but once I was with Lord Talon, the burning and pain instantly dissipated.

I move closer to Lord Talon, 'I began burning and sweating as I fled from the underground. When you came and rescued me. You were in the same state as me. Why was that?' I ask him.

'Remember how I told you that you weren't a prisoner, but I had no choice but to keep you at the castle?'

I nod.

'It was because I knew this would happen if we were separated. I couldn't let you go. Otherwise, we would burn up. You see, when you find your Blood Flame, you can't be apart from each other for long periods, nor can you go a long distance away from each other. The God's chose us to be together because we are meant for each other. We are fated for one another. Going against their wishes and trying to leave your Blood Flame will result in both of us burning until there is nothing left of us but ash. The only way to stop it is to be together again.'

I panic at the realisation that I can't return home to live with my family unless Lord Talon is to leave the coven and live with me.

'This means I can't stay there. I can't go home to live with my family again?' I say to him.

Lord Talon looks away with guilt. 'I'm sorry, Lylah, but we can visit them together as much as you like, and they can also visit us,' he says.

I nod but remain silent.

We are washed and dressed as we're about to make our way to my pack until we see Nadia and Soren approach. Thankfully they're no longer blood lusting after me. They smile as Lord Talon takes my hand, kisses it, and holds my hand by his side. They can tell straight away he has finally been able to feed from me. The fang marks are also obvious on my neck.

'Lylah knows everything now. I need you both to rally the coven and have them here ready to fight. Lylah and I will gather the werewolves and meet back here. We are going to defeat my brother once and for all.'

They smile and nod before racing back into the distance.

It takes us a day and a half to reach my pack house. I close my eyes and breathe in the air as we walk towards the heavy front doors. Before I enter, it swings open. I see my father. He holds in a cry, and his lips almost tremble as his eyes well up. Within a flash, we are in each other's arms.

'My baby girl, my baby is home. Your back and you're okay,' he says, looking me up and down. His eyes pause on the two sets of fang marks on my neck.

'It's okay, Dad. I know it doesn't look good, but it's okay. I'm okay now. I missed you so much,' I tell him as I pull him in to hug again.

My mother, brothers, Amara, Bill, Nathan, Kayla and everyone else in the pack runs toward the front door and can't believe I'm here. We all hug and cry.

My mother, Hope, cups my face. 'I thought I'd never see you again,' she sobs.

'Oh, Mother,' I say, trying to sound casual, 'You know more than anyone that my stubbornness could never stop me from seeing again.'

She chokes on her cry, which changes into a laugh. Everyone else begins to laugh at the trueness of my words.

Theo and Leo glare at Talon, who stands cautiously a small distance behind me.

'It's okay. Lord Talon isn't the enemy,' I assure them.

I approach Talon, take his hand with a reassuring smile, and lead him back to my family.

'I want you all to meet Lord Talon again, but this time on good terms,' I smile.

Talon steps forward, 'It's a pleasure to meet you all again,' he says sincerely, but everyone is unsure about him, except for Kayla smiling at us.

I frown. 'You never came after me. You never tried to find me or save me,' I say to them.

'I told them not to,' Kayla says.

'What! Why?'

Kayla walks up to me and takes my wrist. 'Because of this.' she says and traces her finger over it. 'I knew what it meant. I knew the moment Lord Talon's eyes were red that he was Blood Flamed. I knew the moment he marked you that you were his Blood Flame, but I also knew it meant you would be safe and protected by him. I explained to your family what had happened and what it meant, and removing you from Lord Talon would result in your death. They knew there was nothing they could do but hope and pray to see you again, and here you are again, but with your Blood Flame,' she smiles.

'It's true then? You and Lord Talon?' my father says.

I place my hand on his forearm, 'Yes, and I'm in love with him, Dad. Although I will never truly be at peace until I have killed Lord Atticus. Talon has helped to heal my heart and soul again.'

My father smiles at me, then turns to face Lord Talon and extends his hand out to shake his hand.

Talon accepts it with a smile. 'Alpha Maximus, it's a pleasure and a true honour to be blessed with your daughter as my Blood Flame.'

My father smiles and nods, and we enter the packhouse.

Chapter 41

'Alpha Maximus, Luna,' Talon says to my parents as we face them in the dining hall. 'We have to put Lord Atticus to an end. Over one hundred years ago, he went on a murderous killing spree. He even killed our father as well as beloved members of our coven.'

'Your brother is who's responsible for all of these deaths? For Micah's death?' Theo asks.

'Unfortunately, yes. He is my brother. We had managed to send him through a portal into an abyss of darkness. Since he freed himself over a year ago, he began where he had left off, continuing to kill and murder whilst growing in strength by feeding off his victims. He knows Lylah is my Blood Flame and, unfortunately, has managed to taste her blood. He would have figured out not long after we escaped from him that the small taste of Lylah's blood he had, has greatly strengthened him much more than anything else he has ever fed off. Lylah's blood is unlike anyone else's. Just one cut, one drop, can send any vampire within a distance into a blood-lusting craze. Her blood wreaks of pure power.'

My father stands from his seat. 'If you and my daughter can put your differences aside and learn to love each other. Then our races can put our differences aside and fight together as one. Nathan, Alex, Theo and Leo. Contact all the packs. They are to prepare themselves and join the fight against Lord Atticus immediately. Make sure Alpha Varan and Alpha Greg are contacted first. I will organise our warriors now, he says, leaving the room.

Nathan, Alex, Theo and Leo also leave the hall.

'So what do we do, now?' Amara asks.

'We prepare ourselves,' I say, grabbing Talon's hands and leading him to my bedroom.

He looks around my chambers, taking in everything and touching everything in curiosity. He smirks when he sees my table covered in dozens of daggers as I place the one Micah made me amongst them. The wand my mother gifted is also there. I open my drawer and pull out a fresh pair of my black leggings, baldric, black tank top and a hair tie, placing them on my bed. I gesture for Talon to untie the back of my dress. I let it slide from my shoulders and drop onto the floor. I put fresh underwear on and then my leggings. Talon hands me my black crop top. I take it and put it on, then take my baldric, draping it over my shoulder. I sit on my bed, pull my knee-high cavalier boots on, and lace them up tightly. I walk over to my dresser and brush my hair before tying it in a high ponytail. Talon then hands me my special dagger that I kiss before sheathing it into my baldric. I turn my head enough to see the exposed scars on my back through my mirror and frown. As I grab my hoodie, Talon places his hand over mine.

'Do you want to wear it, or is it to hide the scars from everyone?' he asks.

'To hide them,' I reply.

'Lylah,' he says, tossing my hoodie aside and gently grasping my chin with his thumb and index finger. 'These scars are part of who you are. These scars tell a story of how strong and courageous you are. These scars show everyone no matter what comes your way. You will never be defeated. These scars are reminders of someone you love and should never be forgotten. So, show them proudly like the armour these scars have become.'

'You're right,' I reply as I face myself in the mirror. 'I'm ready now,' I say with determination.

Talon takes my hand, and I look around my room, knowing this is no longer my home now. I leave my room for the last time. Memories of Micah climbing through my window with a smile on his face flash through my mind. The moments we cuddled up and giggled in my bed. The pillow fights and the moments we fell off the bed together, laughing on the floor. 'Lylah,' I hear Micah whisper. I grip Talon's hand tighter and smile at him as we walk down the stairs together.

My father has the warriors gathered outside, ready to disembark. It's not long until all the surrounding packs arrive, including Alpha Greg and Alpha Varan.

I make eye contact with Alpha Varan. He looks as depressed as the day I last saw him. Alpha Greg breaks our eye contact, stepping in front of me and pulling me in for a hug.

'Lylah. I'm so pleased to see you, and who is this strapping young lad?' he asks, eyeing Talon up and down.

'This is my Blood Flame, my mate, Lord Talon,' I tell him.

'Blessed with a second mate, hey? Well, I'll be damned by the stars,' he says. 'Most will never witness anyone in their lifetime having the blessing of a second mate. It's incredibly rare. I'm happy for you, Lylah. I supposed this means you won't become a warrior for the pack, though?'

'No, but I could perhaps become a warrior for the coven?' I say, now staring at Talon.

'You're supposed to be the lady of the coven now,' Talon says.

'Talon! You even agreed that I wasn't a lady when I said I wasn't one!' I argue.

'Hmm, did I? I don't recall,' he smiles teasingly.

'Let me help you recollect your memories then, Talon. It was moments before I tried to kill you for the fiftieth time by throwing a blunt butter knife at your head!'

Theo and Leo burst into laughter behind us.

'That definitely sounds like our sister,' Leo laughs.

'It sounds like our dear little sister kept you well and truly on your toes?' Theo adds.

'You have no idea,' Talon says to them.

'Everyone ready yourselves! We will be heading east any minute now,' my father shouts.

'Talon, before we leave. There is one last person I need to see.'

He nods and follows me. I enter the garden outside my window and kneel on Micah's grave.

'Micah,' I say, staring at his gravestone. 'I wish you had told me your secret. I wish I'd known that you knew you were going to die by protecting me. I miss you so much, Micah. It still hurts every time I think of you.'

A tear drops from my face and lands on his grave. My dagger begins to flicker, giving off light. 'Lylah,' I hear Micah whisper, but Talon flinches as if he had also heard the whisper and stares at my dagger in awe. I look down and withdraw it. The eye above the fuller, Micah carved. It now looks and moves like a real eye. I recognise it immediately as Micah's eye.

'Micah?' I say.

A heavy wind suddenly flows through me. 'Micah! I love you so much!'

I close my eyes. I'm suddenly brought back to the moment I held Micah before he died in my arms.

'Don't cry, my sweet princess,' Micah whispers, 'I will always be here with you. I will always be by your side in spirit and have my happily ever after with you. But Lylah. Your life doesn't end here with me. More is waiting for you, and I want you to find it. You will go on adventures. I know you will find someone and fall in love all over again. I want you to find happiness. I want you to live again and know it's okay to be happy without me,' he whispers.

I lean down and kiss Micah's lips for the last time.

'Forever in spirit, by your side always,' he whispers.

'Lylah! Lylah!' I can feel hands on my shoulders, shaking me as my mind returns to the present time being on Micah's grave. Talon is kneeling in front of me with worry.

'Talon?'

'Yes, it's me. What happened? Your eyes and the eye on the dagger suddenly glazed over silver. You couldn't hear me, and you stopped moving.'

I look down at the dagger to see the sable eye moving and blinking. 'It's Micah. I saw him again. He said he would always be with me by my side in spirit. I get it now!' I say, standing with a smile. 'Part of Micah is in this dagger. Micah wasn't kidding when he said he had carved his eye in the dagger so he could always keep his eye on me. He said he would always be by my side! Don't you get it? The dagger is always by my side, whether it's tucked in my belt or sheathed in my baldric. Micah has always been with me from the moment he died, here in this very dagger. His spirit has always been with me! This is why I could hear him whisper my name all those times. It was him, after all, who helped lead me out of the labyrinth!'

'Wait. I wondered how in the wands you were able to find your way out of there!' Talon says.

'Micah said he knew I would find love again. He knew you and I would meet and that we would also be fated mates. Micah must have seen how happy you had made me in the future, which was why he was at peace with dying. This is why Micah didn't tell me he could see the future because he didn't want me to stop him from dying. He wanted me to live my life on with you,' I explain.

Talon and I stare at each other in shock.

'I don't know what to say. If Micah had never died, you might never have become my Blood Flame. He must have been able to see my life as well. Micah must have known all I wanted in life was to find my Blood Flame, to love her and cherish her as if she was the most precious thing in this entire universe. Micah died for us to be together, for us to find love and happiness with each other,' Talon says.

Talon looks down at my dagger and glides his fingers across the blade of the Moon Stone. 'I won't let your death be in vain, Micah. You sacrificed your life knowing Lylah would learn to love again and that I would love her just as much as you did and no less. There will never be a day I will ever let Lylah feel she isn't loved and appreciated. You have my word,' Talon says.

Micah's eye looks at Talon and blinks. I kneel back on his grave, kiss my fingers and then press my fingers on his gravestone. 'I will always love you, Micah, now and forever. I love you always,' I say.

I stand, sheathing the dagger back in my baldric and take Talon's hand.

'All in order!' I hear my father shout.

Chapter 42

Talon watches, intrigued, as the werewolves shift into their wolf forms while my father and brothers shift into their Lycans. Talon gestures for me to climb onto his back. I wrap my arms around his neck as he holds my legs. Together with the pack, we run forward for many hours until we meet the coven of vampires awaiting us.

'Lord Talon, Lady Lylah,' All the vampires say, bowing as they greet us.

Nadia and Soren approach and stand by our sides as if to guard us. I look over at my father and nod to indicate we're ready. We head in the direction of the mountain we last saw Lord Atticus. It becomes dark very suddenly before we even approach the mountain. Hundreds of black whisps whip by us and then circle us. They are extremely fast, and I know exactly what they are. 'Blood Dwellers,' I mutter under my breath.

'He's here!' Talon shouts, warning everyone.

'I see you brought the entire coven and even the wolves to watch you pledge your allegiance to me, along with my dinner,' Lord Atticus says, smiling at me. 'I must say tasting your blood not only was delicious, but it has increased my agility and power. Imagine how much more powerful I'll be after I feed off you properly. I could take on the largest city of humans, armies even,' he smirks.

'I'll never pledge my allegiance to you. You have destroyed all these lives! You're not worthy of being a leader. You're twisted and evil and deserve to rot in the depths of hell with your demonic dogs. And you will never lay a finger on, Lylah, ever again!' Talon shouts.

'That's a shame, brother, as you leave me no choice but to kill you and take Lylah for myself by force!' he yells, and the Blood Dwellers attack us.

The vampires and werewolves fight against the Blood Dwellers. There are hundreds of them. Every time a Blood Dweller is defeated, it flickers and reappears in full health again. Vampires and Werewolves are being injured, and some lay dying. My mother is running from one to another, trying to heal as many as possible. Kayla throws vials toward the Blood Dwellers to poison and disorientate them, but it does not affect them.

'Talon, the Blood Dwellers can't be killed. They are illusions from Lord Atticus's mind. Although they become real, he can resummon them each time they are killed. The only way to stop them is by defeating Lord Atticus himself. If we do that, then the Blood Dwellers will disappear forever.'

'Then you stay here, Lylah. I'll go for my brother.'

'No, not on your own! You can't defeat him on your own. I'm going with you!'

'I'm sorry, Lylah. I won't let any harm come to you,' he says. I look at him, confused, as he nods to some over my shoulder, 'Keep Lylah safe,' he says.

Soren wraps his arms around me, pinning my arms down as Talon races towards Lord Atticus. 'No! Talon!' I scream.

Talon and Lord Atticus hiss and circle around one another before attacking. They are fighting to the death. They claw, bite, punch, and shred each other with their now elongated sharp claws. I elbow Soren and ram the hilt of my dagger into his thigh, allowing me to break free of his grip. I run toward Talon and Lord Atticus and come to an abrupt halt as I see Talon covered in wounds and lying limp. Lord Atticus pulls him up by the scruff of his shirt, and as he is about to rip Talon's heart out from his chest. I scream.

A massive ball of light erupts within me, sending everyone flying back, including Lord Atticus. Everyone looks at me in shock and surprise. There is an aura, a powerful glowing light flaring from all around me. I slowly walk toward Lord Atticus and withdraw my dagger, holding the blade to my wrist.

'Father!' I shout to him, 'Don't kill the vampires, just keep them back,' I say.

He is confused by what I mean. I slit my wrist and hold my arm up, sending every single vampire, including Lord Atticus, into a blood-lusting craze. As they come towards me, my father, brothers and pack form a line behind me and fight back the blood-crazed vampires.

'If this is what you want, Lord Atticus, come and get it!' I say to him.

He hisses and races toward me. As he reaches out to grab me, I hold my hand out, making him freeze like a statue. He stares at me, stunned. Talon struggles to sit up in immense pain and stares at me in awe.

Holding my dagger firmly in my other hand, I step closer to Lord Atticus and stab him in the heart. He cries out in pain, and the Blood Dwellers begin to disappear. I don't withdraw the knife yet. Instead, I stare Lord Atticus in the eyes, and to his horror, I twist the knife causing unimaginable pain.

'The pain you feel right now is nothing compared to the pain you caused me when you killed Micah.'

Lord Atticus laughs as blood begins to dribble profusely from his mouth.

'My only regret,' he says, choking on his blood, 'Was not being able to finish him off before your pack arrived,' he smiles and flings his head back, laughing.

He heaves for air as I push my dagger in deeper. I lean forward and whisper in his ear, 'Inferno Flamo,' I say.

Everyone gasps and steps back as he erupts into flames, wailing and screaming until he becomes nothing but a pile of ash at my feet.

I stare at my dagger and breath with a sense of relief and happiness I hadn't experienced for a very long time. I did it, Micah. I killed Lord Atticus. I hug my dagger close to my heart before hearing Talon struggle for air. I sheath my dagger back in my baldric and run to Talon.

I kneel beside him and see the dozens of wounds, gashes and open flesh.

'Lylah, you did it,' he says breathlessly.

'Shh, don't move. You're making the blood loss quicken.'

My mother kneels beside me and nods that she can heal him.
'Wait! I say as she goes to heal him. 'Let me do it,' I say.
I hover my hands over his chest and close my eyes. A ball of light forms above his chest and explodes into millions of tiny particles that sparkle as they slowly land on him. All his wounds begin to heal, not even leaving a mark. Then I realise it has even removed the scar on his chest and arm. I heal the cut on my wrist, removing the vampires from their blood lust craze. The scars on my wrists also fade.
'What about the scars on your back?' Talon says.
I smile and shake my head. 'These scars are part of who I am. These scars tell a story of how strong and courageous I am. These scars show everyone no matter what comes my way. I will never be defeated. These scars are reminders of someone I love and will never be forgotten. So, I will wear it proudly like the armour the scar has become.'
Talon smiles, nods and swiftly pulls me into his chest. We hug, laugh and kiss until Alpha Varan approaches.
'Lady Lylah,' he says and gets down on one knee, bowing his head. 'I want to apologise for how I've treated you and for blaming you for Micah's death. You meant the whole world to Micah, and he loved you wholeheartedly. I should have respected his feelings towards you. I'm so sorry for the hurt I caused you and because of your determination and your love for Micah. You were able to give him the justice he deserves, and now Micah can be at peace, and because of that, you have given my heart peace. You have my utmost honour and respect. I hope you can find it in your heart to forgive this old fool?' he says.

I gaze into his watery eyes and fling my arms around his neck. 'I forgive you,' I say.

He begins to cry and hugs me tight.

I hug my mother, father and brothers goodbye.

'We will visit you each month, okay, sweety,' my mother says.

'I would like that,' I reply.

'It's going to suck not having our baby sister around to trick and play pranks on,' Leo says.

'Well, you and Theo need to focus on finding your mates to become Alphas anyway, and besides, you'll always have Amara to prank,' I smile.

'That's true,' Theo says, 'Leo and I have already made plans to begin expanding our search for our mates. Maybe with luck, we will find them sooner rather than later.'

I fling my arms around my father one last time. We hug tight, not wanting to let go.

'I'm going to miss you the most,' I say to him.

'I'm going to miss you the most too,' he says. 'Now remember what I taught you. If anyone tries to harm you again, what do you do?'

'Kick them right where it hurts the most and say to them, I am Lady Lylah, daughter of a Lycan, and you've just met your worst nightmare!'

'That's my girl,' he smiles.

Chapter 43

We arrive back in the underground and enter the castle.
'Tonight, we will celebrate our victory and our official lady of the coven, Lylah,' Talon shouts.
The coven cheers and dissipates to prepare for the celebration.
I face Talon, Soren and Nadia. 'There is something I need to do first before we celebrate. Can you take me down to the crypts?' I ask them.
They give each other a confused and unsure glance.
'Cedric should celebrate with us,' I tell them.
'Lylah,' Talon says, 'You know he doesn't want anyone to see him in this state. You know he has gone mad?'
'I know, but I need you to trust me on this,' I say, my eyes pleading with his.
'You know you always have my trust. Come on then, let's go down to the crypts.'
Nadia carries a fire torch as we descend through an abundance of stairs and narrow passageways. As I enter

the crypt, I gesture for them to wait at the entrance as I slowly approach the shadow in the corner.

'Cedric,' I say and watch the shadow flinch. 'We've met before, but I never got to introduce myself to you. I am Lady Lylah, Blood Flame to Lord Talon, daughter of a Lycan and your friend,' I tell him.

He slowly creeps across the ground and into the light, looking curiously at me. This time I'm not scared of him. I don't scream, and I don't run. Instead, I smile kindly at him and extend my hands out for his. Cedric glances at my hands and then back at me. He hesitates, but he reaches up, places his frail hands in mine, and stands.

I smile and hug him. He is unsure and doesn't know what to do. I break the hug and cup the bones on his face.

'I lost my mate too. I'm sorry you lost Alanis. I know you miss her. I miss Micah every single day too,' I say to him. 'Unfortunately, I can't heal your heart, Cedric. I can never take away the pain you feel from losing her. No magic in the world can heal the loss of a loved one. I can heal your mind and body, but I cannot heal your broken heart,' I say to him—light forms from my hands.

Cedric's face of exposed bone begins to regrow skin. His body is no longer hunching over and instead straightens. He is no longer severely underweight, and his natural skin colour has returned. I continue to watch as lips form along with his nose and eyelids. The rest of his face develops skin, and I step back.

Cedric looks down at his hands and then touches his face in shock before he looks up to see his friends.

'Talon, Soren, Nadia?' he says.

They smile and wipe away their tears of happiness before they lunge toward Cedric and pull him in for a group hug, laughing and patting him on the back.

They break the hug and all gaze at me before nodding in agreement for some unknown reason. Suddenly they're all racing toward me and all hug me at once.

'Guys, you're squashing me,' I laugh.

'That's the whole purpose,' Nadia smiles.

'Thank you, Lylah. Thank you for everything,' Soren says.

We part from the hug.

'Let's get you ready for the celebrations, Cedric,' Soren says to him.

Nadia follows behind them.

Talon scoops me up and carries me into our chambers.

'Lady Lylah, daughter of the Lycan. There is one thing I need to do to you before we get ourselves ready for the celebrations.'

'Oh, and what might that be?' I ask him.

Talon kicks the chamber door shut and playfully throws me onto the bed. 'Show you how much I love you,' he says, ripping his shirt off with a mischievous grin.

ABOUT THE AUTHOR

Jazz Ford is a wife and mother of three children. She was born in Bendigo but lives in Geelong, Victoria, Australia. Jazz is a former Personal Care Attendant with a background in nursing homes and in-home care. She loves writing full-time from home. In her spare time, she enjoys photography, graphic design, photoshop, and spending time with her husband and children. Jazz Ford's other works are 'The Alpha's Mate Who Cried Wolf,' 'The Alpha Who Cursed His Mate ', 'The Alpha's Mate And The Vampire King,' 'The CEO,' 'The CEO 2.' and many more. You can find Jazz on TikTok, Facebook and Instagram.

Printed in Great Britain
by Amazon

38526809R00172